SAMHAIN
SECRETS

SAMHAIN SECRETS

Jennifer David Hesse

KENSINGTON PUBLISHING CORP.

www.kensingtonbooks.com

KENSINGTON BOOKS are published by

Kensington Publishing Corp.
119 West 40th Street
New York, NY 10018

Copyright © 2018 Jennifer David Hesse

All Kensington titles, imprints, and distributed lines are available at special quantity discounts for bulk purchases for sales promotions, premiums, fund-raising, educational, or institutional use. Special book excerpts or customized printings can also be created to fit specific needs. For details, write or phone the office of the Kensington sales manager: Kensington Publishing Corp., 119 West 40th Street, New York, NY 10018, attn: Sales Department; phone 1-800-221-2647.

KENSINGTON BOOKS and the K logo are Reg. U.S. Pat. & TM Off.

ISBN-13: 978-1-4967-1771-9
ISBN-10: 1-4967-1771-6

First printing: September 2018

10   9   8   7   6   5   4   3   2   1

Printed in the United States of America

First electronic edition: September 2018

ISBN-13: 978-1-4967-1772-6
ISBN-10: 1-4967-1772-4

For Lucille Provinzano,
who continues to share her love of autumn, nature,
and Halloween fun. I love you, Grandma!

Samhain (sou-en): A cross-quarter holiday on the Wheel of the Year, beginning at sundown on October 31. A time for celebrating the final harvest, honoring the dead, and communing with spirits.

On Samhain we seek to understand ourselves and our spiritual journeys as we enter the dreamtime. . . . in the midst of realms of spirit where form no longer exists, we seek a dream, for all new life begins first with a dream.

—From *Witch Crafting: A Spiritual Guide to Making Magic* by Phyllis Curott

CHAPTER ONE

"You know there's no such thing as ghosts!" My words came out in a raspy whisper. I was trying to be forceful enough to get through to the hysterical woman on the other end of the line, while avoiding the attention of the small crowd of business people milling about in front of the converted barn. I failed on both counts.

All eyes looked toward me with blatant curiosity. Among them were those of the park district supervisor, the head of the Chamber of Commerce, and the senior partner at my law firm, all of whom were awaiting the start of their VIP tour through the Fieldstone Park haunted barn. Every year, Edindale's town leaders recruited local businesses to create spooky displays and a funhouse-style maze inside the emptied-out storage barn. This was the law firm's first year participating. As one of the newest partners, I was roped into playing a costumed volunteer. As if that weren't embarrassing enough, now I'd unwittingly placed myself in the spotlight.

With my cell phone pressed to my ear, I looked for an escape route. Instead, I saw Pammy Sullivan, one of the associates at the law firm. She broke off from a small group that included our boss, Beverly Olsen, and made her way toward me with a gleam in her eye. An incorrigible gossip, Pammy probably just wanted the scoop on my strange phone call. On the other hand, maybe Beverly had sent her over to chide me for taking a call right when the tour was about to start.

I offered an apologetic grimace and squeezed out from behind the makeshift ticket booth. Scanning the park for a quiet spot, I landed on a cluster of maple trees beyond the pavilion. As I made my way through the throng, past picnic tables filled with laughing kids and rowdy teenagers, I kept my head down and listened to my client fret on the other end of the line.

Scratch that. She was beyond fretting. She was freaking out.

As soon as I reached the relative privacy of the maple grove, I allowed myself to interrupt. "Mrs. Hammerlin! Wait a minute. Just think about what you're saying. I'm sure there's a perfectly logical explanation—"

She cut me off, leaving me to pinch the bridge of my nose. I took a slow breath in and out and tried again. "Okay," I finally said. "You're right. I agree. We don't know for sure what happens to our spirits after we die. But, really, it's highly unlikely that the noises you're hearing—"

"Keli?" I felt a tap on my shoulder and turned to

see a tall man in an old-fashioned tuxedo and flowing black cape. He had slicked, coal-black hair and a matching trim beard. Most striking, though, was the glowing white powder, which rendered his normally pale face even more anemic. Not to mention the two pointy false teeth protruding from his blood-red lips.

In spite of the Dracula getup, there was no mistaking the impatient scowl. It was my fellow junior partner, Crenshaw Davenport III, Esquire.

I nodded and rushed to end the call with my client. "I have to run now, Mrs. Hammerlin, but I promise I'll stop by later this evening. Okay? Okay. Good-bye."

I sighed loudly as I stuffed my phone into my purse.

"I trust everything is under control?" said Crenshaw around his plastic canines. "You gave me quite a start. When I saw you leave your post, I was afraid you were going to abandon your ticket-selling duties."

"I wouldn't do that. I just had to take this call. This client is driving me crazy. We closed on her new house last week, and she's called me every day since—several times each day."

"Ah. Buyer's remorse?"

"I don't know. It's the weirdest thing. She insists the house is haunted, and she wants to go after the seller for failure to disclose."

Crenshaw raised his eyebrows. "You do attract the most interesting people, don't you? But there's no time for that now. Doors will open soon, and those tickets won't sell themselves."

"Fine," I grumbled. "Though I still can't believe we have to do this. I have better things to do with my Friday night."

He ignored my complaint and gave me a nudge. We'd already been through this earlier in the evening, when he'd met me in the parking lot near the ball field. He must have been watching, waiting for me to pull in, because he pounced the moment I opened my car door.

"At last!" he'd said.

"What's the rush?" I asked, checking my watch. "I'm not late."

"People are already starting to arrive, and we need to get changed. Come on."

"Changed? What are you talking about?" I stepped out of the car and stared at his hair. It was different from how it had appeared at the office earlier in the day.

"Here." He thrust a garment bag into my arms and tossed another over his arm. "I brought our costumes, so we can arrive at the barn in character."

"Costume? What costume? I'm not wearing a costume."

He glared at me under heavy dark eyebrows that were normally ginger-colored. "Of course you are. Don't be ridiculous."

Ridiculous? A grown man who dyed his hair for a silly haunted house gig is calling me ridiculous?

"Come along now," he said.

I shook my head and dug in my heels. "I'm only

selling tickets at this thing. I don't need to be in costume."

Crenshaw looked down his nose. "You do understand the concept of a haunted house, do you not?"

"I do. But I'm not going to be *in* the haunted house." I had to trot to keep up with him as he led the way toward the restrooms. I realized it was futile to keep arguing. As an amateur actor involved in the local theater scene, Crenshaw fancied himself a true thespian. He loved playing dress-up.

I unzipped the garment bag as we walked. "What is it anyway?" I asked, trying to look inside. "Please tell me I'm not the Bride of Frankenstein."

"Where's your Halloween spirit, Milanni? More to the point, where's your community spirit? You know Beverly's on a big push to raise the firm's visibility. As partners, you and I have a vested interest in promoting—"

"I know, I know. Hey, what is this? A *witch* costume?"

"What's wrong with a witch costume? It's a classic Halloween character."

"Never mind. Here we are. Wait for me?" I dashed inside the ladies' room without waiting for a response.

Luckily, the facilities at Fieldstone Park were well-maintained. Still, I wasted no time in switching outfits. In spite of my protests, I didn't want to disappoint our boss. As it turned out, the gauzy black dress with jagged trim and bell sleeves wasn't too terrible. But the accessories were another story. I cringed as I pulled the bushy, Elvira-style wig over my own chestnut-colored hair. The artificial black mop made my face appear wan and washed out.

Or, I realized as I peered into the mirror above the sink, maybe I just needed to get outside more. Now that I thought about it, I couldn't remember the last time I'd sat outdoors in the sun. What kind of Wiccan was I? I'd been so busy at work; I had let the entire summer pass me by without a single trip to a lake or swimming pool. If I didn't make a change soon, the last mild days of autumn would pass me by, too.

I grabbed the garment bag, now containing my business suit, and joined Crenshaw, who had just emerged from the men's room in full creature-of-the-night formal wear. I did my best not to laugh, but he looked none too happy. "Where's the rest of your costume?" he demanded.

"This is good enough."

"Well, at least put on the hat." He gestured toward a pocket on the outside of the garment bag. "A witch isn't a witch without a pointy hat."

Ha! I thought. Out loud, I muttered, "Shows how much you know."

"I beg your pardon?"

"Nothing," I said, as I donned the pointy hat.

The truth was, in all my years of being Wiccan, from the time I discovered and embraced the path at age sixteen to now, I had never been offended by the image of the Halloween witch. Some might disagree, but I didn't view the stereotypical witch's costume as demeaning to my religion—or even some kind of cultural misappropriation. How could it be, when the "wicked witch" archetype predated Wicca by hundreds of years? Besides, fictional witches came in all stripes. Considering all the pop-culture teenaged witches, not to mention the Harry Potter franchise, witches were as likely to be seen as cool rather than scary. After all, we could wield magic!

Even so, I had to draw the line at the warty rubber nose and sickly green face paint. A girl was entitled to a smidgen of vanity.

Now, as we left the maple grove and made our way back to the entrance of the barn, I was glad to see the business crowd had already gone inside. I took my place behind the cash register. Crenshaw paused at the counter. "Say, do you happen to have a mirror in your handbag? I'd like to check my stage makeup."

"Sure," I said, reaching into my purse. "But it won't do you much good, if you can't see your reflection."

Crenshaw stared at me, evidently not getting the joke. I waved a compact mirror in front of his face as if to clue him in.

While we bantered, a side door opened and a middle-aged man in a charcoal-gray suit came barreling out of the barn. I recognized him as Tadd Hemsley, a local business owner who advocated for small farmers. He was usually pleasant enough, but now his lips curled above his grizzled soul patch as he glared at his cell phone. I could relate to the sentiment. My own phone had buzzed in my handbag at least three times in the last five minutes.

As Tadd passed us, he bumped into Crenshaw

and glanced up. His frown turned into a smirk. "I always knew lawyers were bloodsuckers," he drawled. "I guess this proves it."

Crenshaw flushed beneath his white makeup, and I suddenly felt sorry for him. *That was a cheap shot*, I thought. With a strange sense of almost-parental indignation, I stood taller, ready to defend my over-eager colleague. But it was too late. Tadd Hemsley was already halfway down the sidewalk with his phone pressed tightly to his ear.

I looked at Crenshaw and tugged lightly on his cape. "Still want the mirror?"

"Never mind that. I need to join the monsters inside." He straightened his stiff high collar, then disappeared behind the ragged strips of black cloth that blocked the main entry to the "haunted barn."

I shook my head as I peeked at my own reflection, then tossed the mirror back into my purse. While I appreciated the fun factor, Crenshaw was right that my spirit was lacking tonight. Halloween was usually one of my favorite holidays, especially since it coincided with Samhain, one of Wicca's most important festivals. I was probably just too tired to be in the mood tonight. I still had a week before the big day. I'd find the spirit before then.

As I unlocked the cash register, I became aware of a man loitering near the picnic tables. He appeared to be alone, some distance apart from the group of teens clustered a few feet away. He caught me eyeing him and ambled up to the counter.

"Open for business?"

"Uh, sure." I glanced at my watch. "Doors will open to the public in about five minutes."

"I'll take one ticket," he said.

I took his cash and handed over a ticket. He accepted it but didn't leave right away. He seemed to be studying me, which made me slightly uncomfortable. He had a friendly enough face and wasn't bad looking—with his blue-gray eyes and smattering of freckles, he reminded me of my mother's Irish cousins—but wasn't it odd for a forty-something-year-old man to hang out at a place meant for kids?

Perhaps he read my mind. He cleared his throat and looked away. "I haven't been to one of these things in ages. Guess I'm feeling a little nostalgic." He flashed me a small grin. "Is it very scary?"

"Oh, I'm sure it's a fright fest in there." I smiled. "You'll be fine."

A small line had formed behind him, so he finally stepped aside. I sold tickets to several teenagers and a number of giggling tweens, then looked up in surprise at the last two people in line—a bubbly blonde with a large smile and a sharply dressed man with a glint of amusement in his warm brown eyes. If I didn't know better, I might have mistaken them for a couple.

"Hey, you two." I looked from my best friend, Farrah Anderson, to my colleague, Randall Sykes. Although Farrah was a lawyer, too, she had left the traditional career path to become a legal software salesperson, which perfectly suited her outgoing personality. Randall, on the other hand, was cool and laid back with a wry sense of humor. Catching a glimpse of Randall's single gold earring, it occurred to me that he and Farrah might not be a bad match after all. "What are you guys doing here?"

"Oh, my God," said Farrah, lifting the ends of my black wig. "This . . . is . . . awesome."

Randall chuckled. "Your friend stopped by the office just as I was heading over here. How is everything?"

"Peachy," I said drily. "There's nowhere I'd rather be right now."

Farrah whipped out her cell phone and snapped a picture of me. She probably had several shots before I realized what she was doing and held up my palm. She laughed. "What's the matter? You make a perfectly lovely witch. There's something so, I don't know, *natural* about seeing you this way."

I wrinkled my nose at her. Farrah loved that I was Wiccan and that she was privy to my secret. While I trusted her like a sister, I sometimes feared that, with her overabundant enthusiasm, she might inadvertently spill the beans. Given how judgmental some people could be about unconventional lifestyles and lesser-known religions, I felt I had to be discreet to protect my job. Not that I thought Randall would care, but he wouldn't be above some good-natured teasing. And that wasn't the kind of attention I wanted at work. Heck, even my family back in Nebraska didn't know I was Wiccan.

Luckily, at that moment a skeletal arm beckoned the group inside, and I was left alone with my thoughts. I exhaled softly as I gazed across the empty ball field at a line of trees in the distance, the shadowy branches swishing in the breeze. It was a quiet evening. The low rumble of ghostly sound effects emanating from the barn, punctuated by the occasional bloodcurdling shriek, made for an eerie backdrop. My mind flickered briefly to Mrs. Hammerlin and the strange noises she'd been hearing in her new home. I was sure they'd turn out to be as innocent as the ones within the barn.

Thinking of Mrs. Hammerlin, I reached for my phone to check my messages. Sure enough, I had missed another call from the anxious woman. The other missed calls were from my office and from my boyfriend, Wes. I felt a twinge of guilt for not checking in with Wes sooner, but he knew I was working tonight. I shot off a quick text to let him know where I was. I would have added that I planned to stop by Mrs. Hammerlin's on my way home, but I was distracted by another person coming up the sidewalk. She wore a colorful kaftan with matching head scarf and walked with short, deliberate steps. For a moment, I wondered if she was another volunteer.

"Keli Milanni?"

"Yes?"

"I was told you would be here. I recognize you from your photograph." She spoke with a Caribbean accent and gazed at me with earnest ebony eyes. "I must speak with you. Please. It is urgent."

I glanced around the empty barnyard. *Who told her I'd be here? And where did she see my photograph?*

"What can I do for you, Ms. . . . ?"

"My name is Fredeline Paul. I need to speak with you about Josephine."

Josephine. Ms. Paul didn't provide a surname, but she didn't have to. There was only one Josephine she could mean: Josephine O'Malley—Josie, to her old friends, Aunt Josephine to me. The name brought up a rush of conflicting feelings: affection, curiosity, exasperation. Coating it all was a sense of frustration. Aunt Josephine was a mystery. I had never met her, yet I felt like I knew her—or at least a part of her. At one time, I'd even thought I might take after her. But, for some reason, she never let me find out.

"What about her?" I asked.

"She is missing."

CHAPTER TWO

Josephine O'Malley was my mother's older sister by five years. When my mom was twelve, Josie packed her bags, kissed her sister good-bye, and snuck off in the middle of the Nebraska night. She met up with her boyfriend, a college dropout who wrote beat poetry, boarded his 1969 Volkswagen Bus, and headed for the highway. She never looked back.

When I was growing up, not a whole lot was said about Aunt Josephine, especially around my grandparents. Although she did send cards and letters sometimes, they were few and far between, only adding to an overriding sense of disappointment and heartache. It was understood that Josie was the black sheep. Any references to her were usually accompanied by shame-filled terms such as *ungrateful, irresponsible,* and even *traitor.* Now and then, someone outside of the family laughingly called her hippie-dippie or, more kindly, free-spirited.

As I got older and found myself diverging from the

religious and ideological beliefs of my upbringing—
and toward magical practices such as Wicca—I
became more and more fascinated by Josephine.
The postcards she sent to my mom came from all
corners of the world and were often sprinkled with
Latin sayings, which seemed so poetic and sophisti-
cated to me. I moved to Edindale, Illinois, partly
because I knew she had once lived here. And I was
always delighted when I received my own cards
from her. They were always warm, cheerful, and
personal, as if I were her favorite person in the
world. I even got to speak to her directly one time.

It was about eight months ago, on New Year's Day.
She had tracked me down at a nightclub (which
proved my suspicion that she had been keeping
tabs on me), and left a phone number—a local
number, no less. I called it, and a man answered.
But when I asked for Josephine, I was immediately
rebuffed.

"There's no one here by that name. You must
have the wrong number."

That's when I remembered that the person who
had called the nightclub had left initials instead of
a name. "How about AJ?" I quickly asked, before
the man could hang up.

His voice softened. "Ah. You must be Keli.
Hold on."

A moment later, she was on the other end of the
line. Her voice was clear as a mountain stream, her
manner sweet and disarming. "Keli, love!" she had
said, as if this weren't the first time she'd spoken to
me in all my thirty-two years.

I had so many questions for her, and she patiently answered them all. Well, the first ones, at least.

Why had she left home at seventeen? She was young and in love, craved adventure, and felt stifled by small-town life. Why didn't she ever go back? Her parents were unforgiving. Her father had threatened to disown her if she didn't come home, which only strengthened her resolve. (I hadn't known this about my late grandfather. I wondered if my mother knew.)

And what had she been doing all these years? Why the sporadic postcards with no return address? Why all the intrigue? She'd laughed at this last question, but answered without hesitation. "I had found my calling, love. I read *Silent Spring* and knew my mission in life."

Silent Spring. I was familiar with the book, an instant bestseller when it was released in the early 1960s. I knew that the author, Rachel Carson, was considered the mother of the environmental movement. "You became an environmentalist?" I asked. This wasn't a surprise given that my aunt had once lived in a commune called the Happy Hills Homestead.

"Absolutely!" she replied. "As soon as I learned that all of nature is interconnected, and that chemical pesticides are so destructive, I was inspired to spread the knowledge. My goal is to promote organic farming as far and wide as possible—which brings me to the help I need from you. I have some deliveries for the Edindale area that must be made as soon as possible, and I can't do it. My train leaves early tomorrow morning. Gil can't do it, since he's going to Tibet. There's no one else I trust, besides you. I know I can trust you."

At that point, my head was spinning. Deliveries? Tibet? Gil? "Wait. You're leaving? But I was hoping to meet you. Where are you going?"

"Oh, you're a dear. We actually have met, though I'm not surprised you don't remember. I've so enjoyed following your life and your career. But, really, it's safer—better this way."

And that's where all her previous candor evaporated into thin air: Did she have a cell phone? No. Was there another number where she could be reached, or a forwarding address? No and no. Could she tell me when she'd be coming back? No.

A couple days later a package appeared on my doorstep. There was no note, but I knew it was from her. Inside was a box filled with a dozen or so large manila envelopes, and on each envelope was the address of a small farm. Over the next few weekends, I drove all over the county dutifully delivering the envelopes. At one of the farms, a woman opened hers in front of me, so I was able to see the contents: several packets of heirloom seeds. However, at every single place I visited, not one person had ever heard of Josephine O'Malley. Or Josie, or AJ. They only knew that the packages were from Sister Seeds, a nonprofit that provided open-pollinated vegetable seeds to any farmer who pledged to grow the plants organically and save the harvested seeds at the end of the growing season. They also agreed to send back part of the seed harvest, which could then be given to other farmers. The circle of life in action.

At each farm, I also asked if anyone knew of a man by the name of Gil. After a string of nos, I finally got lucky: someone asked if I was talking about Gil Johnson, the owner of a canoe shop a few miles outside Edindale. I looked him up and, sure enough, his phone number matched the one Josephine had used the one time I spoke with her. As it happened, Gil was out of the country for the winter, but as soon as he returned in the spring I called him.

Gil Johnson was a pleasant, talkative guy. In fact, he was so chatty I found it difficult to ask about Josephine. After introducing myself, I made the mistake of opening the conversation by mentioning that I understood he had spent the winter in Tibet. This launched him into an impassioned speech about the plight of the Tibetans and his work on their behalf. I learned all about his travels to India every year, where he stays in an ashram, and how he teaches English to the villagers. Every time I interjected a question about Josephine, Gil managed to change the subject.

"Do you know where she went when she left Edindale, or where she is now?" I asked.

"Oh, someplace out west. Could be Arizona, or New Mexico, or California. Probably Arizona. There's a reservation there she likes to visit. Do you know that Native Americans are still fighting for their lands to this very day? From loggers and cattle ranchers to oil companies, somebody is always trying to steal their sacred land. Most recently—"

"Do you know when Josephine will be coming back to Edindale?"

"It's hard to say. She's not one for planning. She likes to be spontaneous and drop in on you like a surprise party. You might say her migratory habits are as unpredictable as the weather. Speaking of the weather—"

"But what if someone needs to reach her?" I asked, feeling increasingly frustrated. "What if I'd like to send her a message?"

"Well, now, that's a tricky proposition. Josie likes to lay low. She's not one to pin down. I think it's best if you just let Josie be Josie. You be you, and I'll be me. As Buddha said, 'It is better to conquer yourself than to win a thousand battles. Then the victory is yours. It cannot be taken from you.'"

In other words, mind my own business. Terrific.

So, that's why I wasn't particularly concerned when Fredeline Paul told me that Josephine was missing. *Missing* was her regular state of affairs.

"I'm afraid I don't know where to find her, Ms. Paul. And, to tell you the truth, I don't think Josephine wants to be found. I'm sorry."

Fredeline's brow wrinkled as she slowly shook her head. "She was to meet me at the airport. It was all arranged. She said she would hire a car service, but there was no car. I had to pay for a taxi. It was very expensive."

"Oh. Well, that does seem odd. But I don't know how to reach her. Except . . . wait a minute." I consulted my cell phone, then wrote down two names and phone numbers on the back of my business card and gave it to Fredeline. "These are friends of Josephine's. They've never been particularly help-ful to me, but maybe you'll have better luck."

She took the card with a perplexed look and mentioned she was staying at Gayle's Guesthouse, a quaint inn on the edge of town. "Please call me if you hear from her."

"Uh, yeah. Okay." I knew that wasn't likely.

CHAPTER THREE

I was still thinking about Josephine when I headed to Mrs. Hammerlin's house later that night. I couldn't seem to get my aunt out of my mind. It had been six months since Gil Johnson gave me the brush-off, and I hadn't heard a peep from Josephine. Reflecting back on my conversation with Gil, it seemed clear that he was trying to protect her. Or at least protect her privacy. But why? Why would she want to "lay low," as Gil had put it? He almost made it sound like she was a fugitive or something.

Gil's was one of the names I had given to Fredeline Paul. I wondered if Ms. Paul was able to reach him. *Maybe I should call him again myself,* I thought, as I parked my car along the curb on Hamilton Street.

After leaving the haunted barn, I changed out of my costume before retrieving my car from the parking lot. All my friends had gone home, so I was alone as I walked up the dark sidewalk to Mrs. Hammerlin's new house. With the bright moon spotlighting wispy clouds overhead and the intermittent breeze skittering dried leaves across my path, it felt like the perfect October night for telling ghost stories.

Like the other homes on this street, Mrs. Hammerlin's was a tall, graceful Victorian with gingerbread trim, steep gables, and a broad wraparound porch. She had decorated her porch with a cluster of fat pumpkins and colorful mums. The autumn wreath on the front door shook when it swung open.

"Oh, thank goodness you're here! Please come in. Follow me."

Grace Hammerlin, still willowy and vibrant in her seventies, led me through the elegant foyer, past the formal dining room, and directly to the kitchen at the back of the house, where a large bay window provided a nice view of the cemetery next door. I wondered if this was the cause of her overactive imagination. The old graveyard behind the backyard fence had been a selling point when the house was on the market: "Guaranteed peace and quiet . . . A perpetual, open view of nature out your back door." But I knew it wasn't for everyone. The houses on either side of hers had both sat vacant for quite a while. Perhaps living so close to the nonliving was getting to her.

Then I noticed the small rectangular table on one side of the kitchen. It was set for two, with plates, cups, bowls, a tea tray, cheese and crackers, a dish of grapes, and a plate of cookies.

"Sit, sit! Have a snack. Is hot tea all right, or would you prefer coffee or cocoa?"

"I can't stay long," I said apologetically.

"You can eat while we chat. Aren't you hungry? You look like you could use a meal. You're so thin." She laughed nervously, and I felt a pang of sympathy. Watching her flutter about, pouring ice water and taking cold cuts out of the refrigerator, I realized the poor woman must be lonely. She had been widowed for less than a year, and now she was in a huge, unfamiliar house all by herself.

"Tea sounds good," I said. "Can I pour you a cup?"

She joined me at the table. To be polite, I ate a grape and tried not to think about the late hour. "How's the unpacking going?" I asked.

"I have only a few boxes left, and a couple things yet to buy for the guest rooms. But with everything that's been happening, I don't see how I'm going to be able to open by Thanksgiving—which is what I promised Father Gabe." I recalled that she intended to open her home as a temporary safe house for abused women through a program run by her church. She twisted her napkin nervously. "I can't have my guests being tormented by restless spirits. Those poor women have been through enough already."

"You know," I began, "strange noises are common in old houses."

"It's not house noises. It's something *inside* the house." She looked around. "I was hoping it would happen while you're here, but it's so unpredictable. Sometimes I hear sounds coming from the basement." She cast a fearful glance toward a closed door in the corner. "Sometimes I hear it upstairs.

And sometimes it appears to be coming in from outside, as though carried in the wind."

I frowned. "What do the inside noises sound like? Creaking? Clunking?"

"Clunking, banging. Scratching."

"Scratching? Maybe you have an animal. Mice in the walls or a squirrel on the roof."

She shook her head. "I haven't seen any droppings. And, like I said, the sounds are all over. The whistling is the worst." She shivered. "It's always at night. Wakes me up at all hours."

"Whistling like a bird? Or a person?"

"It's like . . . a banshee. An otherworldly, moaning banshee."

She'd stumped me there. I sipped my tea as I tried to imagine something mundane that might sound like a whistling banshee.

"There have been other things, too," she continued. "Doors opening by themselves. Things moving on their own or disappearing, like my gloves—there one minute, gone the next."

"You don't think you misplaced them? I do that all the time."

"No." She shook her head firmly. "I'm telling you, there is *something* in this house. Something uneasy, restless. Father Gabe came over and blessed the house, but I don't think he used enough firepower, if you know what I mean. I've been doing some research, and I found this outfit out of St. Louis, a paranormal society. They have a medium who specializes in clearings—that's what they call it when they rid your home of unwanted spirits. But it's not cheap. That's what I wanted to talk to you about. I think the seller ought to foot the bill."

I fought the urge to raise my eyebrows. There was no way we'd get the seller to pay for a "spirit clearing," especially since the title had already transferred to Mrs. Hammerlin. Besides, in Illinois, sellers are not obligated to disclose any deaths that occurred in the house—if that was what she was driving at.

"A neighbor told me about the people who lived here a few years ago," she went on, "before the fellow who sold the house to me. It was an older couple who had one grown daughter who'd moved away. Well, first the wife died in the house, then a week later, the husband died. Also in the house. Two deaths! That might explain why the noises are all over the place."

I could tell there was no point in arguing with her. Instead I nodded. "I have an idea. I have a friend who might be able to help. She's a gifted psychic, skilled at tapping into other planes beyond the physical. She could walk through your house and see if she senses anything unusual. She can also perform a spiritual space cleansing if you'd like."

Mrs. Hammerlin readily agreed. "That would be wonderful. Can she come tomorrow?"

"I don't know, but I can certainly speak with her tomorrow." I pushed back my chair. "Thank you for the tea."

"Let me wrap these cookies for you," she said. "You can take them home."

While she rummaged in the pantry for a plastic

container, I took our cups to the sink. I peered out the window at the headstones glowing in the moonlight. It was a peaceful sight, though melancholy and a little eerie. I wasn't sure if I'd choose to live so close to a cemetery myself.

As I gazed at the silent gravestones, a movement caught my eye. I couldn't be sure, but I thought I saw a shadowy figure flit beneath the trees and disappear behind a mausoleum. I shivered involuntarily.

Maybe it was just my imagination. Mrs. Hammerlin's superstitions were rubbing off on me.

It was after midnight when I finally unlocked the door to my town house and let myself in. All was quiet and dark, the only illumination coming from a night-light in the kitchen—providing just enough light to see the note on the counter.

Sorry I couldn't wait up. I'm beat—and will be up at dawn again tomorrow. But the rest of the day can be ours—I hope. —W

I sighed. Wes and I had been a couple for nearly two years, but we'd been living together for only a month and a half. After we made the decision on New Year's Eve, we realized it made the most sense for Wes to finish out the lease on his apartment and then move in with me. I spent the intervening months cleaning out closets and making space for a housemate. I was thrilled to finally have him here. He was everything I ever wanted in a man: honest, thoughtful, interesting, and kind. It didn't hurt that he also had rock star good looks and eyes that could still smolder. And yet . . . all was not bliss.

What was the problem? I pondered this question as I brushed my teeth and undressed in the bathroom. Was I hung up on petty domestic complaints—socks on the floor, volume too high on the TV? Or had I lived alone for so long that I was finding it hard to let go of my deep-rooted sense of independence?

All I knew was that we seemed to be out of sync lately, especially with our schedules. In order to pursue his passion for photography as an art form and not just a job, Wes had been getting up early to take advantage of the golden hour shortly after sunrise. I, on the other hand, had been working late, both at the office and at home.

That must be it, I decided. Work-related stress was spilling over at home. For the past few weeks I'd been spending extra hours at the office preparing for a custody hearing. With children at stake and a client on edge, I wasn't about to show up underprepared. Fortunately, my hard work paid off and we had a happy outcome. I should have been out celebrating, or taking a much-needed breather. Instead, my boss piled on networking events and community service.

I tiptoed into the bedroom and slipped under the covers next to Wes. I supposed the truth was a combination of things. I had to admit I was still getting used to the idea of sharing my home and my life with another person. But I had no regrets. As I snuggled up against Wes's warm body, I was grateful that the next day was Saturday. I could sleep in and spend a deliciously languid day hanging out with my man.

Unfortunately, it wasn't to be. My plans fell apart with the ring of the phone at 7:00 a.m. It was my boss, Beverly Olsen.

"Keli, sorry to call you so early," she said, not sounding sorry at all. "The photographer wants to do our group photo this morning at the office. Do you think you can be here by nine? Wear your navy suit and a white blouse. And maybe a string of pearls, if you have any."

"Photographer?" I rubbed my eyes and tried to remember.

"From the Bar Association magazine," she said impatiently. "For my profile, remember? They want to include a photo of all the partners."

"Oh, right. Okay. No problem."

I hung up and looked at the empty space in the bed next to me. Then I heard a sound in the doorway. Wes came in and leaned against the jamb. Even through my bleary eyes, he looked incredibly sexy with his dark, tousled hair and unshaven jawline. He had his camera around his neck and a scowl on his lips. "You're leaving?"

"It won't take long," I said. "Just a quick little photoshoot at the office."

"Right." He knew there was no such thing as a quick photoshoot. He also knew I never took quick trips to the office. This wasn't the first time I'd been called in on a weekend.

So much for my lazy Saturday. I dragged myself to

the shower and got ready for work, grumbling to myself the whole time. A little while later, I arrived at the office dressed for success—or at least the appearance of success—in a pressed suit, sensible pumps, and smooth French twist.

My boss took one look at me and shook her head. "Hair down, Keli. Pulled back is a bit too severe. Let's not hide your lovely locks. We're going for approachable here. Trustworthy."

I opened my mouth to respond but found myself at a loss for words. Beverly's own silver-streaked auburn hair was piled high on her head. I supposed that was different. Her trademark coiffure was like a crown, marking her as the boss lady.

I slipped into my private office to brush out my hair—and to suppress the negative feelings that threatened to reveal themselves in my expression. I seemed to be doing that at work a lot lately, tamping down feelings of discontent.

After a quick round of *ujjayi* breathing, which I had learned in yoga class, I returned to the lobby with my game face on. The photographer was still conferring with Beverly and adjusting the lights, so I joined the other partners, Kris, Randall, and Crenshaw, at the coffee bar in Beverly's private lounge. Crenshaw was reading something out loud from his smartphone.

"How awful," said Kris. "I can't imagine finding—" She stopped midsentence when she saw me.

"What's awful?" I asked.

"A body was found in the woods early this morning,

out near Briar Creek Cabins," said Crenshaw. "A woman, shot once in the back. Evidently the authorities haven't been able to ID her yet."

A feeling of dread coursed through my veins, and I grabbed the back of a nearby armchair to steady myself.

"Yeah," said Randall. "For once someone besides you found the body."

"I'm sorry," said Kris, touching my arm. "This must bring back bad memories for you."

I shrugged and reached for the glass water pitcher. *Right*, I thought. *That must be it.* My past experiences finding murder victims must account for the slight tremble in my hand as I poured a glass of water.

Beverly called us to the lobby. I put the grim news out of my mind and plastered a smile on my face. It was time to look happy. And trustworthy.

The photoshoot proceeded along fairly smoothly, though the photographer had to keep telling Crenshaw to lower his chin. After several shots, we took a short break while the magazine people set up a new location. That's when I heard my cell phone ring. I dug it out of my purse, expecting it to be Mrs. Hammerlin again. To my surprise, the display said *Edindale Police.*

"Hello?" I answered, my heart already beating faster.

"Keli Milanni? This is Detective Adrian Rhinehardt."

I swallowed hard. Adrian Rhinehardt was a homicide detective. Our paths had crossed more than once over the past couple of years. "Hello, Detective," I said. "What can I do for you?"

"I'm sorry to have to ask this, but could you please meet me down at the medical examiner's office? There's a body here I'm hoping you can identify."

Chapter Four

My colleagues offered to accompany me to the ME's office, but I turned them down. There was only one person I wanted at my side. Wes made it to my office in record time, and we drove to the county building together. Detective Rhinehardt met us at the entrance.

Stocky and muscular, with a buzz cut that de-emphasized his receding hairline, Adrian Rhinehardt was a man who inspired confidence. In all my previous encounters with him, he'd been cool and serious, but today he seemed warmer. I noted his rumpled dress shirt and the lines around his eyes and wondered if, like me, he'd been called in to work on his day off.

He led us to a small, private room decorated in soft blues and greens. "Please sit down," he said, motioning to a pair of upholstered chairs situated on one side of a large table-like writing desk. He sat on the other side, just as the door opened and a petite woman slipped quietly inside. "This is Amy

Tracy," the detective said. "She's a grief counselor, here to lend her support."

We shook hands and took our seats. I sat on the edge of the chair and squeezed my hands together to keep them from shaking. I had never done anything like this before and didn't know what to expect. The support of Wes's steady hand on my back helped, but only a little.

Detective Rhinehardt gathered a stack of papers in front of him and tapped them together. "First off," he said, "in case you're wondering, we're not going over to the morgue. Nowadays, the ID is done by photo."

"Oh! I didn't know." That made me feel slightly better.

Rhinehardt cleared his throat. "Now then, I am truly sorry for asking you to come here like this. I know this isn't pleasant. But I have to ask—would you mind sharing your thoughts? You didn't seem very surprised when I called." He paused a beat and eyed me carefully. "Do you have any idea who this woman might be? She was found in Shawnee this morning without any identification. She had a purse on her with some cash, but there was no driver's license or any credit cards."

I nodded. "Yes. I—I do have an idea. I have an aunt who was supposed to pick someone up at the airport yesterday and didn't show."

Rhinehardt dropped his shoulders in a subtle gesture of relief. His job had just gotten a whole lot easier. "Okay," he said. "Now I just need to get some information from you." He pulled out a form from his stack of papers and began filling out the top section.

Amy leaned forward. "Were you and your aunt close?"

"Actually . . . not very. I didn't even know she was in town." I turned to Rhinehardt. "How did you know to call me?"

"There was a paper in her pocket," he said. "Here, I'll show you." He retrieved a Ziploc bag from a nearby box and laid it flat on the table. Inside was a handwritten note. It appeared to be a to-do list:

   — *See Ricki*
   — *Pick up Fredeline*
   — *Call Keli*

When I recognized my phone number printed next to the name "Keli," a small cry of sadness escaped my lips. This was really happening.

"Fredeline is the woman who flew in to see my aunt," I told the detective. "She told me she was looking forward to finally meeting her. I guess they had corresponded only by letter and phone." *In typical Josephine fashion.*

I provided Rhinehardt the contact information Fredeline had left with me. Then I told him the details he needed for his form—my own contact information, as well as Josephine's full name, age, and next of kin. When he finished writing, Rhinehardt sat back and peered carefully at me once again. "How are you doing? Would you like a glass of water? Coffee?"

"No, thank you." I appreciated his solicitude, but I was anxious to get on with it already. I was also hoping he would answer some of my own questions when we were through.

"Okay." He pulled a manila envelope from the evidence box, set it on the table, and touched it with his finger. "There's a single photo in here," he said. "It's the face only. There are no marks, no indication of trauma. Are you up for taking a look? Just to confirm it's her?"

Amy leaned in and spoke gently. "You can take your time. There's no rush."

I took a deep breath. As distressing as it might be, I did want to see the photo. I hated the circumstances, but I wanted to see her face. For years I had wanted to meet her, and I was curious about what she looked like. There was only one problem. Since I *didn't* know what she looked like, I wouldn't be able to provide a positive ID.

I thought for a moment, then had an idea. "Is it okay if I call someone to join me? It's someone else who knew Josephine, perhaps even better than I."

Rhinehardt agreed. I stepped out of the room and placed the call to Fern Lopez, an old acquaintance of Josephine's from her commune days. In spite of Fern's past reticence whenever I asked her about my aunt, I felt sure they were still in touch. Her reaction when I explained where I was, and why, confirmed my hunch. She said she'd come right away.

Half an hour later, I was seated across from Rhinehardt once again, with Wes on my left and Fern Lopez on my right. She wore a paint-splattered smock over faded jeans, and had her long, gray-streaked black hair pulled back into a loose ponytail. Specks of blue paint dotted her sun-browned face.

After Rhinehardt took her information, writing "friend" for relationship to the deceased, he brought out the dreaded envelope once again. This time, when he asked if we were ready to see the photograph, we both nodded. He slid it out of the envelope and placed it in front of us.

It was an 8 × 10 portrait of her head and shoulders. Her eyes were closed, her skin colorless and waxy. If not for the pale blue sheet at the bottom of the picture, I might have thought the photo was in black-and-white. Short gray hair lay in tumbled waves around her flat, lifeless face.

"That's her," said Fern.

Tears sprang to my eyes. Amy handed me a tissue, which I took and squeezed between my fingers. What got me, I realized, was not so much the confirmation that the dead woman was Aunt Josephine. Or even the picture itself. It was the shape of her face. The squarish angles, the wide mouth, and even the small nose—these were my mother's features. In a few more years, this could be my mother's face.

Rhinehardt put the photo away. After a moment of silence, he thanked us and offered his condolences. Then he pulled out a pad of paper. "If you don't mind, I have a few more questions. Ms. Lopez, when did you last see Josephine?"

Fern's eyes flicked to me, then down at the table. "May," she answered.

I knew it. Whenever I had questioned Fern about Josephine, she'd always said they had lost touch years ago. I knew she was holding back.

"And where was this?" Rhinehardt asked.

"At my place. She stayed with me for about a week."

"On vacation?"

"She liked to travel. She was passing through Edindale, heading east."

"How often did she pass through?"

Fern lifted her arms in a slow shrug, but Rhinehardt continued to look at her, his expression impassive. Finally, she relented. "Two or three times a year, maybe."

"What?" I blurted the word before I could stop myself. If Josephine visited Fern two or three times a year, that meant she'd been to Edindale at least twenty times since I'd lived here. And she never once stopped by to see me.

Wes reached for my hand and gave it a squeeze. Rhinehardt regarded me for a minute, then returned his attention to Fern. "Did you know she was in town yesterday?"

"No."

"Where else might she have been staying?"

"I couldn't say."

At that moment, a cell phone jingled loudly.

Wes jumped up and quickly quieted the phone in his pocket. "Sorry about that."

I took advantage of the interruption to change the subject. Recalling the newspaper article Crenshaw had read, I said, "Detective, is it true that she was shot in the back? Is that how she died?"

He hesitated, apparently reluctant to discuss an ongoing investigation. Then he seemed to remember why we were there—to identify the body of a loved one, not to be interrogated.

"That's correct," he said. "She had been shot only once. I can't tell you the distance or type of weapon. The medical examiner hasn't completed her report yet."

"Where exactly was she found?" I asked. "Had her body been moved after she was shot?"

Rhinehardt closed his notebook and stood up. "We don't think she was moved," he said. "I believe she died on the spot where she was found, a short distance from a hiking trail near Briar Creek Cabins. A guest in one of the cabins is the one who found her."

"And she was just found this morning? She was supposed to be at the airport yesterday afternoon. Isn't it odd that no one found her sooner? Also, did anyone hear a shot?"

Detective Rhinehardt smiled. "Ms. Milanni, I think you're in the wrong business. You should have been an investigator instead of an attorney." He opened the door, so we all stood and gathered our things. Amy Tracy gave Fern and me her business card and said to call anytime. Rhinehardt assured us that the police would be making all the inquiries I could think of, and more. He also promised to be in touch when Josephine's body and personal effects were ready to be released to the family, including some rings and a necklace she'd been wearing.

The family. I was going to have to call my mom with this terrible news. I wished I had more information to give her. She would have so many questions.

I turned back to the detective. "How long do you think it will be? Will you have to keep her until the case is solved?"

"No, that won't be necessary. Only until the autopsy is complete. It shouldn't be more than a week or so."

I nodded. "Okay."

"Do you need some help with funeral plans?" asked Amy. "There are two funeral directors here in town. Here, let me give you their numbers."

I squeezed my eyes shut tight. Funeral plans. One more thing I'd have to talk to my mom about. "Thanks, Amy." I took the paper from her and dropped it into my purse. Then I accepted Wes's outstretched hand.

As we left the building, my mind returned to Fredeline. The poor woman had been frantically trying to track down Josephine since the day before. I felt bad for not taking her more seriously. *I should call her,* I thought, *before the police seek her out for questioning.* Maybe I'd even invite her to join me for dinner. Wes would be working at the newspaper office this evening, and I had already made plans to hang out with Farrah at one of our favorite local wineries. I decided to extend the same invitation to Fern.

"No," she said bluntly. "I need to get home. I have things to do tonight."

"Oh," I said. "That's okay. I understand. Maybe another time."

Without answering, she reached into her patchwork purse and pulled out her car keys.

"Thank you for coming," I said. "I'm sure this must have been very difficult."

She paused and stared into the distance. "I liked Josie," she said. "I'm sorry this happened. But I can't say I'm shocked. Josie was a risk taker. She made sacrifices, she took risks, and, along the way, she made a number of enemies." Fern shook her head. "No. I'm not shocked at all."

CHAPTER FIVE

When I related what Fern had said, a few hours later at the Hillside Winery, Fredeline Paul wrinkled her brow. "Josephine was kind and generous. I don't know how she could have had one enemy, much less many."

"Fern Lopez." Farrah tapped her pink fingernails on the metal café table. "She's always been a little paranoid, right?"

"True." I sipped my wine, a warm, luscious burgundy, and eyed the view from the winery's patio. Rolling hills sloped toward a colorful tree line in the distance, where brilliant golden yellow and burnt orange leaves had an uplifting effect, even as several of them fluttered to the ground. After the difficult phone call with my mom, I was more than ready to have a drink or three.

I turned back to the group of women chatting companionably and nibbling on cucumber and watercress triangle sandwiches. Besides Fredeline, who was grateful to join us, and Farrah, who was happy to expand our gathering, I had invited my friend Mila Douglas. As a Wiccan high priestess and owner of my favorite occult gift shop, Mila had become something of a mentor to me, as well as a surrogate big sister. I found that she often lent a calm, reassuring presence.

"How long will you be in town, Fredeline?" Mila asked.

"It was supposed to be one week. My flight back to Port-au-Prince is next Friday. I don't know what I will do now." She fingered the strand of pastel clay beads that hung from her neck.

"Can you tell us about the program that brought you here?" I asked. "How did you become acquainted with Josephine?"

"She was a godsend," said Fredeline, her eyes brightening. "I had a dream to start a farming business in my village. I would employ women, and we would raise crops to feed our families and to sell. I applied for a microloan through an organization that collects donations from all over the world. Josephine selected my application and sent the money. But that was only the beginning."

"I've heard of organizations like that," said Farrah. "What a great service."

I nodded in agreement and made a mental note to look into it myself. I had donated money to relief efforts after the big earthquake in Haiti years ago, but I imagined the need was still vast.

"After she transferred the money, she began writing to us. She sent us nice letters filled with encouragement and advice, sometimes with extra checks. And I sent her pictures of our farm."

I sat up in my seat. "She gave you her address? Where did she live?"

Fredeline gave me a strange look before she answered. "I don't know where she lived. All our correspondence—the letters, the donations—came through her business, Sister Seeds. The address was a post office box in Arizona."

"Sister Seeds," I echoed. "I tried to look them up a few months ago when Josephine asked me to deliver seed packets for her. I couldn't find anything about the company. It seems surprising that they don't even have a website. Did you ever deal with anyone in the company besides Josephine?"

"There was a secretary who signed the checks. Her name was Jesse O'Mara, I believe. But your aunt was the heart and soul of the business." Fredeline shook her head. "I don't know anything about websites and such things. All I know is that Sister Seeds saved us. There was another company, a big multinational corporation that donated seeds to other farmers in Haiti. They said they were doing this wonderful thing, feeding the poor, but they weren't. Their seeds were bad. They were mutant, impotent, poison!" She scowled.

"You're talking about GMOs," said Mila. "I've read about this. Small farmers are upset because they become dependent on the corporations to provide new seeds every year. These crops don't produce their own seeds, so the farmers can never become self-sufficient."

"That's right," said Fredeline, her eyes flashing. "The farmers become prisoners, forced to always use the products of these giants, their herbicides, their chemically treated mutant seeds, all of it."

"So, with the money from Sister Seeds, you were able to buy heirloom seeds?" I asked.

"No, the money was for other expenses. The seeds she gave us for free. For two whole seasons, we grew beautiful plants from her seeds and harvested the seeds for the next year."

"That sounds right up her alley," I said.

"She was a good woman. She sent me money for a plane ticket, so I could come here and learn from her. She was going to teach me more about seed collection, as well as ways to expand to other villages. In essence, she was going to teach me to be a teacher."

She grew silent then, as she gazed into the bottom of her wineglass. I didn't know what to say. I looked helplessly from Farrah to Mila.

Mila patted Fredeline's arm. "It seems to me that you are already a teacher and a leader. You're leading by example. You also have a deep thirst for knowledge. You'll continue to learn and grow, I'm sure of it."

"You are very kind," said Fredeline.

"I'm so sorry she died before you could meet her," said Farrah, glancing from Fredeline to me. "Both of you." She sniffed and dabbed her eyes with her cocktail napkin.

"Don't be sad," said Fredeline. "At least, don't be *only* sad. Death is a natural transition. In Vodou, we believe that our spirits leave our bodies at death, but they do not depart the earth. For one year and one day, they stay in the air around us, before proceeding to the afterlife. I believe Josephine's spirit is still here, in the treetops and the grassy fields, on the breeze."

At that moment, the wind kicked up, lifting our hair and fluttering our dresses. Farrah's eyes widened, while Mila clapped her hands in delight. "Perfect!" she exclaimed.

I smiled in spite of myself.

We watched the sun set over the vineyard as we finished our sandwiches and tasted a few more varieties of wine. Mila switched to grape juice, since she was our designated driver, but the rest of us became increasingly relaxed as the evening wore on. At one point, Farrah became emboldened enough to ask the question I knew she had been dying to ask.

"Fredeline," she began, "what you said before, about your religious beliefs and spirits lingering after death, I thought that was really beautiful. But I have to ask: do you really practice voodoo?"

"Vodou, yes," said Fredeline. She didn't appear to be fazed by the question. "I heard some Americans are afraid of Vodou, no? They think it's hocus-pocus. Strange, evil stuff. They know so little."

"I'm not afraid," Farrah declared. "I'm just curious. I've never met a voodoo practitioner."

"There's a lot of misunderstanding about it," Mila said. "But Vodou really isn't that different from other mystical religions. Vodou practitioners believe there's a spiritual realm, where magic occurs, which can affect what happens to us in the physical realm. They also believe in one God who has many intermediaries, called Loa, who are sort of like spirit guides. Is that right, Fredeline?"

Fredeline looked impressed. "Very good. Yes. We honor the Loa. They are spirits, each with a particular specialty. We also venerate our ancestors." She shot Farrah a coy look. "We do *not* stick pins in dolls to punish our enemies."

Farrah laughed nervously. "I know. I didn't think that was real."

"Movies and TV spread a lot of false information," Mila said. "I don't think there's any non-mainstream religion that doesn't suffer some level of misunderstanding because of pop culture."

"For sure," I agreed. "Like witchcraft. It's precisely because of all this misapprehension that so many witches like me hide out in the broom closet."

Fredeline's eyes grew wide. "You practice witchcraft?"

For a moment, I froze. Had I made a mistake in outing myself in front of a new acquaintance?

"I practice witchcraft," Mila said cheerfully. "But you have to understand that 'witchcraft' is neutral, just like all forms of energy and energy manipulation. It can be used for good or evil." Her eyes twinkled as she spoke. "I use my power with a great sense of responsibility and gratitude."

I decided to own up. "I practice witchcraft, too. It's a particular type called Wicca, and it's definitely a good kind of magic. It's all about being attuned to nature."

"Ah. I see." Fredeline turned to Farrah. "And you? Are you a witch too?"

Farrah shook her head. "Not me. I'm too chicken to mess around with magic stuff. If I tried to cast a spell, I'd probably goof up and turn myself into a toad." She saw Fredeline's astonishment and laughed. "I'm only joking. Mostly."

Mila smiled and turned to Fredeline again. "You should stop by my shop sometime this week. I carry a few books on Vodou, as well as some statues and beads. I'd love to show them to you and hear more about your tradition."

"Thank you. I would like to come."

A waiter stopped at our table to light the candle centerpiece. Farrah checked her watch and exclaimed, "Oh, gosh! I gotta go soon. I have to get home and change into my dancing shoes. I have a late date at the Loose Rock. Don't want to keep Randy waiting."

I signaled for the check and grabbed my purse. "Who's Randy?" I asked.

"Randy Sykes."

I stared at her. "Randall? So, you *are* dating Randall! Since when?"

"Since a couple weeks ago, when I stopped by your office and you were too busy to take a break. He's super nice." She paused and gave me a plaintive look. "Isn't he? He's not going to turn out to be a jerk, is he?"

"No, no. He's fine. He's a nice guy. I just feel so out of the loop, that's all. Do you like him a lot?"

"So far, so good. He's really funny. Tells the best stories." Farrah waggled her eyebrows mischievously. "Plus, if we ever run out of things to talk about, there's always you. You'll give us loads of conversation fodder."

"Great." Just what I needed, my law partner hearing embarrassing stories about me from my best friend.

Then I had a worse thought. What would happen if Farrah dumped him? She'd been known to break a few hearts in her day. It was practically inevitable. That could make things a little awkward at work.

I sighed. *Oh, well.* There was nothing I could do about it.

As we headed to the parking lot, I began to brighten. Soon I'd get to finally spend some quality time with *my* favorite date.

Alas, for the second night in a row, the house was dark when I got home. This time, Wes wasn't in bed. According to the note on the counter, he'd come home from his newspaper job only to be called in to his second job as a backup bartender at his friend's nightclub—the very same club where Farrah was meeting *Randy*. I had half a mind to head there myself, but then I thought better of it. I could take advantage of having the house to myself.

I had been waiting for an evening alone like this.

I hurried to the bedroom and unlocked the cedar chest at the foot of the bed. *Let's see. What will I need?* I filled my arms with as much as I could carry—white altar cloth, silver chalice, book of spells, magic wand—and hurried to the spare bedroom where I'd moved the wooden console table that once stood under my bedroom window.

It wasn't that I couldn't perform spells with Wes in the house. When I closed the door to the spare room, he never disturbed me. He respected my privacy and my religion. Still, I felt freer and more relaxed with no one else at home. This way, if I felt moved to chant or raise my voice, I didn't have to feel self-conscious.

The spell I had been planning—and postponing—in recent weeks seemed frivolous now. I had intended to call upon Saturn for some assistance with time management, but there were more important things on my mind now. The loss of my aunt was starting to sink in.

I cleared off my altar table and covered it with the white cloth. As I gathered candles and arranged them on the table with the items from the chest, I thought about Aunt Josephine. For so long, she had been an almost mystical presence in my life, like a guardian angel or spirit guide. But she wasn't a spirit all those years. She was a flesh-and-blood human being. I had built her up in my imagination, but I never really knew her at all.

The way Fredeline had described her made my aunt seem like a really lovely, altruistic individual.

I was sure I would have liked her. And yet . . . what kind of person cuts herself off from her family—her loving, worried family—with no explanation? My mom was heartbroken when I told her I'd identified Josephine's body. Thinking of it now filled me with sadness once again. Her pain was double what it might have been: she lost not only a sister, but also the last vestiges of hope that they might one day be reunited.

Suddenly, my sorrow turned to anger. I stood before my altar and stared blindly at the cover of my spell book. Was Josephine really that selfish? That heartless? Why couldn't she have written a nice, long letter to my mom, instead of pithy postcards every few years? Apparently, she kept up a substantial correspondence with Fredeline Paul in Haiti, but she couldn't make an effort to connect with her only sister?

I dropped my head and blew out a frustrated breath. I was so conflicted. I supposed I shouldn't judge my aunt. As I'd already realized, I didn't know her. I didn't know what secrets she carried, or what internal demons she battled. All I could really do right now was to pray. In my own way, of course.

I picked up my wand, a tool I'd made myself from the branch of a willow tree. The smooth, carved wood felt good in my hand. With the fingers of my other hand, I traced the delicate vines that spiraled toward the tip, where I'd fastened a tiger's eye with copper wire—all the better to harness and direct magical energy. With a deep inhalation and measured exhalation, I walked slowly around the altar, using the wand to draw a circle in the air. At each cardinal direction, I paused to call the quarters:

> *Come now, guardian of Air, watcher from the*
>   *East,*
> *Breath of inspiration,*
> *Winds of knowledge,*
> *Poetry of the Pagan priest.*

> *Come now, guardian of Fire, watcher from the*
>   *South,*
> *Power of will,*
> *Heat of passion,*
> *Flaming from the dragon's mouth.*

> *Come now, guardian of Water, watcher from the*
>   *West,*
> *Drops of love,*
> *Stream of tears,*
> *Wash me in the rivers blessed.*

> *Come now, guardian of Earth, watcher of the*
>   *North,*
> *Peaks of strength,*
> *Trees of growth,*
> *Grounding roots send forth.*

Once the circle was cast, I paused before the altar and thought for a moment. Something was missing. To honor my aunt, I should have something to represent her.

Taking my athame, I cut an invisible doorway

in the air and stepped through it to exit the circle. I went straight to a stack of folders I'd left on a side table and found what I was looking for: a photo of Josephine. I had copied it from a book on Edindale history. The section on the 1960s and 1970s included a short description of the Happy Hills Homestead alongside a snapshot of three smiling hippies at the entrance to the commune: Josephine in the center, with flowers in her hair and freckles on her cheeks; Fern Lopez, in braids, to her left; and a long-haired man with a scraggly beard to her right. I'd blown up the photo back when I was asking around about Josephine, all to no avail.

Now, I found an empty frame in the closet and placed the photo in the frame. Then I reentered the sacred circle, closing the "door" behind me, and stood the framed photo on the altar. After a few centering breaths, I considered what I wanted to do. What did I want?

Peace.

Above all, I wanted peace. For my mom and our family. For myself. For Josephine. I hoped her soul was at peace, free from earthly worries.

With this in mind, I picked up a white candle and scratched the outline of a dove into the wax. I lit the candle and placed it next to the photo. Then, I opened the slim drawer below the altar table and rummaged through the bottles, vials, and jars until I found one that suited my intent: powdered vervain. Known as "the witch's herb," vervain was handy for many purposes, from pain relief and stress reduction to the promotion of peace and harmony. It was even known to enhance dream questing. I sprinkled the herb into my chalice, added water from a small pitcher, and swished it around. Perhaps I'd make a proper tea later, but this would do for now. I raised the chalice in a toast to the heavens and took a sip.

As I set the chalice back on the table, I closed my eyes. After three purposeful breaths, I murmured words that came from my heart:

> *Like the birds that fly so high,*
> *Above the trees, into the sky,*
> *Like the stream that flows to sea,*
> *Gently, dreamily, just to be . . .*
>
> *Peace shall come in its time,*
> *No wars to fight, no hills to climb,*
> *Peace at last, calm and free,*
> *As I will, so mote it be.*

I fell silent and remained standing with my eyes closed. Images began to appear in my mind. I saw Josephine as a girl, younger than the flower child in the photo. She was laughing, pushing a playground swing holding a smaller girl—my mom.

I saw her in flashes then, at different times in her life: a young woman, barefoot in a garden; then as an older woman, hiking through a desert. I saw her in all aspects women share with the Triple Goddess: maiden, mother, and crone. Josephine had lived a full life. She had lived to reach maturity.

But, no. That wasn't good enough. This wasn't right. Her life had been cut off too soon. Someone had ended it before her time.

I sighed and dropped my arms. There would be no peace for Josephine, nor for me. At least, not until I could figure out why she had been killed.

Clearly, Josephine had some unfinished business.

Chapter Six

Sunday morning, I awoke early with one thought in mind: *I need to go into the woods.* I wanted to find the spot where my aunt had died, and maybe even figure out why she was out there in the first place.

Not surprisingly, Wes had left before me again. This time, the note on the counter said, "Be back by noon." I shook my head, as I flipped it over to leave my own note for him, to tell him where I was going. *This can't be healthy,* I thought. *How long can a couple survive a relationship-by-note?*

Pushing aside that dreary thought, I hopped in my trusty silver-blue hybrid and headed to the country. Twenty minutes later, I parked near the office at Briar Creek Cabins and made my way to the trailhead behind the farthest log cottage.

I was familiar with this place. I'd stayed in one of the cabins before and found it to be charmingly rustic, though modern and comfortable. But the grounds were the real attraction. The woodsy, secluded property provided a nice, easy access point to Shawnee National Forest, and the owner of the cabins was welcoming to day visitors. Since he didn't advertise his open-door policy, the trails were generally quiet and tourist-free. One of the trails, I knew, had a partially hidden offshoot, which led to a large clearing, perfect for bonfire rituals.

But I wasn't here for a ritual today. Today's purpose was much more somber. As I walked through the cool, still forest, dried leaves crunching underfoot, my eyes searched the underbrush on either side of the trail.

Where was Josephine found? There were so many possibilities. Was it there, behind that fallen tree? Or there, in that tangle of wildflowers and ivy? Or down that ravine in the creek bed below?

I shuddered. I doubted if I'd ever feel peaceful in these woods again.

After crisscrossing the area for half an hour, I realized my quest was hopeless. If there had been any police tape out here, it must have been removed already. And apparently, I wasn't going to pick up any cosmic vibrations. *I should have made a divining rod,* I thought, half-seriously. I imagined myself holding a forked stick out in front of me like a wild-haired mountain woman and laughed out loud at the image.

"What's funny?"

I jumped and whipped around to see who had snuck up on me. I recognized him immediately. It was the solo guy from the haunted barn.

"What are you doing here?" I pressed my hand to my thudding chest.

He walked up to me, sporting a rueful grin. "Sorry

if I startled you. I thought you saw me when you turned around before. I've been behind you for the past ten minutes or so."

I narrowed my eyes. He'd been following me? I must have been so preoccupied peering into the trees that I'd failed to notice him. That wasn't good.

He stuck out his hand. "I'm Levi Markham. I'm staying at Briar Creek Cabins."

I hesitated for a beat, then shook his hand. "I'm Keli."

"You're the witch from the haunted house, aren't you? I thought you looked familiar."

I nodded. Though it was a little disconcerting to be alone in the woods with a strange man, I had to admit he didn't seem the least bit threatening. He wore nice blue jeans and a clean flannel shirt, and his sandy hair stuck up on one side as if he'd left the cabin without looking in a mirror. It was kind of funny, actually.

Then his earlier words sank in.

"You're staying at the cabins? Did you hear about what happened here yesterday?"

He nodded soberly. "You could say that. I'm the one who found the body."

"You are? Could you show me where?" It would seem my luck had turned.

"Well," he began.

"I'm not trying to be morbid," I hastened to say. "I'd just like to know what happened. The woman you found—she was my aunt."

"Oh. I'm sorry for your loss." He looked down

the trail behind me. "I should be able to find the spot again. It's probably half a mile from here, I think."

We headed down the trail together, side by side. He had several inches on me and probably twice the weight, which seemed to be all muscle, from what I could tell. Once again, I became conscious of how vulnerable I was. I'd come to the woods by myself many times in the past, but things were different now. It was as if Josephine's death had opened up a terrible possibility that hadn't existed before.

I cast a sidelong glance at Levi and caught him looking at me. He opened his mouth, then closed it and looked away. It seemed he wanted to make conversation but didn't know what to say. Or maybe he was just shy.

"So," I said, "are the other cabins occupied?"

"Not anymore. There were a couple families and a pair of honeymooners here over the weekend. They were supposed to check out today, but they all left yesterday as soon as the police had finished questioning them."

"I can't say I blame them." Considering the circumstances, I was surprised Levi hadn't left, too. "How long will you be staying?" I asked.

"As long as it takes," he answered.

I glanced at him again. "What do you mean?"

"Oh, I'm, uh, working on a book. I'm a writer. I find I can be more productive when I'm away from my usual routine and all its distractions."

"That makes sense." I knew all about distractions. "What kind of book are you writing?"

"Um. A thriller," he said vaguely. He slowed his steps, then stopped and pointed to the left of the path. "There. See that grouping of stones, about ten to fifteen feet from here? I thought it might be an old Native American cairn. I was checking it out when I saw . . . well, you know."

I left the trail and picked my way through the brambles to the pile of rocks. I supposed it might have been an ancient marker of some kind. I searched the ground around the stone, while Levi hung back, giving me space.

There was nothing to see, really. I didn't know what I expected. It wasn't like there could have been a chalk outline or anything. I couldn't even detect any broken twigs or flattened grass.

I paused. On second thought, there was a clump of weeds that seemed to have been cut back. I wondered if there had been blood spatters in that spot.

I straightened and turned slowly in place, looking all around. Why had Josephine left the trail? Or had she even been on the trail to begin with?

Levi sneezed, startling me out of my reverie. "Allergies," he muttered, as he pulled a handkerchief from his pocket.

I rejoined him on the trail, but I continued to stare at the spot he'd pointed out. "What time did you find her?"

"It was about six thirty or so. I was taking an early morning walk. I like to wake up with the birds, watch the sun rise. I sure didn't expect to find . . ." He trailed off and shook his head. "Poor lady. I'd just seen her a couple days before, too."

"You had?" I turned to him in surprise. "Where did you see her? Did you speak with her?"

"Yeah. Out here. We crossed paths a few times, earlier in the week. The last time was Thursday afternoon. She was real friendly. Said she was a bird-watcher. She was trying to spot some rare bird, I can't remember what it was called. She wanted to get a picture of it."

I glanced back at the rock pile. Was that why Josephine was out here? She was trying to capture a rare bird? Detective Rhinehardt didn't say anything about a camera. "So," I asked, "she was carrying a camera when you saw her?"

Levi smiled. "She had this huge, old film camera around her neck. It had a really wide, brown strap." He held his hands out to show how wide. "I don't know where she was gonna get the film developed, unless she had her own darkroom. I haven't seen a camera like that in ages."

"Did you see the camera when you found her body?"

"No. It wasn't there. I guess she didn't have it with her."

"Hmm. What was she wearing?"

"Oh, I don't know. A tan jacket, I think, and jeans. Hiking boots."

"I don't suppose you heard the gunshot, did you?"

Levi shook his head. "It might have happened when I went into town Friday evening. I needed a break from my writing, which is why I decided to check out the haunted house."

"Ah," I said. At least that was one mystery solved.

"Or," he went on, "it might have happened overnight. I was talking with Carl, the owner of the cabins. He said suppressors aren't legal in Illinois, but if it was a poacher, he was already breaking the law anyway."

"Wait. What's a suppressor?"

"A silencer. It muffles the sound of the rifle to protect the hunter's ears."

"You think Josephine was shot by a hunter?"

"It's possible. He might have been lost and didn't realize he was on private property, or maybe he was trespassing. Either way, he could have mistaken your aunt for a deer."

I squinted, as I gazed into the forest once again. Something didn't quite add up.

As soon as I got home, I gathered together everything I had on Aunt Josephine: all the cards, letters, and notes; her photograph; and even her old book about Johnny Appleseed, which my grandmother had given me when I was a little kid. I plopped down on my bed and spread everything out around me.

First, I picked up the postcards she had sent to me on my birthdays. Well, three birthdays to be exact: my tenth, twentieth, and thirtieth. Josephine was born in July, too, a few days and exactly thirty years before me. She had already left the commune and was apparently gallivanting around the country when I was born in Nebraska. Still, she seemed to get a kick out of our shared birthday month. In her brief messages to me, she called us "kindred spirits" and "two of a kind." I had always wondered why she wrote to me only once per decade. Was it because of some superstition?

Next, I picked up a piece of paper so old and fragile that I'd placed it in a plastic sleeve for safe-keeping. It was the original letter Josie had sent to her parents right before she left the commune. My mom had given it to me when she found it in my grandmother's things a couple years ago. She was hoping I might be able to find a clue as to where Josie went.

I tried, Mom, I really did. But I wasn't successful. Maybe I should have hired a private eye. Now it was too late.

I brushed away a tear and read the letter, for the thousandth time.

Dear Mom and Dad,

First off, I am doing well, so you can stop worrying about me. I hope you're all doing well, too. I miss you, but I have to live my own life.

Secondly, I won't be writing again for a while. We've been forced off our land, so I'll be hitting the road soon. I can't tell you exactly where I'm going, because I've been entrusted with a secret undertaking. But once my mission is complete, and once it seems safe again, I'll be returning to Edindale. This is where my heart belongs.

I'll keep in touch as I can.

Love,
Josie

P.S. Roger moved to Canada to avoid the draft. You may have been right about him after all.

Just then, there was a tap on the bedroom door, which I'd left ajar. I looked up to see Wes standing in the doorway. "Mind if I come in?"

I moved the papers over to make a place for him to sit.

"Did you get some good pictures this morning?" I asked.

"Yeah. Not bad. I still need to look through them and see how much I can use. But I think I'm getting close." He was working on creating a portfolio to shop around at all the area's art galleries.

"That's great." I reached over and turned down the right-side collar of his brown leather jacket to match the other side. He caught my hand and kissed my fingers.

"How are you doing?" he asked, searching my eyes.

"I'm okay. I just—" I broke off and dropped my eyes. "I feel like I let my mom down, you know, by not finding Josephine all this time—especially when she was right here, in my own town."

"Hey, don't think like that. I'm sure your mom doesn't blame you. She knows how flighty her sister was."

I shrugged helplessly. "Still, there are a lot of unanswered questions."

Wes looked at the papers on the bed. "So, that Haitian woman, Fredeline? Was she able to shed any light on what your aunt was up to? Or why she was in Edindale?"

"It had to do with her business, Sister Seeds. When I asked Fredeline about it, she couldn't tell me much. Apparently, the business address was a

P.O. box in Arizona. But, get this. When I asked Fredeline if she knew anyone else involved in the business, she mentioned that the donation checks weren't signed by Josephine. They were signed by someone else that Josephine said was the business's secretary, a woman named "Jesse O'Mara."

Wes cocked his head. "Jesse O'Mara? That sure sounds a lot like Josie O'Malley. Coincidence?"

"I don't think so. When I pressed Fredeline, she conceded that the signature on the checks might have been similar to Josephine's signature on her letters. She said she didn't think anything of it, though."

Wes narrowed his dark eyebrows. "Your aunt's behavior has always been a little sketchy, hasn't it? The way she always took off without leaving a forwarding address. It's like she was on the run or something."

I nodded slowly. The same thought had crossed my mind: Josephine didn't want to be found.

"I wish I knew what she was hiding." I picked up a postcard from California and turned it over in my hands. "Fern said Josie took risks. . . . I can't imagine she had much money to live on when she left the commune. Maybe she turned to a life of crime. Could she have committed shoplifting or robbery? Or some kind of fraud or embezzlement?"

Wes shook his head. "I don't know, babe."

I sighed. "As mysterious as she was, I never thought of her as a criminal." The problem was, I knew so little about Aunt Josephine. When it came right down to it, all I knew for sure was that she was free-spirited and passionate about the environment—especially planting seeds. I picked up the Johnny Appleseed book and flipped through the pages. "I wonder . . ." I said, half to myself.

"What is it?"

"Could Josephine have been involved in something illegal related to protecting the environment?"

"Like what?"

I set the book down and reached for my cell phone. "I don't know. But I do know someone who might."

CHAPTER SEVEN

Zeke Marshal was a cocky young millennial, who, nonetheless, wasn't completely devoid of charms. I'd met him back when we were both trying to dig up dirt on a businessman-turned-mayoral-candidate-turned-murder victim. Zeke had proved useful in the end—in spite of his propensity to flirt like James Bond and play games like the Riddler. He was a bit of a rogue character, who somehow seemed privy to all manner of information, both above- and belowground. When I asked him to meet me for coffee on the square, he said he could be there in five minutes.

"Let's make it thirty," I said.

When I hung up, Wes didn't exactly look thrilled. "Should I be jealous?" he asked.

"Don't be silly. I'm just gonna go gather a little intel. Hopefully." I looked down at what I was wearing—the same jeans and light sweater I'd worn on my hike in the woods—and decided it was good enough. I ran a brush through my hair, slipped on my brown boots, and promised Wes I wouldn't be gone long.

A short time later, I entered the Cozy Café and spotted Zeke at a table by the windows.

"Keli Milanni! It's about time you called me." He stood up and approached me with open arms.

"Hello, Zeke." I let him kiss my cheek as we briefly clasped hands, then took opposite seats in the red, vinyl booth. I had to smile as I assessed his outfit—black skinny jeans and a designer hoodie over a T-shirt featuring a garish skull face. His gelled hair stuck up in trendy spikes.

"Thanks for meeting me here." I turned over my coffee cup and waited while the waitress filled it. Zeke had already ordered a soda and a plate of fries before I arrived. "Where are you working these days?" I asked. "Still in IT?"

"Yes, ma'am. I work for the city now, at the Edindale library across the street. I take care of all their computer needs."

"I bet you do." *The little hacker.* He probably knew more about each one of Edindale's citizens than the tax authorities and advertisers combined. "So, have you seen Fern Lopez lately?"

He shrugged. "Now and then. How about you? How have you been? Are you enjoying your new gig as a big-shot law partner?"

"I'm not exactly a big shot, but I'm fine." I took a sip of coffee and decided to cut to the chase. "Hey, I have a question for you. Hypothetically speaking, if someone were to be 'on the lam,' for, let's say, committing an unlawful act in defense of the environment, what would come to your mind? Is there any—"

"Sorghum."

"Sorghum?"

"Yeah. The Sorghum bombing of seventy-eight. There was a series of bombings in the 1970s, culminating in the destruction of the headquarters of Sorghum, Inc., in Texas. You know, the chemical company? Years ago, they manufactured Agent Orange, and now they make GMOs. Real nice company."

"I've heard of them. I don't think I've heard of the bombing, though. Was anyone hurt?"

He nodded. "Two security guards were killed. The responsible parties were never caught. GEO was blamed at the time, but it wasn't them. They're not that obvious."

"What's GEO?"

Zeke stared at me without answering, until I remembered. "Oh, right." The Green Elf Organization was an underground network of eco-activists. Zeke had never come right out and told me, but I had gathered that the group was still alive and well in the Edindale area, and that he and Fern Lopez were key players. "So, GEO didn't take credit for the bombings?"

"No. They don't want trouble with the law. It might have been an offshoot, though. I don't know. Rumor was the feds had a line on some possible suspects at the time. I guess the trail grew cold, or they didn't have enough evidence, or whatever." He played with his soda straw, stirring the ice in his glass. "Why do you ask?"

"No reason." I said it automatically and immediately felt silly, especially when Zeke looked up with a smirk. If I expected him to keep feeding me information, I'd have to show a little trust. Besides, if anyone could keep a secret, I was sure Zeke could. At least, I was pretty sure.

I looked around the half-empty restaurant to make sure no one was within earshot, then kept my voice low. "Did you hear about the woman who was found in Shawnee yesterday, shot in the back?"

"Yeah. Shot by a hunter, right?"

I frowned. "Did someone come forward?"

"Not that I know of."

"Then why does everyone keep assuming she was shot by a hunter?" I recalled Levi saying the same thing.

Zeke shrugged. "I heard there was no evidence she'd been assaulted or robbed."

"How did you hear that?"

He ignored the question and said, "Why else would anyone shoot an old lady in the forest, except by accident?"

I crossed my arms and looked out the window. Zeke propped his chin on his hand and leaned in. "Who was she?"

I met his eyes. "Her name was Josephine O'Malley. Ever heard of her?"

He shook his head.

"She was a friend of Fern's. She lived in Edindale back in the early seventies, but then took off and moved from place to place. I'm not sure what she was doing exactly, except she had a business called Sister Seeds."

I thought I detected a flicker of recognition in Zeke's eyes, but he only grunted. "So, what's your interest?" he asked. "Did you know her?"

Did I know her? Not at all. I sighed. "She was my aunt. I suspect she might have been involved in Fern's . . . network. But Fern won't tell me anything."

Zeke regarded me thoughtfully, then tossed back the rest of his soda. "I'll talk to Fern and see what I can find out. Then I'll give you a call."

"You will? Thanks, Zeke. I really appreciate it."

"No sweat. But next time we meet, let's make it dinner and drinks. My treat."

"Um, yeah. Maybe. We'll see."

After leaving the café, I decided to walk over to Moonstone Treasures to say hi to Mila. She always went all out for the Samhain season, and this year was no exception. Her shop windows were decked out like a Gothic Halloween dinner party, with crystal beads draped over black candelabra, gold-rimmed obsidian goblets, painted skulls, and candles galore. On one side, a cauldron bubbled with manufactured fog, while on the other, a spooky raven perched on gnarly tree branches. It was delightfully chilling.

Inside was just as enchanting. I was greeted with the warm scents of pumpkin spice and cinnamon and the sight of vintage witchy art alongside cheery harvest decor. Soft Baroque music added a touch of refined drama to the atmosphere.

"Don't you just love October?" said Mila, as she descended the iron staircase from the second floor. She carried a black sequined sorceress gown, which she hung in a prominent place up front. She, herself, was wearing a black satin jumpsuit with an orange and purple paisley scarf, wine-colored suede boots, and silver skeletons dangling from her ear-lobes. I just loved her funky style.

"This is a busy time for you," I said, as the door jingled behind me and a trio of young women entered. Mila winked at me and went to say something to her assistant, Catrina, who was ringing up a customer at the register. Then she beckoned me through the gauzy curtain that led to her divination parlor.

"Never too busy for tea with a friend," she said, waving me to sit down at the round table in the corner. Today it was adorned with a lacy, web-patterned cloth and a heavy vase of purple carnations.

"I had coffee right before coming here," I said, declining the tea. "I was just in the neighborhood and thought I'd pop in for a minute. Has Fredeline been by yet?"

"She came in this morning and we had a nice chat. She's an interesting woman. Proud of her heritage and loyal to her homeland, but also eager to learn new things."

"It's too bad there isn't someone else from Sister Seeds who can help her out. I'm going to try speaking with Fern Lopez again. I'll ask her about it."

Mila straightened a deck of tarot cards on the dresser next to the table before pouring herself a cup of tea and sitting down across from me. "Fredeline said something else I think you should know."

"What did she say?"

"She seems to be worried about money. I got the impression that part of her purpose for coming here was to obtain another donation from your aunt. I don't know if Josephine had stopped sending checks, or if Fredeline thought she could send more, but I believe Fredeline viewed this trip as a fund-raising mission. And since that's no longer an option . . . well, let's just say she might be exploring other possibilities."

"What do you mean?"

"I mean, she might be hitting you up. It seems that she views you as your aunt's heir or successor, someone to pick up the mantle of her charity work."

"That's an awful big assumption, isn't it?"

"She also asked about what you do for a living and whether you're well-off—which could be nothing more than natural curiosity. But I wanted to give you a heads-up anyway."

"Thanks." I wasn't sure what to make of this information. For some reason, it didn't sit well with me. On the other hand, I couldn't forget that Fredeline came from a place with astounding rates of poverty. I couldn't blame her for having money on her mind.

I fingered the lace on the edge of the table cloth and looked around at the exotic decor on the walls and tables in Mila's parlor. She'd added a couple new pieces since I'd last visited.

"It's been a while since I've been here, hasn't it?"

"Yes, it has," said Mila. "You're the one who's been busy. How are you holding up?" She searched my face as if she could read the truth without my saying a word. In fact, she probably could.

"I'm fine. Except . . ."

"Yes?"

"I had a vision of my aunt. I saw her living a happy life, but something was off. It felt incomplete to me, like something was missing."

Mila nodded. "Of course. Her life ended in a very sudden, unexpected way."

I bit my lip. As someone who wholeheartedly believed in unseen forces and magical synchronicities, I was a little embarrassed at the question on the tip of my tongue. Seeing Mila's open, nonjudgmental face, I decided to go ahead and ask.

"Mila, do you believe ghosts are real? I mean, do you think it's really possible for spirits to stay behind? It seems almost clichéd to me. In every book, TV show, and movie about ghosts, there's unfinished business to take care of. The troubled ghost is confused or angry or regretful, and can be helped by only that one special person, the one with the 'gift' to 'see dead people.' But that's all fiction, you know?"

Mila tipped her head in acknowledgment. "It's a common storyline, no doubt. But perhaps there's a grain of truth in all fiction. Perhaps these ideas have taken such hold on our imaginations because deep down, we know they are true."

"Or," I countered, "these stories reflect our deepest fears. People fear death and the unknown. They can't abide the thought of death being a permanent end, so naturally they prefer believing our spirits live on. In that case, it would make sense for ghosts to have the same fears and needs as the living. In other words, imaginary ghosts are just projections of our own feelings."

Mila raised her eyebrows ever so slightly and didn't say anything.

"I'm sorry. I sound cynical, don't I?"

"You sound like someone who's never experienced a ghost firsthand."

"I suppose so." I glanced over at the storage side of the back room, partially hidden by Japanese folding screens, and remembered the night I'd found a dead man in that very spot. Later, Mila, Catrina, and I performed a space-clearing ritual in the room, and I eventually helped bring the man's killer to justice. But I never felt the presence of his spirit—at least, not in any way more substantial than as a memory.

As if guessing my thoughts, Mila touched my hand. "You know, I happen to believe that our souls do move on after death. I think there's truth in all those stories, myths, visions, and dreams: We'll be greeted by angels or loved ones, follow a white light, and enter a place of love and understanding.

We'll join the oneness and then, most likely, transition to the next phase in our spiritual evolution."

I leaned forward, taking in her words. She sounded so wise.

"And yet," she continued, "sometimes a part of us does stay behind. It might be no more than an impression, a strand of memory, or a feeling. Sometimes this lingering energy attaches itself and becomes a part of the place where it was felt the strongest. It's like an echo, what some call an etheric imprint. Anyone can feel it if they're open, but sensitives and psychics feel it more."

I thought of Mrs. Hammerlin—whom I'd put out of my mind since learning of Josephine's death. Maybe she really was feeling some sort of ghostly energy in her house. Still, I couldn't help thinking it seemed far-fetched to attribute knocking sounds to residual energies.

"What about poltergeists?" I asked. "Or the idea that ghosts are trying to communicate with the living? How does that fit in with this idea of psychic imprints?"

"Remember what happened at the winery yesterday? The wind rushed over us at the exact moment we were talking about spirits in the air. It is absolutely possible to manifest on the physical plane that which has been imagined on the spiritual plane. You know this. You practice magic."

"You're saying we caused the wind to kick up? It wasn't spirits, separate and apart from us?"

Mila hesitated, as if selecting her words carefully.

"I think it's a little bit of both. In most cases, strange, seemingly unexplainable occurrences are probably caused by our own influences. Shattered lightbulbs, electronic equipment going haywire, objects falling off shelves—people cause these things with their own invisible, strong vibrations, both positive and negative."

"I get that. As the ancient saying goes, 'As above, so below.'"

Mila nodded. "Exactly. But that doesn't mean intelligent apparitions don't also manifest from time to time. Whether they have yet to cross over, or they've come back to deliver a message, why not believe spirits could be among us?"

I groaned and smiled sheepishly. "I don't know why I have such a hard time relating my magical experiences with the idea of ghosts. I mean, I have no trouble feeling the presence of the Divine in nature. But the concept of what happens after death is more ineffable, like a larger mystery I'm not ready to grasp."

"Or, maybe, you just haven't had the need," suggested Mila. "Here's another thought: The experience of ghosts is highly personal. Perhaps it's not the dead who have unfinished business. It's the living. It is the living who have the need to understand, the need for closure. We wish to lay spirits to rest—or set them free—not for them, but for us."

"Yeah," I agreed. "That makes sense."

My phone buzzed, and I dug it out of my purse

to silence it. When I saw the number on the display, I had to laugh. It was Mrs. Hammerlin.

"Mystical forces are converging again," I said. "Or maybe it's the universe's sense of humor. How would you feel about going on a ghost hunt with me?"

CHAPTER EIGHT

I waited while Mila took care of a couple things in her store and made sure Catrina had everything under control. Then she filled a basket with an assortment of energy-clearing supplies, from basic salt to bundles of dried sage. I returned Mrs. Hammerlin's call to let her know we were on our way. She met us at her front door, as giddy as a schoolgirl.

"Thank you for coming!" she gushed. "I can't tell you how much I appreciate this. I'm at my wits' end. The whistling happened again last night. I think it was coming from the cemetery. Who knows how many ghosts haunt this property? It might be teeming with spirits!"

Mila set down her basket, so she could shake Mrs. Hammerlin's hand while touching her opposite arm. I knew she was sending calming vibrations to the older woman. "It's lovely to meet you," said Mila. "Why don't we chat for a bit before getting started? I brought some chamomile tea, if you don't mind putting on the kettle."

Mila does love her tea, I thought with a smile, as I followed the women to the kitchen. This time I accepted a cup and warmed my hands over the steam, while Mrs. Hammerlin went over everything she'd been experiencing in the house.

"You must be a keenly intuitive person," said Mila. "Not everyone is. Tell me, Mrs. Hammerlin, have you always had the ability to feel psychic energies?"

"Please, call me Grace," said Mrs. Hammerlin, patting her silver hair. I was happy to see the sparkle in her eyes. Mila had succeeded in putting her at ease. "And, yes, you know what? I do believe I *have* been able to feel things that others haven't. I easily pick up on people's moods and even the mood of a room. For example, if there's negativity in a place, say if two people have been arguing, I feel a sort of heaviness in the air."

"That's what I thought," said Mila, nodding her head. "You're a clairsentient."

"I am?" Mrs. Hammerlin looked pleased, but then her face fell. "Then why didn't I feel anything when I first walked through this house?"

Good question. I looked at Mila and waited for her answer.

"I'm guessing your own positivity outweighed any negative vibes," she offered. "Or perhaps the stagnant energy, and possibly old spirits, weren't stirred up until you moved in. Either way, there are lots of steps we can take to cleanse the energy in here—ghostly or otherwise."

Mrs. Hammerlin looked on eagerly as Mila pulled

out her bag of tricks. "We'll go through the house room by room, top to bottom, with a smudging stick," said Mila, "paying special attention to corners, cubbyholes, and anyplace you've heard or felt anything unusual. We'll open all the windows to release the old energies. We'll also use sound to clear the space and salt for protection. Oh, and we'll talk to the spirits as we go. It's very important to use your voice with authority to let the spirits know they are not welcome here."

"Oh, my," said Mrs. Hammerlin, slightly breathless. "I must say, I'm very glad *you're* here."

"I am, too," I said, standing up. "Mila is the best. While you two are smudging the house, I think I'll take a look outside."

Mrs. Hammerlin directed me through a small solarium off the dining room to the back door, which led to a pleasant little porch with a rocker and a swing. I stepped carefully down the concrete steps and into the lush backyard, replete with late-blooming flowers, aromatic herbs, and kitschy garden ornaments. I wandered to the side of the house, where an old cellar door caught my eye. The padlock was old and rusty, but when I gave it a tug, it didn't budge.

When I returned to the backyard, the sound of tinkling bells drifted down from an upper-story window. At the same moment, I heard a scuffling sound under the back porch. I went over to investigate, bending down to peer in a hole where the latticework was broken. As soon as I brought my face to the opening, a dark shape bounded out,

causing me to lose my balance and land on my
bottom. I swiveled my head in time to see a black
cat leap onto the low brick wall separating the yard
from the cemetery.

"Well, there's a pretty sight," I said, admiring the
cat. It was a beautiful creature, perched on the wall
like a sentinel, guarding the tombstones behind it.

On a hunch, I peeked in the hole under the
porch. Sure enough, there was a foundation window
that presumably led to the basement. It was missing
a glass pane.

I turned back around and spoke to the cat. "Are
you the one who's been causing all the trouble,
scratching and knocking things about? Well, I guess
we'll find out if a little window repair puts an end
to the Haunting of Hammerlin House."

The cat stared at me with big, yellow eyes, and I
felt my heart melt a little. "Only, then what will
happen to you? Do you have someplace else to go?"

I took a step closer to see if the cat wore a collar.
It didn't. As I moved near, the cat took one step away,
still eyeing me closely. It seemed thin, I thought,
though its coat was shiny and full. "You're on your
own, aren't you? Are you a stray? A wild child?"

Again, the cat backed up one step, with every step
I took toward it. We continued this dance until we
reached the end of the wall, where the cat suddenly
jumped down onto the cemetery grounds. I realized
there was an opening in the wall there, so I slipped
inside. The cat seemed to be waiting for me.

"Really?" I said. "Okay, then. Lead on."

By this time, I believed the cat was a she, and that she must be one smart kitty. Maybe she hoped I'd feed her, though she didn't show any indication of approaching me. She kept looking over her shoulder as she zigged and zagged between the tombstones.

Oak Grove Cemetery was larger than I'd realized. It was situated on hilly terrain, with a new section some distance away from the older graves near Mrs. Hammerlin's house. As I followed the cat, I looked around, taking in the beauty of the evening. The sun was low in the sky, painting purple, pink, and orange swaths across the horizon. Trees and monuments cast long shadows that would soon disappear into the darkness.

"Why do I get the feeling you're toying with me? This better not be a setup." I laughed softly and glanced at my watch. It had been about forty minutes since Mila and Grace began the house clearing. "Well, Kitty, as fun as this has been—"

I stopped short as the cat suddenly jumped to the top of an old, tablet-shaped tombstone. She gave me her inscrutable look as I drew near.

"What's this?" I peered at the stone, which was crumbling and worn. When I reached out to brush off some dirt, the cat jumped down and ran away, disappearing into the gloom.

"Well, good-bye to you, too." Turning back to the headstone, I wiped it off with my hand and read the names of the deceased. The family name was Joseph, and beneath that were two names,

Ricky N. and Ina Mae, probably husband and wife. They had lived and died in the 1800s.

I scratched my head as I stared at the inscription. The name *Joseph* naturally put me in mind of Josephine—especially with the name Ina so close by. And the name *Ricky* reminded me of the note found in Josephine's pocket. What had it said? *See Ricki.*

"How odd," I muttered. "What does this mean?"

I looked around at all the nearby headstones, silent and unhelpful in the growing dusk. The black cat was nowhere to be seen. I thought about what Mrs. Hammerlin had said about feeling invisible energies. Would she sense a heaviness in the air here? Should I?

As I headed back to the house, I couldn't say I felt the presence of any ghosts in the graveyard. But the more I thought about my experience with the mysterious cat, the more certain I was that I had been given a sign. Now, among all my other questions, the one I most wanted answered was this: Who was Ricki?

It was nearly 8:00 p.m. when I finally trudged up the steps of my town house. My stomach rumbled with hunger and my head was beginning to ache. As I fumbled with my key ring under the soft glow of the porch light, the door swung open and Wes stood aside to let me in.

"Hey. Thanks." I walked past him, kicked off my

shoes, and tossed my purse on a chair. "How's it going? Have you had dinner already?"

When Wes didn't respond, I turned to look at him. His cold expression hit me like a punch in the gut. *Uh-oh.*

"What's the matter?" I asked, though I had a sinking feeling I knew. I'd been so preoccupied, I failed to check in with him all evening.

"How's what's-his-name?" Wes said flatly. "*Zeke.* That must have been some 'damn fine coffee,' huh?"

"Wes, I wasn't with Zeke all this time. I was with Mila."

Wes lifted his eyebrows as if he didn't believe me.

"I mean, yeah," I amended. "I was with Zeke at first, at the café. But only for a little while. Then I stopped in at Moonstone. And then . . ." I trailed off, feeling annoyed at Wes's accusatory glare. His crossed arms didn't help either.

"Come on!" I said. "Do I really have to account for my whereabouts every single minute of the day? I thought we trusted each other."

"This isn't about trust."

"No? Then what? Why are you giving me such a hard time?"

Wes dropped his arms and turned his back on me. He headed into the kitchen.

"Fine. Don't talk to me." I stalked off to the bathroom to wash my face and freshen up. This was so not the evening I had anticipated.

When I came out, Wes was gone. There was no note on the counter. *Terrific.*

For the next hour, as I prepared and ate a quick meal of sautéed spiced greens and cannellini beans, I grumbled to myself about independence and trust and the general childishness of all men. But underneath it all, I was starting to feel pretty rotten.

Later, as I was getting ready for bed, I grabbed my phone from my purse to plug it into the charger. That's when I saw the text messages I'd missed earlier in the evening. All from Wes.

The first one was sent around 4:30 when I was at Mila's shop:

Hey, Babe. How does grilled pizza sound for dinner? We gotta fire this thing up while we still can. I'll get everything ready.

An hour later, when I was probably following a cat in a cemetery:

Coming home soon? Cold drink waiting for you here!

And yet an hour later when I was telling Mrs. Hammerlin and Mila about the broken basement window:

Everything okay??? I miss you.

"Dammit," I said to the empty room. "I am such a heel."

I hovered my fingers over the keypad to text Wes back, then stopped. A texted apology seemed curt and inadequate, and, in any case, I was too exhausted to come up with the right words. It had been a long day. Plus, I had to get up early for work in the morning. *We'll have to work this out tomorrow.*

I left a note on the counter with only two words: "I'm sorry." Then I went to bed.

* * *

I awoke with a start. The bedroom was pitch-black. As the memory of my argument with Wes surfaced in my mind, I quickly checked the space next to me in the bed. He was there, asleep, with his back to me. I sighed in relief.

But what had woken me up? It must have been something outside, I decided. Maybe an animal or a neighbor coming home.

I lay my head back on the pillow and closed my eyes. Seconds later, a loud thud pierced the silence. I bolted upright, and Wes rolled over.

"What was that?" he murmured.

"I don't know. I think it came from the front door."

"The paper?"

I checked my bedside clock and saw that it was 2:00 a.m. "Uh-uh. It's too early."

Wes hopped out of bed and darted out of the room. I followed him. Together, we peeked out of the living room window. There was no one to be seen.

Wes unlocked the door, opened it a crack, then pulled it all the way open. I stood close behind him and held onto his arms, as I peeked around his shoulder. "Anything?" I whispered.

He started to shake his head, then looked down. I followed his gaze and saw what caught his attention: a fat, brown envelope. The name "Keli" was written in black marker across the front. He bent down and examined the package, then picked it up and turned it over.

I stepped out onto the porch and looked up and down the street. It was empty, except for the neighbors' cars parked along the curb. Across the street was a minivan bearing the name of a cleaning service, but it was dark. Whoever had thrown the package was long gone.

"Do you want to call the cops?" asked Wes. "It's probably not wise to open a suspicious package."

"I don't know," I said doubtfully. "It's not lumpy, or stained, or anything, right? And it's not ticking."

Wes looked at the package again. "The corner is ripped. It probably happened when it hit the door. There's no powder coming out of it."

My curiosity got the better of me. "I'm going to open it." I reached for the package.

"Wait," said Wes. "Go get some scissors."

I complied and handed him the scissors. Carefully, he inserted the tip in the ripped part of the envelope and cut off the end. Then he emptied the contents onto the doormat. It was a book. I picked it up and read the title: *Silent Spring*.

Goose bumps prickled the bare skin of my arms. I opened the cover and flipped through the pages. The book was worn and dog-eared, but there were no apparent markings. And no note.

"Is there anything else in the envelope?" I asked.

"No," said Wes, as he shook it. "Is that the book your aunt told you about?"

I nodded. It was the book that had changed her life, the one that set her on a course of fierce dedication to the environment. Something told me this wasn't just a copy of the book, but the *actual* book my aunt had owned.

Who left this for me? And in the middle of the night, no less?

I had no idea. One thing was for sure, though. Whoever threw this book was not a ghost.

CHAPTER NINE

Monday morning came sooner than I would have liked. I slapped my ringing alarm clock and rolled over with a groan. Wes's side of the bed was empty. I wasn't worried, though. After all the excitement in the small hours of the night, we kissed and made up. We didn't exactly have a heart-to-heart and discuss all our issues—we'd still have to find the time to do that. But at least we were friends again. He told me he had to leave early for a work assignment, taking photos of a pumpkin patch at dawn.

I took a quick shower, threw on a robe, and headed straight to the coffeemaker. While the coffee was brewing, I made myself a big bowl of cinnamon oatmeal with sliced apples and walnuts. Then I took my breakfast to the table facing the patio door and watched the birds while I ate. The whole time, I kept thinking about young, idealistic Josie, the girl who ran away from home to live in a commune. She was the earth child who read *Silent Spring* and was inspired to . . . do what, exactly?

In the letter she'd sent to her parents all those years ago, she said she was leaving to undertake a "secret mission." What in the world did that mean? She also said her heart belonged in Edindale. Thinking about that now, I heard in my mind the melody for "I Left My Heart in San Francisco." Did Josie fall in love with the small city of Edindale in the short time she lived here? Or was there a person here whom she loved? And, if that was the case, then why did she leave without that person?

I mulled over the possibilities as I sipped my coffee. Maybe that was the real reason she passed through town so many times over the years. She came back to see her lover. Was it Gil? She seemed to be staying with him, not Fern, when I spoke with Josephine at the beginning of the year.

I had tried calling Gil several times, and he never answered. When I asked her about it at the winery, Fredeline told me he didn't answer when she tried either. Where was this guy? Still out of the country? Or was he like Josephine and just didn't want to be found?

As I took my bowl to the sink and poured another swig of coffee, an idea started to take shape. Gil was a business owner. Surely, he kept tabs on his business even when he was out of town. Maybe someone at his canoe shop could let me know how to reach him.

I looked up the number and dialed. A few rings

later, a recorded voice informed me that the shop opened at 10:00, but that, even during business hours, they'd probably be out back or else driving customers to and from the river. I was welcome to leave a message.

Shoot. I hung up and headed to the bedroom to get dressed. *Maybe I should just drive out there and speak to someone in person.*

As I stood in front of my closet staring at my business suits, the possibility of tracking down Gil started to sound better and better. Before I knew what I was doing, I reached into the other side of my closet and selected a pair of cargo pants, a long-sleeved T-shirt, and a lightweight field jacket. I pulled them on, and then called my office to let my boss know I'd be in late today. Given the death of my aunt, I figured a little bereavement time was understandable. Next, I called Farrah.

"Hey, gal pal. Do you have anything going on this morning that you can't ditch?"

She laughed. "Are you asking me to play hooky, Madam Partner?"

"Just for a couple hours. It takes two to canoe, and I need a second. Though, I'd really just like your company."

"Did you say Tippecanoe?"

"Yeah, right. And Tyler, too." I rolled my eyes at our silliness and filled her in. Just as I figured, she was more than game. She was working from home today and only had to be back for an afternoon conference call. A short time later, I picked her up at her apartment, punched the address for Gil's Canoes into my phone's GPS, and headed to the countryside.

It was a beautiful day. The brilliant autumn foliage shimmered against a vivid blue sky. As we cruised down the rural highway, we listened to indie folk music and chatted lightly about movies, TV, and the latest celebrity gossip. Actually, Farrah did most of the talking, since I had had zero time for entertainment in recent months. As we got closer to our destination, I asked her when she'd last been canoeing.

"Not that long ago," she said. "I went a couple times over the summer."

"But you've never been to this place, right?"

"Right. When I go, it's usually 'cause the guy I'm dating owns his own boat. I've seen signs for this shop, though. I think they must do a pretty decent business, at least when the water level cooperates."

"Speaking of signs, there's one now."

Following the arrows, we turned onto a dusty lane and soon pulled into a gravel parking lot next to the office for Gil's Canoes. It was a gray, wooden structure that resembled a beach hut and doubled as a bait shop. Other than two pickup trucks holding an assortment of kayaks and canoes, the only other vehicle in the lot was a beat-up Jeep.

The screen door slammed behind us when we entered, prompting a young guy to emerge from a back room and take his post behind the counter. Wearing a tie-dyed T-shirt and a shy grin, he looked barely old enough not to be in school.

"Hi," I said. "Is Gil around?"

"Nah. Haven't seen him. Can I help you?"

Farrah opened a refrigerated soda case and selected a glass bottle, then perused the sparsely stocked snack shelves.

"Do you think he'll be in soon?" I asked. "I was hoping to talk to him."

The boy shrugged. "Maybe this afternoon. I think he said he was gonna work on his deck this morning."

I felt a small surge of hope. At least now I knew he wasn't in Tibet.

Farrah set her soda and a bag of trail mix on the counter. "Are you still renting canoes? It seems like it's getting to be a little late in the season."

"We're open 'til the end of the month, weather permitting."

"So," I interjected, "does Gil live nearby?"

The boy paused in the middle of ringing up Farrah's purchases and gave me a sidelong glance. I worried I'd gone too far. Now he thought I was a stalker.

"I'm only wondering how soon he might be here," I said. "I really need to talk to him. It's about a mutual friend of ours who recently passed away."

"Want to leave him a message? I'm pretty sure he'll be in later. He said he was gonna fix the broken trailer out back. Plus, he needs to restock the bait."

I glanced at the fish-shaped clock on the wall. It was only 10:15.

"Hey," said Farrah, tugging my shirt tail. "Why don't we rent a canoe? It's gorgeous outside, and this is probably our last chance this season. Besides, you could use the sun. You're looking more like a vampire than a witch these days."

"Am not!" I protested, though I had to admit she was probably right. "Are you sure you have time?"

She waved away the question. "Let's do this."

We paid the kid behind the counter, and he supplied us with life jackets and safety instructions. He led us to one of the pickups in the lot, and we piled in for the bumpy backroads ride to a crude boat launch a couple miles upstream. Once we were settled in the canoe—with me in front and Farrah in the rear—the kid gave a shove to the stern, and we were on our way.

The water was deep and the river flowed easily. Carried along by the current, we had to use our oars only to steer around bends and maneuver around the occasional rock or fallen tree.

"This is better than being out here in the summer," remarked Farrah. "Less bugs."

"Mm-hmm." I watched the terrain slowly pass by: towering cliffs, shimmering trees, ancient rocks, and swooping birds—it was like a picture postcard for Southern Illinois. It wasn't hard to imagine that Josephine really had fallen in love with this area.

Every now and then we passed small beaches along the shore where boaters before us had apparently stopped to picnic or explore. I had my eye on one such spot up ahead when I noticed a painted wooden sign at the tree line beyond the sand. "What does that say?" I asked, shielding my eyes with my hand.

"What are you looking at?" called Farrah behind me.

"Steer left," I replied, digging my oar into the water. "Up to that sandbank."

We navigated the canoe to shallow water, then hopped out and dragged it inland. The sign, which was shaped like an arrow, read *Briar Creek Cabins*.

"That's what I thought. Mind if we go for a little walk?"

"As long as we don't get lost," said Farrah. "Maybe we should leave a trail of pebbles." She scooped up a handful of rocks from the beach.

"I wonder how far we are from the cabins."

As we strolled into the shadowy forest, I told Farrah about meeting Levi Markham the day before and seeing the place where he found Josephine's body. When I mentioned that he said Josephine might have been shot by a hunter, Farrah froze.

"But it's not even deer season yet. Do you think there are poachers out here?"

"If it was a hunter, I doubt if he'd go off shooting in the forest again after such a horrible accident," I reasoned. "Anyway, I don't think that's what happened."

After walking a few more minutes, we came to a fork in the path. Another sign, pointing left, directed us to the cabins. The right-hand path wound deeper into the woods. I hesitated.

"What do you think?" asked Farrah. "You know these trails basically go on forever."

I couldn't explain it, but something about the unmarked trail called to me. "Let's see where this goes, at least a little ways."

"Okay. But I'm gonna start dropping pebbles."

It was a scenic path that grew wilder and rockier as we went. As the terrain sloped upward, I glanced to the side and caught sight of a chain-link fence a little distance away.

"I wonder what that's for?" I left the path and hiked up to the fence.

"Hey!" yelled Farrah. "That is *not* staying on the trail."

The fence was about eight feet high and topped with a coil of nasty-looking barbed wire. It seemed to be well-maintained. Other than that, there wasn't much to see. The land on the other side looked the same as on my side. Still, I was curious.

"You stay on the trail," I called down to Farrah. "I'll follow the fence. Let's see how far we can go while keeping each other in sight."

That plan worked for only a few yards, when the fence angled away from the trail.

"What now, boss?" said Farrah.

"I really want to see where this goes. I can't say why. It's just a feeling I have."

"Hang on," said Farrah. She scrambled up the

slope to join me. "Let's tie something to the fence here, so we'll know where to find the trail."

"Okay." We scanned one another and came up empty-handed. Neither of us was wearing a belt, scarf, headband, or any extraneous articles of clothing.

Farrah shrugged and reached under her shirt. "I can spare my bra for a few minutes."

"Wait! You nut. You don't have to do that. We can stick a small branch between the links here." I chuckled. "Though I should have let you hang your bra here. That would have been way funnier."

"Hey, I do what I gotta do. Remember that time we got lost in the forest at night?"

"I'll never forget it."

We picked our way through the trees and brush along the fence for several minutes. Finally, the ground leveled off and the trees opened up to reveal a dirt road. The fence ended at an electric keypad-access gate, beyond which were a number of metal buildings and a fleet of semitrailers. A sign on the gate said NO TRESPASSING. PROPERTY OF HAPCO.

"What's HAPCO?" asked Farrah.

I tried to remember. "I've heard of it. It's owned by the Hemsleys—that's what the 'H' is for. Do you know Tadd Hemsley? He was at the haunted barn the other night. Anyway, I think it has something to do with agricultural chemicals, like fertilizers or animal feed or something."

Farrah shrugged and pulled out her phone to look it up, then made a face. "No signal."

"Of course. Oh well, we can find out later."

I took a parting glance at the tall security gate and the plain buildings, and wondered what Josephine would have thought of the products stored back there. Would this business have offended her values?

More to the point, what would she have done about it?

CHAPTER TEN

Farrah and I retraced our steps and found our way to the beach. By this time, the sun was high overhead. Farrah shared her trail mix with me before we pushed off and continued down the river. Half an hour later, we approached another sandbank where a colorful flag waved from a metal pole. We turned in, left our canoe upside down in the designated spot, and climbed steep wooden stairs, which ended at a point behind Gil's canoe shop.

As we neared the little hut, we heard the ringing sound of a hammer on metal. Following the noise, we went around to the side of the shop, where we found a broad-shouldered older man fussing with the coupler on a steel utility trailer. Intent on his work, he didn't notice us approaching.

I studied him for a moment. With his Bermuda shorts and sleeveless T-shirt, showing off leathery, suntanned skin and sinewy muscles, he looked like he could have come straight out of Margaritaville. I tried to imagine this burly, gray-haired sixty-something as the scraggly-bearded fellow who once posed for a picture with two girls in front of the Happy Hills commune.

I cleared my throat and he finally looked up, squinting as if he was trying to place us. He put down his tools and wiped his hands on his shorts.

"You the gals who were looking for me earlier?"

"You must be Gil Johnson," I said, stepping forward. "I'm Keli Milanni, Josephine O'Malley's niece. You and I have spoken on the phone. This is my friend, Farrah."

He grasped my hand with a large, calloused grip, and we exchanged condolences.

"Sad news," he said, shaking his head. "Sad, sad news."

"Yes. And shocking. Have the police spoken with you?"

"Oh, yes, yes. Of course, I couldn't tell them much. I hadn't seen Josie in months. Didn't even know she was in town."

He sounds like Fern, I thought, but decided to let it go. I was just grateful for the opportunity to finally speak with him in person. Gil led us to a trio of lawn chairs on a patch of scrub grass next to the canoe shop.

"There's something I've been wanting to ask you," I said, as soon as we were all seated. "I have a picture of Josephine and Fern Lopez at the commune where they lived. There's a guy in the photo with them. Could that be you?"

He grinned like I'd brought up an inside joke.

"Can you believe it? What a baby I was, huh? Those were the days."

"What was it like living in a commune?" asked Farrah. "Was it like a great big campout? Did you work all day and sit around singing songs at night?"

"It was great," said Gil, with twinkling eyes. "We worked the land, shared our chores, made lots of mistakes." He let out a hearty laugh. "We learned a lot and had such fun. We were giddy with freedom! Everyone should have such an experience, at least once in their life. In fact, folks are still trying shared living in some places around the country. Experimental communities, I think they're called."

I remembered Gil's tendency to go off on frequent conversational tangents and resolved to stay on topic. "How did you meet Josie?"

"Well, now, let's see. Some buddies and I started Happy Hills in sixty-eight, I think it was. And we'd get all kinds of folks passing through. We were a welcoming place, always had a tent ready for anybody who needed a place to crash. One night this young couple stopped by on their way out east. A fellow named Roger, and his pretty young lady— Josie. 'Josie June,' we called her sometimes." He laughed at the memory. "Their bus broke down, so they ended up staying longer than they planned. Then they made friends here, saw how great a thing we had going, and decided to stay."

"Josephine once told me she was highly influenced by the book *Silent Spring*," I said. "By Rachel Carson?" I watched for Gil's reaction, hoping to see a flicker of guilt, or a twitch, anything to indicate that he might have tossed the book on my porch. He was the picture of innocence.

"Oh, sure," he said. "We all were. Those were exciting times for the burgeoning environmental movement. In 1970, we had the first Earth Day, which coincided with the creation of the Environmental Protection Agency—under President Nixon of all people. Did you know that? Then we had the passage of all kinds of new laws: the Clean Air Act, the Clean Water Act, the Endangered Species Act. Let's see, what else?"

I nodded, determined not to be sidetracked. "What did Josephine do, specifically, to help the environment?"

"Specifically? Well, we grew our own food at Happy Hills, of course. And we tried to use sustainable practices, composting our waste, recycling our gray water, that sort of thing. But we had a bigger vision, too. We cared about the planet beyond our little neck of the woods." He gazed into the distance, chuckling to himself. "Josie was all gung ho to clean up pollution. She'd pick up litter in the parks and try to restore blighted land through guerrilla gardening."

"Gorilla gardening?" asked Farrah. "As in apes?" She screwed up her face as if imagining monkeys with rakes and hoes. Smiling, I kicked her softly with my toe.

"Guerrilla, as in covert ops," said Gil. "Josie made these seed packets—seed bombs, we called them. We'd hurl them over fences, onto barren vacant lots, so wildflowers would grow there."

"Ohhh," said Farrah. "How cool."

"Was that the start of Sister Seeds?" I asked.

Gil gave me a funny look. "I suppose you could say that. Josie was always a seed planter, and the farther and wider the better. She was our own little Josie Appleseed."

"Ha! I get it," said Farrah. "Keli, didn't you tell me you have a book about Johnny Appleseed that used to belong to your aunt?"

I nodded. Evidently, spreading seeds was a passion Josie had nurtured her whole life, from Nebraska to Illinois to Haiti.

I turned to Gil again. "Do you have any idea why she might have been out in the woods on Friday night?"

"She was always at home under the trees. She was probably just going for a walk. Wrong place, wrong time."

"So, she wasn't staying with you over the weekend?" I knew he'd already answered this question, but I couldn't help asking again.

He shook his head. "She had friends everywhere, but she never wanted to impose. She'd bounce from place to place. Sometimes she'd show up on my doorstep, out of the blue. Maybe she'd stay, maybe she wouldn't. She'd blow in on the breeze and blow out just as suddenly."

He smiled sadly as the imagery took on a more poignant meaning. We all fell silent, listening to the rustle of nearby tree branches. But I was still thinking about Josephine's last hours. If she hadn't been staying with Fern or Gil—and if she really did have friends everywhere—then was there someone else out there with information about what she had been up to?

"Gil, I'm sure the police asked you about this, but do you know anyone named Ricki? Josephine had that name on a piece of paper in her pocket."

Gil leaned over, picked up a stick from the ground, and began stripping off the bark. "Nope. The cops mentioned the paper. I guess that's how they found you, huh? What a shock it must have been. I know Josie wouldn't have wanted that. She cared a lot about you, talked about you often over the years."

Farrah and I exchanged a glance. It seemed obvious he was trying to change the subject.

"It was *Ricki* with an *i*, wasn't it?" said Farrah. "With that spelling, it's probably a girl. And it's not the most common name; I'm sure the police will track her down before too long."

"Did Josie ever mention anyone named Ricki?" I pressed.

Gil threw down the stick and looked me in the eye. "All right, I'll tell you. I didn't see any point in telling the fuzz, because Ricki Day had absolutely nothing to do with Josie's death."

Now we're getting somewhere. "How can you be sure?" I asked. "Who is she?"

"I just don't care for the idea of the fuzz poking around in Josie's affairs." Gil pulled a bandanna from his pocket and wiped the perspiration from his forehead. Then he gave me a pained look. "But Josie trusted you. So, I'll tell you."

I nodded to give him encouragement. "It could be important, Gil."

"Okay . . . but leave my name out of it, will you?"

"Agreed."

"Ricki Day is a county environmental officer. She inspects factories, cites polluters for violations, that sort of thing. I told you Josie cared about cleaning up pollution. If she had concerns about local businesses not following the rules, she'd give Ricki a call. That's probably why she had her name. Nothing fishy."

Maybe not, I thought. But could the same be said about Gil's reasoning? Withholding information from the police seemed pretty fishy to me.

As we drove away from Gil's Canoes, Farrah and I talked about what we had learned.

"Do you think he was telling the truth?" she asked.

"I'm not sure. He held back his knowledge of Ricki Day."

"He did tell us eventually," Farrah pointed out.

"True. And I do think his description of Josephine was probably accurate." I let out a frustrated sigh. "Why did she have to be so mysterious all the time? Sneaking into town without telling anyone; wandering around in the woods by herself, when she was supposed to be picking up Fredeline from the airport . . ."

"I hate to say this," said Farrah, "but have you considered the possibility that she might have had dementia? That might explain why she forgot to go to the airport. Maybe she was lost in the forest."

I let up on the gas, ready to turn around and go back to ask Gil. Then I had a better idea. We weren't far from Briar Creek Cabins.

"Hey, do you mind if we make a quick detour? I want to talk to Levi Markham again. He said Josephine was out bird-watching when he saw her on the trails. It didn't sound like he thought she was lost. But I'd like to find out if he can tell me anything more about how she was acting. Or if he can remember anything she might have said."

I knew I was probably grasping at straws, but Farrah, loyal friend that she was, told me it was a great idea. "Besides," she said. "I've always wanted to meet an author."

We drove into the lane leading to the cabins and pulled up next to the only one with a vehicle parked in front of it. Even the office cabin appeared unoccupied.

"Virginia plates," noted Farrah, as we walked up the narrow stone path.

I rapped on the door and stood back expectantly. Through the open curtains, a face briefly appeared, then disappeared. Then the door swung open.

"Keli!" said Levi. "This is a surprise."

"Sorry to barge in on you like this. We were in the area and—"

"Come on in," he said, without letting me finish. "I'm starved for human company."

He ushered us inside. The cabin was small but

homey, with a living room and kitchen on the first floor and a sleeping loft at the top of steep, ladder-like stairs. Levi quickly cleared some folders and papers from the couch and snapped shut a laptop sitting on an old oak desk. "I think I've been out here too long," he said, running his fingers through his hair. "I don't know how Thoreau did it." He laughed nervously.

Farrah gave him her most dazzling smile and reached for his hand. "I'm Farrah. It's so nice to meet you. I think this is so romantic—a real-live author writing a book in a woodland cabin."

I tried not to roll my eyes, as I nudged Farrah onto the couch.

"It's not really that romantic," said Levi. "Can I get you something to drink? Beer, ginger ale, water?"

"Beer would be lovely," said Farrah, at the same time I said, "No thanks."

"One beer, then." He grabbed a bottle from the refrigerator, twisted off the cap, and opened a cabinet.

"I don't need a glass," called Farrah.

I gave Farrah a suspicious look. She had used her powers of seduction to gain information in the past. Was that what she was doing now? I had a feeling Randall wouldn't appreciate the tactic.

As soon as Levi sat down in the rocker next to the couch, I leaned forward. "I wondered if I could ask you a few more questions. I've been speaking to some of my aunt's friends, and no one seems to know where she was staying during her visit to

Edindale. Since she wasn't a guest at the cabins, did you happen to ask where she was staying?"

Levi shook his head regretfully. "No, sorry. I didn't think to ask that."

"How was she acting?" asked Farrah. "Did she seem to be lost or confused?"

"No, I don't think so. She was friendly, pleasant. I think she was excited at the prospect of finding this certain bird she was looking for."

"She seemed excited?" I asked.

Levi thought about it. "Yeah. Excited, eager. She smiled a lot."

"And when was this again?"

"I saw her a few times. Once on Wednesday, and twice on Thursday—in the morning and in the afternoon."

Farrah tapped her nails on the side of the beer bottle. "Can you remember any other details? Like, what were the exact words she said to you?"

Levi wrinkled his forehead. "I don't recall her exact words. She said, 'nice morning,' I think. And, 'Good weather for photographing birds.'" He turned to me. "I take it you didn't know she was into bird-watching?"

"Um. Not really."

"And she didn't tell you where she was staying?"

"No."

"Where did she live?"

I hesitated, not sure how to answer, when a cell phone rang from the kitchen counter. Levi jumped up to answer it.

"Would you excuse me for a minute?" He brought

the phone to his ear and said, "Hey," as he opened the front door and let himself outside.

"He's adorable," said Farrah. "Too bad he doesn't have any useful information."

"I'm not so sure," I said, standing up. "Watch out the window, okay?"

"What are you gonna do? Snoop?"

"I want to check out these folders. I thought I saw a name . . ." I trailed off, as I began rifling through the papers and folders Levi had scooped up from the couch. The papers appeared to be photocopies of old newspaper articles, but I didn't take the time to read them. I was more interested in the folders. Each one was labeled with a name, most of which I didn't recognize. "Davey Winslow, Allen Smith, Jane Marlowe . . . Josephine O'Malley!" I looked up at Farrah. "I was right. I thought I saw her name."

"He's coming back! He's coming back! Quick!"

I dropped the folders back into the stack and dove for the couch. Farrah was still standing, so she grabbed the doorknob just as it swung open. "Oh!" she exclaimed, in mock surprise. "I was just coming outside to find you. Unfortunately, we have to leave. I've got an appointment and Keli has work."

I hopped up and joined Farrah in the doorway. "Yeah, sorry. We'll try to come back again, though. Think you'll still be here for a while?"

"Oh, uh, yeah. I think so. This memoir is taking a lot longer to write than I expected."

"Isn't that always the way," said Farrah breezily. "Well, thanks for the beer!"

We wasted no time, and before long we were in the car, barreling down the dusty lane. I tried to make sense of the folders I'd seen.

"Isn't it more than a little weird?" I asked. "Why does he have a file on Aunt Josephine?"

"Hmm," said Farrah. "It might not be as weird as you imagine. I mean, think about it. He's an author. He's probably always collecting bits of information to include in his stories, right? And he stumbled upon a dead body, for crying out loud. That's definitely going to make it in the memoir. It'll probably get its own chapter."

I shook my head. "I don't know what he's up to, Farrah, but I do know one thing: Levi Markham is not being truthful. Just now, he said he was writing his memoir? The other day he told me he was writing a thriller. He's lying, Farrah. And not very well, I might add."

CHAPTER ELEVEN

After dropping Farrah at her apartment, I decided to go straight to the office without going home to change first. By the time I stepped into the law firm's lobby, it was nearly 3:00 p.m.

"I didn't think you were coming in today," said Julie, from behind her reception desk. "You should have stayed home."

"I didn't want to fall too far behind. What did I miss this morning?"

"Not much. The briefing meeting went on longer than usual, because Crenshaw picked up a new client over the weekend—the Barnsworth estate. You know Barnsworth Stables? Mrs. Barnsworth owned that high-end horse-riding school out on Rural Route 3."

"Sure. Wow. Good for Crenshaw."

"Good for the firm," said Julie. "Oh, and he also reported on the opening of the haunted barn. He said you did a good job. Way to represent."

"Thanks." I glanced down at my wrinkled cargo

pants, which had picked up a mysterious dirt stain somewhere along the morning's adventures, and my old field jacket, which was covered in cockleburs. Now that I thought about it, my hair was probably a tangled, windblown mess, too. I wasn't exactly representing the firm very well at the moment. "Julie, I'm going to hide out in my office for the rest of the day. If anyone comes looking for me, please take a message."

"You got it," she said.

I closed the door to my cozy, little private office and dropped into the chair behind my desk. For a brief moment, I stared out the window at the fading light and contemplated the surreal events of the past few days. Aunt Josephine was dead. And everyone I spoke with about her seemed unable to be completely straightforward. Why all the secrets?

I shook myself. It was time to get busy. I swiveled in my chair and turned my computer on, fully intending to check my email. But first . . . , I couldn't resist a quick online search for Levi Markham. As I typed in his name, my intuition told me what I'd find: a big, fat nothing. I soon found I was right. There was no author page, no blog, no books for sale. I supposed he could be an aspiring writer—he never said he was published. Still, it seemed odd that a guy his age wouldn't be on at least one form of social media.

Next, I called Detective Rhinehardt and told him I thought I knew who Ricki might be. I kept my promise and didn't mention Gil as the source of my information. Luckily, the detective didn't question me about it.

"Great work," he said. "There are dozens of Rickis in the local directory—hundreds if you count all the Richards, Fredericas, Ericas, and other spellings of Ricki. If your tip pans out, you've saved us a lot of time."

"Detective, I also wanted to ask you about the guy who found Josephine. Levi Markham? I met him and he said he's a writer, but when I looked him up online, I couldn't find anything."

"I wouldn't worry about it. We questioned him, and he checked out."

"Oh. Okay." I debated whether I should tell Rhinehardt about the folder I saw in Markham's cabin. I knew he wouldn't approve of my snooping. I also imagined he'd come to the same conclusion Farrah had—that Markham was collecting story ideas. Before I could make up my mind, Rhinehardt spoke again.

"Listen, Ms. Milanni, I'm glad you called. I was going to give you a ring anyway. The medical examiner's report is going to be another couple of days yet. The bullet fragments retrieved during the autopsy were sent to the lab, but the lab is short-staffed. This is the way it goes sometimes. If you don't mind, I'd like to keep your aunt's body until the report is finalized."

"So, there's no info on the gun yet?"

"I'm afraid not. However, I can tell you another bit of news. Some hunters who own a house in Shawnee reported that a rifle is missing from their gun cabinet. The house is usually vacant in the off-season, but one of the owners stopped by to check on things and discovered the cabinet lock had been broken. We'll know if we have a match when the lab report comes in."

"A stolen gun? What do you make of that?"

"It's hard to say at this point. But rest assured we're exploring all possible angles."

"Well, was anything else stolen? Was the house in disarray?"

As Rhinehardt answered "no," there was a sharp knock on my office door.

"I've got to run, Detective. Thanks for keeping me in the loop." As soon as I hung up, I called out, "Come in!"

The door opened and Crenshaw strode in. He stopped short when he saw me, his mouth puckering as if he'd bitten into a lemon.

"Hey, Crenshaw. I, uh, went for a long walk in the forest this morning. I was going to go home and change, but . . ." I trailed off, unable to finish my excuse in the face of his critical stare.

"A shower might have helped, too," he said drily. "Never mind. Beverly and I are having cocktails with the new bank president this evening, and she asked me to invite you. I'll pass along your regrets."

"I'm sorry—"

"No," he said, cutting me off. His expression softened. "Don't apologize. It is I who should apologize. Please accept my condolences for your loss. Perhaps you shouldn't have come in today."

"Thanks. I admit I'm a little distracted. I'm the only family my aunt had around here."

"I see." He raised an eyebrow as he continued to peer at me. "Word of advice? Leave the investigating to the police this time. I know you've been instrumental in solving a number of crimes around town, but that is not your job. You should focus on taking care of yourself."

I mustered up a smile and nodded. He meant well. That didn't mean I had to agree with him.

As soon as Crenshaw left, I turned to my computer and looked up the number for the Edindale County Department of Environment. A minute later, I placed the call and asked for Ricki Day. She wasn't available, but I learned she'd be in the office the following morning. I made a note on my calendar and said I'd stop by.

At last, I turned to my real job. For the next few hours, I returned client calls, wrote some letters and memos, and redlined a proposed settlement agreement. When I finally raised my head, I was surprised to see it was after 7:00 p.m. I put away the file I had been working on and rubbed my temples. *Maybe I should cast that time-expanding spell after all.* Of course, first I'd have to find the time to do even that.

My cell phone rang, and when I checked the display, I saw it was my mom. I picked up right away.

"Am I interrupting your dinner?" she asked. "I tried to wait. I know you eat late."

"You're not interrupting. But if you're calling for

an update, I'm afraid I don't have much to report. I spoke to the detective today, and he told me they're still waiting for the medical examiner's report."

"It's just as well. This gives me more time to work on Grandma O."

"What do you mean? Did she take it very hard? Is she okay?"

"She's holding up. The problem is she wants Josie's body brought back here. But I don't think that's what Josie would have wanted. She left Bentlee and never looked back. I don't know if she considered Edindale her home, but it's the only place we know she lived. And it *is* where she died." Her voice hitched.

"She did seem to have strong ties here," I agreed, my heart twisting in my chest.

"Anyway, I told Grandma that funeral arrangements are on hold because of the investigation. But I really think it would be best to have her laid to rest there."

"That makes sense. I'm happy to make the arrangements, Mom."

"Grandma has some money she wants to use for this. Just save all the receipts, and you'll be reimbursed."

"I'm not worried about that. Can Grandma handle the trip?"

"Yes, I think so. Megan said she'll come, too. I don't know if Erin or Alec will be able to get away, but that's okay. Dad and I will bring Megan and

Grandma, and it will be just fine. I don't suppose you know . . . well, never mind."

"What?"

"Nothing. I know you don't know. I was just wondering if she had a house someplace. Any possessions. Or anyone else who might consider her family."

"Those are good questions. I've been asking around. She did have friends, but none of them seem to have known her very well."

"Join the club," my mom murmured. Then, more brightly, she said, "Well, keep me posted. If anyone can uncover Josephine's secrets, I know you can."

"I'll do my best."

When I hung up the phone, I dropped my head into my hands and stared at my desktop. My family was coming to Edindale. My parents, my grandmother, at least one of my sisters—they'd all be looking to me for answers. It's what I was known for. Back home, I was Keli the problem solver: the last kid left at the puzzle table; the referee to my siblings; the legal eagle who resolved family law disputes.

Then, I had an even less pleasant thought. They'd all be expecting a nice Catholic funeral, complete with a religious visitation, a full mass, and a graveside benediction. My mom didn't have to spell it out. That was just how things were done in our family. Of course, none of them knew I was Wiccan.

A sharp knock startled me out of my worried

daydreams. The door opened and Randall stuck his head in.

"Look alive, Milanni. There's someone here to see you."

"What? No! I can't see anyone!"

Randall stepped aside and Wes appeared in the doorway.

"Oh, thank goodness," I breathed. I was still slightly self-conscious about my appearance, even in front of Wes, but he didn't seem to care. He walked over, leaned down, and planted a soft kiss right on my lips.

"I'd apologize for interrupting you at work, except I'm not sorry at all. I just had to see your pretty face and reassure myself you're still part of my life."

"Aw, man. I'm sorry."

"Besides," he said, holding up a Wonder Woman lunch sack. "I figured you might be hungry."

I gasped like I'd won a sweepstakes. "Sweet! Where did you get this?"

He laughed at my enthusiasm. "I saw it when I was picking up a few groceries. It made me think of you."

I opened the bag to find a veggie sandwich and a Honeycrisp apple. "Oh, you are the best," I said, tearing into the sandwich. "Have I told you that lately?"

"Uh-uh. Maybe you should say it again."

"You're the best!" I said, around a mouthful of food.

While I ate, Wes chatted about his job at the

newspaper. His editor realized he'd be wise to make full use of Wes's talents while he could, so the paper was doing more photo spreads. The latest was a new feature called "The People in Our Neighborhood," in which various Edindale citizens were profiled each week.

"You should profile Beverly," I suggested. "She's an interesting person with strong ties to the community. Her grandfather started this firm in the fifties. Plus, she loves any kind of spotlight on her or the firm."

"Are you trying to win brownie points? I thought you were beyond all that since making partner."

"Not necessarily." I told him about my excursion with Farrah, beginning with our jaunt down the river and ending with Crenshaw's reaction upon seeing how I looked.

Wes suppressed a smile. "I didn't even notice."

"Right." I took a bite of apple, then offered it to him. As he bit into the fruit, I was about to suggest we go home when my cell phone rang. It was Mrs. Hammerlin again.

"Darn it. I better take this."

"Oh, Keli," she said, when I answered. "I'm so frazzled; I don't know what to do."

"What's the matter, Mrs. Hammerlin?"

"It's happening again. Everything was calm and normal after you and your friend left. I slept like a baby last night and had a perfectly nice, quiet day. But then the bumping started up again. I was cleaning out the built-in hutch in the dining room, peeling out the shelf liners, when I felt an icy chill, out of nowhere. Then I heard it, this awful, loud thudding. I think the spirits are back!"

I closed my eyes, praying for patience. "Did you fix the basement window, like I said?"

"Not yet. I have a handyman coming over tomorrow. But I really think I'm going to have to call in those professional ghostbusters, after all. Don't get me wrong. Mila is perfectly lovely and wonderful, but, after all, ghosts aren't really her specialty."

"I'll tell you what," I said. "How about if I stop by and see if I can get to the bottom of this?" I glanced up at Wes, who was watching me with curious eyes. "I'll bring my boyfriend."

When I hung up, Wes cocked his head. "Are we going on a ghost hunt?"

"Nope. A cat hunt. But first we need to get some bait."

CHAPTER TWELVE

I knew Mila grew catnip in her abundant herb garden, so I gave her a call before Wes and I left my office. As usual, she welcomed us to come right over. She also let me know she was in the midst of hosting a full-moon gathering of her coven, the Magic Circle. For an instant, I felt a stab of envy mixed with embarrassment. I hadn't even realized that tonight was the full moon.

"We've already performed our ritual," she said, when we arrived. "Now we're sharing libations around the fire pit and making our plans for Samhain. We'd love for you to join us."

I hesitated for only half a second. "Mrs. Hammerlin is expecting us, so we can't stay."

"Right. Be back in a jiff."

We waited for Mila in her large chef's kitchen. As soon as she stepped out her back door, a petite woman with unruly red hair came inside. "Oh, hello, Keli," she said. "I didn't know you were here."

"Hi, Max. Nice to see you." To Wes, I said, "This

is Professor Maxine Eisenberry. She helped me out when I was searching for your grandmother's stolen copy of Shakespeare's First Folio."

"Ah," he said, with a playful grin. "The mystery that brought us together."

"Aren't you two cute," said Max, as she filled a pitcher with water.

Two middle-aged women, in matching white ritual robes, came inside next, saying something about finding their jackets. "Now that my adrenaline has calmed down, I can really feel the chill in the air," said the older of the two. She rubbed her arms, then stopped when she noticed us.

"Well, hi there, newcomers!" she said. "Come outside and have a drink. We have sangria!" Her eyes seemed to linger on Wes's handsome profile. I wasn't sure if I should be irritated, flattered, or amused.

Before we could respond, Mila came back inside, with Catrina at her heels. I noticed they both wore hammered silver jewelry from the shop—Mila in bangles and a round disk hanging on a long, chain necklace, and Catrina in a cuff bracelet and multiple earrings up the side of one ear. I knew silver had a strong association with both the Goddess and the moon.

Mila set a big bunch of catnip on her butcher-block island. "Catrina, grab me that ball of twine, would you?" With twine in hand, she tied the catnip in a bundle. "Drishti just *loves* this stuff," she said.

"Almost as much as Judy loves her sangria," said the younger woman in white. She nudged her companion, presumably Judy, who tore her gaze from Wes to giggle in agreement.

"Where is Drishti?" I asked. Mila's striking gray cat usually greeted me when I visited.

"She's around here someplace, probably hiding. Large gatherings make her shy." Mila handed me the catnip. "I hope this works. I have to say, I really didn't feel the presence of any otherworldly spirits in Mrs. Hammerlin's house. But that doesn't mean they aren't there. Spirits come and go, like people."

"Someone's got a ghost?" Max asked. "This is the perfect time of year to make contact."

"Yeah," said Catrina. "The veil between worlds is thinnest around Samhain."

Wes smiled at Catrina. "Why is that? Do the ghosts have a calendar over there on the other side? Does it flip over to October 31, signaling that it's time to go a-haunting?"

Max shot me an amused look, as if to say, "Really?"

"Very funny," I said to Wes. "Actually, I think we can access the spirit realm anytime if we're in the right frame of mind. Some circumstances are just more conducive. Like now—as leaves die and the air cools, we find ourselves entering the dark, introspective half of the year. And with all the cultural holidays celebrating the cycles of life and death— Samhain, Halloween, the Mexican Day of the Dead—thoughts of death are all around us."

"Precisely," agreed Mila. "The veil is a symbol. It represents the thin, somewhat fluid, separation between the physical and the spiritual. As Keli said, we can always call spirits to us, but there are ways to make it easier. For instance, you might be more effective during a liminal time, such as sunrise, sunset, or midnight, when we're in between day and night, light and dark. And, at this time of the year, we're transitioning between seasons."

Catrina perched on a bar stool and propped her thin elbows on the countertop. The skull tattoo on her inner wrist seemed especially apropos to the conversation. "So many people are calling forth spirits at this time of the year," she said, "you might encounter one even if you aren't the one calling it forth."

"When you say 'calling forth,'" said Wes, with a mischievous glint in his eye, "is that similar to vampires who can't enter your house until you invite them over the threshold?"

A chorus of groans and protests arose from the group.

"Actually," said Mila, cutting through the din, "Wes is not totally off base. While vampire mythology is not typically part of Wicca, there are parallels to be drawn. As for the invitation concept, a wise Witch is careful about what sorts of entities she opens herself up to."

"That's true," conceded Catrina. "I know some kids who messed around with a Ouija board without knowing what they were doing. They ended up bringing in a malevolent spirit. It totally freaked them out."

Wes opened his mouth as if to say something, then thought better of it and remained silent.

The back door opened and another two women popped in. "Is the party in here now?" one of them asked.

Wes stood up from where he leaned against a counter. "I'm starting to feel outnumbered."

"We don't discriminate," said Mila, with a smile. "Men are always welcome to join us."

"Especially men as interesting as you," said Judy, with a shameless wink.

On that note, I waved to Max and Catrina and gave Mila a quick hug. "I'll be in touch," I said.

On our way to Mrs. Hammerlin's house, with Wes at the wheel since I'd left my car at the office, we passed through a neighborhood that had caught the Halloween spirit and then some. Skeletons dangled from porches, cloth ghosts fluttered from trees, and Styrofoam gravestones dotted front yards amid inflatable ghouls and goblins. One yard even displayed a full-size black wooden coffin.

"I see what you mean about death being in the air," Wes remarked. "It's like the whole town put out the welcome mat for the dead."

"Around here, I'd say it's mainly for the spooky fun of it. In other cultures, it's more about honoring your departed loved ones." I thought about Fredeline and wondered if she'd make it back to Haiti in time to celebrate with her family.

Without warning, a white form floated in the street in front of us. I gasped and jumped in my seat. Wes tapped on the brakes. Peering through the windshield, I saw what it was: a piece of white, tattered muslin. It must have detached itself from one of the ghostly trees we'd passed.

"Jumpy?" asked Wes, with a laugh.

"It's all that talk about spirits roaming the earth. It must be getting to me."

When we arrived at Mrs. Hammerlin's place, she met us at the door as usual. I introduced her to Wes, and she informed us that she had known and admired his grandmother. Her welcoming smile soon faded, though, as she took us into the dining room. Tonight, there was no invitation for tea or cookies.

"Here's where it happened," she said, hugging her arms to her chest. She appeared smaller than I remembered, almost swallowed up by the long, cable-knit cardigan hanging from her shoulders.

We looked around. The old-fashioned dining room was sparsely furnished and chilly. A brass chandelier cast a dim light over an oval table and eight Chippendale-style antique chairs. On the far wall, the built-in hutch stood abandoned, with pulled-out drawers and splayed glass doors. I noticed an ornate square cast-iron grate on the wall near the floor and put my hand on it. The smooth, cold metal made me shiver.

Wes peeked in the adjacent solarium, which was filled with hanging ferns and potted plants of all sizes. Then he looked at me as if waiting for instruction.

"Okay," I said. "Let's start in the basement and work our way up."

Mrs. Hammerlin showed us to the basement door in the kitchen. "I'll wait up here."

At the bottom of the stairs, we found ourselves in a family room that hadn't been updated since the 1970s. Wall-to-wall shag carpet, wood-paneled walls, and a curved corner wet bar reminded me of my grandparents' old basement—minus all the license plates, 1950s posters, and sports memorabilia they'd had hanging on their walls during my childhood. Wes checked the closets, while I investigated the other half of the basement, behind a heavy, wooden door.

This section was unfinished and dusty. There were several rooms, all with concrete floors and cracked, stone walls, including a utility room, laundry room, and shelf-lined storage room. In the back of the house, above a workbench scattered with ancient tools, I found the window with the missing pane.

"Here, kitty, kitty," I called into the empty room.

To my surprise, I thought I detected a faint mewing sound behind me. Following it to the dingy utility room, I flipped on the overhead light—a bare, flickering bulb—and called again. "Kitty? Are you in here?"

"Any luck?" said a voice behind me.

I started and spun around. "Wes! Don't sneak up on me like that."

He suppressed a chuckle. "Sorry. Hey, guess what I found behind the bar? An old dumbwaiter. The ropes are nearly frayed, but it still seems to work."

"Cool," I said absently, as I turned back to the utility room. Next to the gas water heater, a mean-looking furnace dominated the room, its asbestos-wrapped pipes snaking to the ceiling like Medusa's hair. "I wish I'd brought a flashlight," I said, straining to peer into the cobweb-filled corners.

At that moment, Mrs. Hammerlin yelled down at us in a quavering voice. "Keli! Wesley! I heard something up here!"

"Will you go, Wes? I really want to find this cat."

He ran up to join Mrs. Hammerlin, leaving me alone in the basement. Something creaked behind the furnace. With the light from my cell phone, I inched my way to the back of the room where I found a small opening. Shining my phone in the space, I realized it must be an old coal chute, angling up into darkness. Could a cat have climbed up there? If so, where would she come out?

My nose began to tickle, so I made my way back upstairs. Wes and Mrs. Hammerlin were nowhere to be seen. As I wandered around the first floor, I realized the solarium must have been added on to the house in later years. Sure enough, when I looked under a table pushed up against what would have once been the exterior to the house, I found the opening to the coal chute.

I took out the catnip and waved it in the air like a wand. "Here, Kitty! Come and get it!"

There were lots of hiding places in the solarium, but the cat didn't seem to be in any of them. I was about to go back into the main house when I noticed a slim, floor-to-ceiling, oak storage cabinet in the corner of the room. The door was ajar. I pulled it open, expecting to see shelves of potting soil and gardening tools. Instead, it turned out to be an empty closet with a door in the back. Feeling like the child who entered a wardrobe to another world, I climbed inside.

The narrow entrance opened into an irregular-shaped cubby with a sloping ceiling. I realized I must be under the staircase. Again, shining my phone like a flashlight, I made out some small shapes on the floor. I knelt down and, looking closer, observed a glove, a pair of nylons, a handkerchief, and a coin purse. *Aha! The kitty's lair.*

But no kitty.

I backed out of the secret closet and went back to the dining room. As I stood near the hutch trying to decide what to do next, I once again heard a faint meow. It was coming from the ventilation grate.

Boy, this cat gets around.

I decided to look upstairs next, but when I reached the second-floor landing, I hesitated. The house was eerily quiet. I couldn't imagine where Wes and Mrs. Hammerlin had disappeared to. Suddenly, a strange wailing noise pierced the silence. It was almost otherworldly, like a ghostly foghorn or an enchanted owl. My body tensed, as my hair bristled on the back of my neck.

The sound seemed to be coming from outside, so I moved toward the window at the end of the hall. Before I could reach it, a crash erupted from one of the rooms off the hallway. I ran to the door and yanked it open.

"Hello? Wes?"

The room was still. By the light of the full moon shining through a window, I made out frilly curtains, flowery wallpaper, and a neatly made bed. I guessed this must be one of Mrs. Hammerlin's guest rooms, though it surely belonged to a young girl once upon a time.

Out of the corner of my eye, I sensed a movement. When I turned to look, my heart jumped to my throat. Floating before my eyes was a woman's face. She had wavy, gray hair, deep-set, shadowed eyes, and a sickly pallor.

I knew this face. It was Aunt Josephine.

I shrieked. Without thinking, I flew out of the room as if chased by demons . . . or ghosts.

CHAPTER THIRTEEN

Wes bounded up the stairs and met me in the hallway. "Keli! What is it?"

Almost immediately, I felt sheepish, though my heart still beat madly in my chest. "I—I saw something. In there." I pointed to the bedroom I'd fled.

Wes pushed open the door and switched on the light. He took a cautious step inside. "I don't see anything. What was it?"

I followed him and forced myself to look toward the spot where I'd seen the face. There, on the wall, was a mirror. An oval, gilt-framed mirror. I approached it and stared at my reflection, pale and drawn. I blinked and let out a shaky laugh. I might not look my best, but I looked nothing like the startling image of Aunt Josephine.

I sat heavily on the edge of the bed. That's when I noticed the wooden cross on the floor. I picked it up and looked at the wall above, where a slim nail stuck out at an odd angle. The cross must have fallen, causing the noise I'd heard.

Mrs. Hammerlin appeared in the doorway, then crossed the room to peer out the window. "It's the oddest thing," she said. "Wes and I went outside when we heard the banshee, but we couldn't tell where it was coming from."

"Banshee?" I looked at Wes, and he shrugged.

Mrs. Hammerlin turned around and drew in her breath. "Where did *that* come from?" she exclaimed.

I followed her gaze and beheld the elusive black feline sitting in the doorway, as serene and poised as the goddess Bastet.

"At last," I said. "It's about time you showed yourself."

As if on cue, the cat leaped into my lap.

By the next morning, I thought I must have imagined Aunt Josephine's visage in the mirror. At least, that's what I told myself. It was the only way I could get through the day like a normal person.

On our way home from Mrs. Hammerlin's house, Wes and I had stopped at Mila's again, just long enough to borrow some cat food and a spare litter box. Her guests had all left, but she invited us to come in for a drink. I could tell she was eager to hear about what happened with our ghost hunt, but I didn't feel like talking. I told her I'd call her later. With an understanding look, she gave us some cat supplies and also recommended a good veterinarian who doubled as a kitty daycare provider.

To my relief, the cat did well overnight. She slept like a princess on the upholstered chair in the

corner of our bedroom. Right after breakfast—
cereal for Wes, avocado toast for me, kibble for the
kitty—we dropped the cat at the vet's office. Then
Wes took me to my office.

For a couple of hours, I buried myself in my work.
At half past eleven, I told Julie I was taking an early
lunch and walked over to the town square, a pictur-
esque block that contained quaint shops and
restaurants on tree-lined boulevards surrounding the Capitol-like county courthouse. I walked
past the courthouse to the less-impressive, plain
brick building that housed an assortment of government offices. The Edindale County Department
of Environment was headquartered on the second
floor.

While waiting for Ricki Day, I browsed through
some brochures on a wall rack. The department's
primary focus seemed to be natural resources con-
servation, with separate divisions concerned with
forestry, water quality, and recreation. Apparently,
there was only a small unit devoted to pollution
control. According to the receptionist, a hawk-eyed
woman who smacked her gum, Ricki Day was the
department's only full-time environmental inspector. When Ricki joined us in the lobby, I thanked
her profusely for taking the time to meet with me.

"You must be very busy," I said.

"It's okay." She shook my hand with a firm grip
and directed me to a tiny meeting room off the
lobby. "How can I help you?"

I sat down in one of the four mismatched chairs
and tried to figure out why Ricki looked familiar

to me. She had short, brunette hair and an open, friendly face. I guessed she was probably in her mid-forties. In her government-approved khakis and navy polo shirt bearing the county logo, she was ready to get down to business.

"I wanted to ask you about Josephine O'Malley," I began, then frowned when Ricki gave me a blank look. "Haven't the police been by to speak with you yet?"

"Police? No."

"I guess I beat them to the punch. You know about the body that was found in Shawnee a few days ago?"

Ricki nodded, and I explained to her about the to-do list in Aunt Josephine's pocket. I also told her I was making inquiries for the family.

"Sorry, but I don't know anyone named Josephine O'Malley. The list must refer to a different Ricki."

Undeterred, I said, "She used different names sometimes. Did you know a Jessie O'Mara? Or someone else with the initials JO or AJ? I was told she reported environmental violations somewhat frequently."

Ricki started to shake her head, then paused. "There is a woman who calls me with tips and complaints sometimes. She's been calling for years, ever since I first started here. For the longest time, she wouldn't leave a name. Finally, one day she said I could call her Shima."

"Shima?" I echoed. That was a new one.

"Yeah." Ricki smiled. "I guess she wanted to remain anonymous. But it's not uncommon for some citizens to take on sort of a neighborhood watchdog role, calling government agencies every time they think they have something to report. Often, it's retired folks who have lots of time on their hands. With Shima, sometimes her tips panned out; sometimes they didn't."

"Did you ever meet her?"

"No. She made all her complaints over the phone."

"Did you happen to note what phone number she was calling from?"

"She called from different numbers. Rarely the same one twice. I figured she did that so I wouldn't screen her calls. She said she didn't want to be a pest, but a lot of times it was hard to get off the phone with her. She liked to talk. Sometimes I wondered if she was just lonely."

Up until Ricki's last comment, I was certain this Shima person must be Aunt Josephine. But I had a hard time believing she'd be lonely considering all the friends she supposedly had.

"When did you last hear from Shima?" I asked.

Ricki looked at the ceiling as she thought about it. "It's been a couple months, I think. Her last complaint was about a CAFO out near Hickton. It was discharging waste into a stream."

"What's a CAFO? Something to do with chemicals?"

"It's a concentrated animal feeding operation—otherwise known as a factory farm."

"Oh." I wrinkled my nose. "What about HAPCO? Are you familiar with that company?"

"Yeah, sure. Hemsley Ag-Pro Company. They do

packaging and storage of agricultural chemicals, such as herbicides and insecticides. Also, fertilizers. I've inspected the facility a few times."

"Is that anything like Sorghum?" I was still curious about the unsolved bombing Zeke had told me about.

"Sorghum is a manufacturer. HAPCO is a distributor for Sorghum's products, among others."

Close enough, I thought. "Did your informant complain about HAPCO?"

"Yes, several times. But it's a pretty compliant company. HAPCO files its required reports and keeps up with its housekeeping. I haven't documented any major violations there."

"Hmm." I seemed to have run out of questions. I also realized Detective Rhinehardt might not be thrilled to find me encroaching on his investigation. I thanked Ricki for all the information and stood up.

As we walked back into the lobby, Ricki said, "I'm sorry to hear of Shima's passing—if it turns out that the woman found in the forest really was her."

The receptionist perked up at Ricki's words. "Did you say Shima is dead? Wow. Pop the cork, huh? That crazy lady took up so much of your time."

Ricki gave her a stern look. "She wasn't crazy. She was just concerned." To me, Ricki said, "I really am sorry. I'm going to miss her calls."

Outside, I stood on the sidewalk and tried not to let my disappointment bring me down. I had hoped Ricki would be able to offer more insight into what had happened to my aunt. Ricki's name on Josephine's to-do list seemed like the most promising lead we had.

An image of the note surfaced in my mind. Something bothered me. It was the wording. As I thought about it, I recalled Josephine's exact words on the paper: *See Ricki*. I was sure that's what it said. Yet the inspector told me she'd never met Josephine—aka Shima. She'd only heard from her over the phone.

Was it possible Ricki wasn't being honest about her encounters with her longtime tipster?

The whoosh of flapping wings startled me from my ruminations. A large crow landed on the back of a nearby bench. When I looked over at the bird, I noticed a man getting out of a black sports car parked along the curb. I recognized him at once. It was Tadd Hemsley, the owner of HAPCO. When I'd last seen him, he was making fun of Crenshaw's vampire costume at the haunted barn. I watched as he held out his key fob to beep the car locked, then took off down the sidewalk.

"Tadd!" I chased after him and stopped short when he turned around, startled. He was a wiry guy, with the sort of swaggering toughness that always puts me in mind of a stuntman or a racecar driver. Something about his piercing, blue eyes and silvery gelled hair screamed Hollywood—not to mention the edgy little soul patch above his chin. He definitely stood out among the farmers he often worked with.

"Hello there . . . Keli. Right?"

"Keli Milanni." I stuck out my hand, feeling somewhat idiotic as I tried to catch my breath. "I'm with Olsen, Sykes, and Rafferty."

"Yes, of course. You're not here to sue me, are you?"

"What? No, I—"

"I'm kidding." He snickered and pulled a pack of cigarettes from his jacket pocket. "It was nice seeing you the other night at that haunted barn thing. You made a great witch."

"Thank you. Um, could I talk to you for a minute? You have lots of contacts in the farming community, right?"

"Sure," he said, lighting his cigarette. "Matter of fact, I'm heading to a Farmers Union meeting right now. But I can spare a few minutes."

"I was just wondering . . . have you heard of a seed company called Sister Seeds?"

He shook his head slowly. "I can check the union membership directory, but that doesn't ring any bells."

"How about a woman named Josephine O'Malley?"

"I don't believe so. She a farmer?"

"I'm . . . not sure. I don't suppose the name Shima means anything to you."

He gave me a cockeyed look that answered my question. I decided to switch course. "Do you spend much time out at your facility near Briar Creek Cabins? I mean, are you there every day?"

"Sure. That's my place of business. It's not that close to Briar Creek Cabins, though. Why do you ask?"

"I'm trying to figure out what happened with that woman who was shot near there. I wondered if you or any of your employees might have seen her walking in the area. She was a relative of mine."

He paused with his cigarette between his lips, mid-puff, then pulled it out and gave me a sympathetic look. "I'm terribly sorry to hear that. No one saw her. I would've heard about it."

"That's okay. I just thought I'd ask. Gil Johnson—he was a friend of hers—he said Josephine was sort of an environmental activist and liked to clean up parks, that sort of thing. I thought you might've encountered her at some point over the years." Tadd shook his head again, and I realized I was barking up the wrong tree. "Well, she didn't even live in Edindale, at least not full-time. So, I guess I'm not surprised."

He took another drag on his cigarette and looked thoughtful. "Are you talking about Gil Johnson, the canoe guy? Now there's an odd character. He volunteered to help out at Farm Aid last year, and then never showed up. He's always been a flaky one."

"Did he give you an excuse?"

"Nah. He just skipped town. Rumor has it he's hiding from an ex-wife. He probably owes alimony or something." Tadd tossed his cigarette butt toward the street. "Maybe the police should question Gil Johnson. If he was acquainted with the dead woman, he'd for sure be at the top of my list."

On my way back to the office, I stopped off at Callie's health food store and juice bar to grab a prepackaged salad. As I stood in line to check out,

I looked at my watch and saw that I'd been out for two hours. *Yikes!* I hotfooted it the rest of the way and burst through the glass doors, only to halt in my tracks at the sight of Beverly standing in the lobby with a client. They both looked up in surprise.

"There you are," said Beverly. "I was looking for you. Mr. Jameson was telling me about a wonderful opportunity I think you'd be perfect for."

Inwardly, I groaned. Lately, all the opportunities Beverly gave me involved after-hours events she didn't want to attend herself. I was saved from having to respond when the door opened behind me. Beverly's smile froze in place, as her eyes betrayed a flicker of alarm. I turned to see Detective Rhinehardt amble toward us.

"Afternoon," he said. "Sorry for the interruption."

"Good afternoon," said Beverly, stiffly. At once, I realized the cause of her discomfort. The last time Detective Rhinehardt had entered the firm's office was to summon Beverly down to the station for questioning. I was sure she didn't relish the memory.

"I was hoping to catch a few minutes of Ms. Milanni's time," he said.

"By all means," she said. "Keli, I'll fill you in later on Mr. Jameson's invitation."

I led Rhinehardt to my office, where we sat at the small round meeting table in the corner opposite my desk.

"Here you go," he said, setting a brown grocery sack on the table. "Your aunt's things."

I reached into the bag and removed a slim travel

purse and a manila envelope. I couldn't resist peeking inside the purse, but it didn't contain much—only a couple of twenties, a ChapStick, an ink pen, a pair of reading glasses, and a few cough drops. I opened the envelope next and emptied out the contents: two rings and a necklace, all made of Black Hills gold. I fingered the delicate grape leaf designs and imagined Josephine wearing the jewelry.

Rhinehardt cleared his throat. "I have the ME's report. Just thought I'd tell you about it in person."

"Any surprises?"

"Not really. Toxicology was negative. No broken bones or contusions. One sprained ankle. Your aunt died from a single gunshot wound to her heart, clean through the back. She was shot at close range, less than 100 yards, with a twenty-two-caliber rifle. I'm guessing she probably didn't suffer long."

I imagined he said that to all victims' families, but I appreciated hearing it nonetheless.

"As for time of death," Rhinehardt continued, "the ME estimates it happened between four and five, the morning of Saturday, October 24."

And Levi Markham happened upon the body an hour or so later, I thought. And he didn't hear the gunshot.

"Twenty-two caliber," I said. "That's a common rifle, isn't it?"

"Yes. It's on the lighter side, often used by beginners and youth hunters. It's usually for small game, but deadly nonetheless."

"Is that the type of rifle that was stolen from the hunters' cabin you told me about?"

Rhinehardt gave me a grim smile. "I knew you'd ask that next. Yes. It's the same." He wrinkled his brow and pursed his lips. "About that—I have some additional information. We lifted some prints from the gun cabinet and in other areas around the house. Forensics informed me this morning that they found a match."

"That's great! Right? Whose fingerprints were they?"

"The victim's. Josephine O'Malley."

CHAPTER FOURTEEN

After Detective Rhinehardt left, I did my best to concentrate on my work. But when Beverly peeked into my office, she found me staring into space. She cleared her throat.

"I have a special request of you, Keli," she said.

The worry must have shown in my eyes, because she held up her hand. "I want you to take the rest of the week off. You've had a death in your family, and you're not at the top of your game."

"Oh, but I don't want to fall behind," I protested. "I'm okay, really."

Beverly shook her head. "Nonsense. Crenshaw informed me that you're the only family your aunt had around here. I assume you're in charge of funeral arrangements, which is not a light burden. We'll manage without you for a few days. I'll ask Julie to reschedule all your appointments."

I relented, and Beverly left me to shut down my computer and pack up. I knew she was right. Now that the medical examiner's report was complete,

Josephine's body could be laid to rest. I'd have to call my mom and let her know.

I was just finishing up one last client email, when my phone buzzed. It was a text from Zeke. He said he had some information for me that would be best delivered over two stiff drinks. I replied at once and told him to meet me at the Loose in an hour. Then I called in my reinforcements.

A short time later, Farrah and I were sitting across from each other sipping wine spritzers at our favorite nightclub. Happy hour had yet to begin, so it was relatively quiet. I filled her in on the news from Detective Rhinehardt.

"Well, that's not incredibly helpful, is it?" she said, stirring the ice in her drink.

I shrugged. "Dunno. One thing I do know, though: Aunt Josephine certainly didn't shoot herself in the back."

"Right. And then get rid of the gun before she died." Farrah rolled her eyes. "There weren't any other fingerprints at that house besides hers?"

"None that didn't belong there. Also, get this— the house wasn't broken into. Only the gun cabinet was busted."

"It was an inside job? Who owns this house?"

"Some guys from upstate who all have solid alibis for last Saturday."

We nursed our drinks as we pondered the possibilities.

"So, Josephine got into this house somehow," said Farrah, repeating the obvious.

"Yep. I'm guessing it's where she was staying.

Rhinehardt said the house was tidy, but her prints were all over—in the kitchen, bathroom, bedroom."

"At least we know Fern and Gil were telling the truth about her not staying with them."

"True."

"And she was the one who stole the gun that killed her."

I nodded. "People can stop assuming it was an accident. She was shot at close range, directly in the back. She must have either given the killer the gun, or the killer took it from her. It was probably someone she knew."

Farrah gave me a sad, sympathetic look, and I shook myself. I was a big believer in the power of one's attitude. Gloominess never helped anyone. This was why I suggested the wine spritzers in the first place. They were light, refreshing, and sparkly— just what I needed. Throw in a little spell in the guise of a positive intention, and you had yourself a magical potion.

I lifted my glass and grinned. "To finding answers."

Farrah brightened. "To finding answers," she echoed. We clinked glasses and took fortifying sips.

"Hello, ladies," said a smooth voice at our elbows. It was Zeke, in full hipster garb, from the top of his high, coiffed hair to the tips of his ankle-high boots. I had to admit, he pulled off slim burgundy pants and a checkered blazer in a way most men couldn't.

"What do we have here?" he asked. "Is it Mary and Rhoda grumbling about the patriarchy? Or Lucy and Ethel plotting a zany scheme? I'm guessing the latter."

"Oh, brother," said Farrah. She scooted over to let him sit down.

"Those references are way too old for you," I said.

Unlike Farrah and me, the young waitress seemed to be impressed. She appeared at our table to wait on Zeke with a finger in her hair and a pout on her lips. He didn't seem to notice.

"I'll have what they're having."

"What?" I said, in mock surprise. "No martini?"

Farrah snorted. Then she asked the waitress to bring some appetizers. Turning to Zeke, she said, "Your treat, slick. Right? Since you called us here?"

"I asked to meet with Keli," he said, looking slightly vexed.

"She's kidding." I shot Farrah a look that said, "Behave," and gave Zeke a reassuring smile. "Now what is it you have to tell me?"

Zeke looked around the room, then leaned in and cupped his hand around his mouth.

"Really?" said Farrah.

I shushed her and drew near to Zeke. "I'm listening."

"You were right," Zeke said. "Fern is part of a network known as the Sisterhood. It's worldwide. I'm not gonna tell you everything they do, 'cause you wouldn't believe me anyway. But your aunt Josie was part of it in the beginning, back in the early seventies."

"Then what?" I asked. "Wait, do you mean *from* the beginning, or only *in* the beginning?"

"Only at the start, I think. She left Edindale to do work for the Sisterhood, but then she went off on her own. Fern wasn't too happy about that. Josie got involved with some other people. Later, she started her own organization, called Sister Seeds."

"I know about that," I said. "At least, a little bit. Is it a nonprofit, or what? I can't find any information about the company."

"That's because it was never legally formed. It's an underground organization."

"But why? What's so secret about distributing seeds?"

Zeke sat back and gave me a coy look. I wondered if he was trying to be cute, or if he just didn't know the answer. The waitress brought his drink then, and a platter of assorted batter-dipped vegetables. Farrah passed out the little plates and filled hers. "What else you got, big guy?" she asked. "Did Fern say anything about who might have wanted Josephine dead?"

Instead of answering, Zeke stuffed a piece of cauliflower in his mouth and chewed it slowly. I recalled his tendency to say as little as possible and wondered if he was reaching his limit. The bar was starting to fill up, and we were losing our privacy.

"Zeke, tell me this," I began. "Fern and Josie must have remained friends even after Josie went off and did her own thing, right? I mean, Fern admitted as much to me. She said Josie stayed with her a few times a year."

"Sure. I guess so."

"Then why won't she talk about Josie? Why won't she tell me what Josie was involved in?"

Zeke took a big gulp of his spritzer, then made a

face. "Actually," he said, setting his glass down. "She will talk to you."

"She will?" I sat up straight. "That's good news!"

"On one condition."

Now my shoulders deflated. "What condition?"

"She said she'll meet with you and talk to you about Josie, if you'll do something for her."

"Do what?"

"She wants to buy the property where the commune used to be. And she wants you to make that happen."

"Oh." I glanced at Farrah, who mirrored my own incredulity. "Is that all?"

I made it to the vet's right before closing time. The tech told me they were prepared to board the cat overnight if need be, but she was glad I made it. She said the cat seemed restless. I peeked in the travel crate and was met with a wary, yellow-eyed stare.

"What's that around her neck?" I asked.

"Oh, it's a collar. Mila Douglas stopped by earlier today. She wanted to check on things and brought a gift."

"How sweet." And how like Mila. I admired the crescent moon charm hanging from the new black collar and decided I'd send Mila a big bouquet of flowers to thank her for all her help.

"The cat is healthy," the tech went on. "And well-socialized. I understand she was a stray, but she's clearly been around humans. She's going to make a nice pet."

I had a feeling the tech was right. I just hoped I'd make a good pet owner. As a kid, I'd helped take care of the family dog, but I'd never had a cat. I wasn't sure if bringing this cat home was the right thing to do, but she seemed to have chosen me. How could I refuse?

When I got home, Wes was in the kitchen sautéing garlic and onions. I set the pet carrier on the floor and opened the door. The cat streaked out and headed for the bedroom.

"Hungry?" called Wes.

"Smells heavenly," I answered, coming up behind him. I helped him finish preparing dinner—pasta and salad—and set the table. As we ate, I told him about my day, frustrations and all.

He listened quietly, then put down his fork. "You know," he began, "just because you keep asking all the right questions, doesn't mean you're gonna get the answers you want. Sometimes mysteries remain unsolved."

I frowned. "How can you say that?"

"I just don't want you to make yourself crazy over this. I mean, maybe it was an accident, maybe it wasn't. Maybe there's someone from your aunt's past who tracked her down, shot her, and then left. That person could be long gone."

"That's not a very positive thing to say. How about some hope? Some optimism?"

"Look, the cops are good at what they do. They're the experts. That police detective, Rhinehardt, he seems pretty good. Why don't you let him sift through the evidence and follow the leads? You don't need to take this on."

"You sound like Crenshaw," I grumbled.

After dinner, I told Wes I needed to be alone for a little while. I found my tarot deck in my cedar chest and brought it to the spare room. As I was closing the door behind me, the cat appeared by my feet.

"You want to join me? Okay, but I'm shutting the door. There aren't any secret passageways or hidden exits in here, like in your old house."

While the cat explored the room, I sat cross-legged on the end of the spare bed and watched her. It had been almost twenty-four hours since I'd taken the kitty—with Mrs. Hammerlin's blessing and gratitude—and I hadn't heard from the older woman since then. I took that as a good sign.

"You gave her quite a fright, you know," I said. "Poor Mrs. Hammerlin heard you knocking things about but was unable to hear your mewing."

Ignoring me, the cat continued to stalk about the room, poking into the closet and sniffing the shoes on the floor. Finally, she jumped to the wide windowsill and settled down.

"What should I call you?" I asked. "Midnight? Spooky? Luna?"

She half-closed her eyes, and I chuckled. "I guess I'll have to get to know you a little better first."

Returning to my tarot deck, I removed the cards from their velvet pouch and held them between my palms. I took a deep breath. "What I need is guidance," I murmured.

Usually, I went to Mila when I wanted a tarot reading. She was skilled at interpreting the cards and all their subtle nuances. But sometimes I liked to draw the cards on my own. It was another way to communicate with the Divine, like a direct line to Spirit. All I had to do was ask the question, then open my heart to receive.

As I shuffled the cards, I thought about what I should ask. My main question, of course, was who killed Aunt Josephine. The second question was *why?* But those inquiries were so specific. I was afraid I'd have difficulty parsing out the answer from the image on a tarot card. With my level of experience, it was probably best to ask for direction. *What should be my next step?*

Closing my eyes, I placed the deck on the bed in front of me and hovered my hand over the top. "What should I do to solve this mystery? What do I *need* to do?"

I opened my eyes and cut the deck. Then I flipped over the top card.

"Knight of Wands." I stared at the illustration on the card. It showed a young, determined-looking knight on horseback, with the horse rearing up on its hind legs. The knight held a big, sprouting stick, his wand, in his right hand. The horse's mane and the plume on the knight's helmet resembled flames, as did the edge of the knight's tunic, which was yellow and decorated with pictures of a salamander. In the background was a desert and three pyramids.

"What is this supposed to mean?" I muttered. "Am I supposed to go on a journey? Am I going into battle?" I tried to recall what I knew about this card. It represented action and adventure. It was a high-energy card, full of passion and heat. It could signify sudden change, or challenges to come.

I tossed down the card in frustration. *How does this help me?* The only advice I could glean here was to hold on tight.

Thunder rumbled in the distance. I glanced over at the cat. She stirred but didn't move from her perch by the window.

I leaned back on the decorative pillows, piled high on the spare bed, and let my eyes drift shut. It had been a long day, following a late night. I felt I should probably cast a spell, or maybe try another form of divination, but I couldn't muster the energy. Ironic, I thought, considering the tarot card I chose.

I was so sleepy. A lot had happened the past couple of days. *And it was only last night that I thought I saw Aunt Josephine's ghost.* Seemed like ages ago.

What was she doing in Mrs. Hammerlin's house?

The next thing I knew, I was transported to a dark forest. It was unfamiliar, unlike any forest I was used to. It seemed to be swampy, with drooping cypress trees and a misty fog. Hidden dangers lurked in the darkest shadows. Snakes, alligators, monsters. My pulse quickened. Suddenly, I heard a noise—footsteps, crashing through the underbrush. It was Aunt Josephine! Someone was chasing her. I ran after them. I wanted to help. But I was on a treadmill, never getting any closer . . . until, out of nowhere, I felt a burst of energy. As if propelled by fire, I rushed forward and grabbed the man who was pursuing my aunt. I whirled him around and looked into his face. It was . . . Levi Markham! The writer in the cabin. But why?

There was another crash, and I awoke with a start, confused. Lightning flashed, and the cat jumped from the windowsill to my altar, knocking a book to the floor.

"It's just a storm," I told the cat. I pushed myself off the bed, as the cat hopped off the altar and darted into the closet. "I didn't know you were such a fraidy cat."

I moved to pick up the book. It was the copy of *Silent Spring* that had appeared on my front porch. I had placed it on the altar next to my aunt's picture. Now, as I retrieved the book from the floor, I noticed it had landed with the pages open. I flipped it over and read the chapter title: "Rivers of Death."

Great, I thought. *Just great.*

CHAPTER FIFTEEN

I tried to sleep in on Wednesday morning, but it was a lost cause. I had too much on my mind. Beverly had told me to stay home in order to arrange my aunt's funeral, so that's what I did. I made an appointment with a funeral director, who, fortunately, was able to see me right away. He helped me select a funeral package within my grandma's budget, and even showed me some ready-made headstones. I placed a rush order on the inscription, so the stone could be placed in time for the burial.

After leaving the funeral parlor, I stopped by Our Lady of Mercy Catholic Church to speak with Father Gabe. Hearing Mrs. Hammerlin mention him the other day reminded me of the time I'd met the priest while investigating the death of an elderly parishioner. Father Gabe was warm and personable and, luckily, available to perform the service. As he explained to me, it didn't matter that Josephine didn't attend his church. As long as she had been baptized, she had a right to a Catholic funeral. That was a relief, since my grandmother was counting on it.

I had no idea if that's what Josephine would have wanted. She'd provided no clues about her last wishes. Would she have preferred to have her body cremated and scattered over field or forest? Or would she have liked a traditional Native American burial—which, as far as I knew, varied widely depending on tribe and geographical location?

Or maybe she didn't have any preference at all. Since the decision was left to me, I chose to honor Josephine in the tradition of our family. In doing so, I hoped to offer a measure of comfort and happiness to the ones she left behind.

Three hours later, I was back home and on the telephone with my mom. I told her I'd booked the date, time, place, and pastor, and she confirmed who was coming. My family would descend upon Edindale in five days.

When I hung up the phone, I paced around my house—from the living room to the kitchen to the study, back to the living room. The cat watched me nervously. "Sorry, Frisky," I said once, as she darted from my path. "No, that's not it. Whiskers? Shadow?" I shook my head and kept walking, from the front window, where I gazed out at the empty street, to the patio door and its view of the backyard that needed to be raked. As I paced, I realized I was avoiding the upstairs for a reason. I was troubled by my failed attempt at divination and my inability to come up with a useful spell. Why couldn't I produce a magical solution? The Goddess had never let me down before.

Circling back to my study, I stopped in the doorway and stared at my dark computer. All at once, I remembered my nightmare from last night. Maybe the Goddess hadn't deserted me after all. I found my phone and called Farrah.

"Hey, superstar. Are you busy today?"

"I'm about to give a legal research demo to the new class of one Ls over here at the law school. You should see them. They're all so cute and anxious. I don't think we were ever so tense, were we?"

"You weren't, that's for sure. Can you stop by later? I'm at home."

"Yes, ma'am."

I busied myself with laundry and vacuuming, but I couldn't escape my own growing anxiety. By the time Farrah arrived, I was ready for action. She, however, was ready for lunch. She raided my refrigerator and made herself a sandwich. Then we sat in the living room, where the cat was playing with a ball of yarn.

"What are you going to call her?" asked Farrah. "How about Cocoa? No, wait. It should be something witchy. Salem?"

"That was the cat's name on *Sabrina the Teenage Witch*, remember? He was kinda snarky, as I recall. Plus, he was a *he*."

"I got it. Sammy, the *Sam Hain* cat."

"Actually, the *m* is silent. It's usually pronounced *sow-en*."

"Right. I knew that. Let's see. Hazel? Dreamy?"

"Speaking of dreams . . ." I told her about my vision of Levi chasing Josephine in a scary forest.

Farrah chewed her sandwich and gave me an appraising look. "With most people, I'd say a dream is just a dream. Knowing you, it's probably a message or something. What do you think?"

"I think I need to get back inside Levi's cabin."

She didn't hesitate. "I'm in. But how? You're not proposing we break and enter."

"No, of course not. He'll invite us in. The problem is, how can we get him to leave long enough for me to go through his papers?"

Farrah crossed her legs and swung her foot as she thought. "What if we say we have car trouble? He comes out to look under the hood and you run inside."

"What if he doesn't know anything about cars?" I shook my head. "I think we're going to have to split up. What if I show up alone, he lets me inside, and then you create some kind of diversion to make him run outside? Like, set off some fireworks or something."

Farrah gaped at me. "Seriously? I'd blow off my fingers or start a forest fire. You want a distraction, let me wear a skimpy top and a short skirt. There's your distraction." She tugged at her suit skirt, which was already on the short side.

"I don't doubt your ability to get a man's attention, but that's only half the problem. How can we get him to leave the cabin with me still in it?"

She had no response. I looked around the room, as if searching for an answer. The cat had abandoned the yarn and was now curled up in a patch of sun beneath the front window. She looked as if she owned the place.

As I gazed at the kitty, an idea began to take shape. I just needed to be as stealthy as a cat.

We parked at the cabin office, so Levi wouldn't happen to see us outside his window. Fortunately, the owner once again appeared to be absent. I cut the engine and turned to look at Farrah. "Are you sure you're up for this?"

"Oh, yeah. No sweat. I'll just knock on his door, tell him I'm helping you out, and bat my eyes. He'll let me in, offer me a drink. I'll ask for a tour of the cabin. When we're upstairs, I'll signal you in the window. You'll sneak in and hide in the closet. Then I'll ask him to show me the spot in the forest where he found the body. You'll come in and snoop around, then call me when you're out. Bada bing, bada boom."

She pulled a compact from her purse and touched up her lipstick. In the jeans and boots she'd borrowed from me, and her own low-cut white blouse, she looked like a model posing as a sexy hiker in a fashion magazine. I tried not to laugh. It was my nerves that were making me giddy. I couldn't believe we were really doing this.

We got out of the car and wished each other luck. While Farrah headed to Levi's place, I darted to the tree line behind the cabins. I crept to a secluded spot with a view of Levi's upstairs window and crouched in place.

It was a cloudy, breezy afternoon. The longer I waited in the bushes, the more my doubts seeped in like a damp chill. There was too much that could go wrong with our plan. What if Levi locked the door after letting Farrah inside? Then I wouldn't be able to get in. Or, what if he declined to show her his bedroom? Stranger things had happened. Or, what if he did, but they weren't up there long enough? How was Farrah going to know when I was safely hidden?

I was about ready to call her and abort the mission, when I saw a movement between the upstairs curtains. It was Farrah, with her back to the window. She raised her hand in a subtle, backward wave.

I sucked in my breath and made a mad dash for the front door. It was unlocked. As quietly as possible, I pulled it open and stuck my head inside. From upstairs, I could hear my friend's cheery voice.

"There's so much room up here! And look at this gorgeous quilt! What kind of stitch is this, do you suppose?"

I let myself in and closed the door behind me. Praying there'd be enough space in the closet to hold me for a few minutes, I tiptoed across the room, grasped the knob, and pulled. It didn't budge. I tried harder, but it was no use. The closet was locked. *Dang it!*

Desperately, I searched the immediate vicinity for a key. Whoever heard of a locked closet in a cabin? What was in there, anyway?

Finding no key, I whipped around and scanned the room for another hiding place. The top step creaked, and my heart skipped a beat. There I was, in the middle of the room, like a deer caught in the crosshairs.

Dang, dang, dang!

"Spider!" yelled Farrah. "I saw a spider! Kill it!"

I let out my breath. It was time to cancel this farce. I hurried back to the front door but paused as the sofa caught my eye. It was situated at an angle, leaving a small gap next to the wall. Could I fit?

"It was just there!" yelled Farrah, sounding hysterical.

Good Goddess. I had to try. I owed it to Farrah, who was giving the performance of her life. I scooted the sofa another few inches from the wall and hurled myself over. Wedged in tight and facedown, I heard the stairs creak again. A few seconds later, Farrah called out in a calmer voice. "Never mind!"

The stairs creaked a second time, and I heard Levi's voice. "I'll keep an eye out before I go to bed. Wouldn't want to wake up next to a brown recluse."

"No doubt. You've already been through enough. Like finding that body. That must have been horrible for you."

"Yeah."

"Would you mind showing me where it was? I know you showed Keli, but she has a terrible memory."

"I don't know. I don't think it'll be very helpful."

"Oh, please? I came all this way. I want to mark the spot on a map."

"Don't you think the cops are on top of it?"

"Who knows? Come on. Let's go before it rains."

I heard the door open. Farrah could be very persuasive when she wanted to be. I imagined her grabbing Levi by the hand. He said, "Okay." The door slammed, and the lock clicked over.

I counted to ten, then shimmied out of my hiding place. Shaking out my hands, which had fallen asleep, I peeked out the window. Farrah and Levi were entering the woods. I swallowed. I really hoped this wasn't a mistake.

Turning to the desk, I observed the same stack of papers and manila folders as before. At this point, I wanted nothing more than to get out of there as quickly as possible. I rushed over and flipped through the folders, skimming labels and skipping past names I didn't recognize—until I came to one I did know. Gil Johnson. I held the edge of the folder, curious about the contents, but then I saw the next file. It was the one I was really after. In the interest of time, I dropped Gil's file back in place and opened up the one bearing Josephine's name.

The top sheet was a newspaper clipping from the *Edindale Gazette.* It was the most recent article about her death, the one that reported a family member had identified the body in the woods as that of Josephine O'Malley, 62, of Bentlee, Nebraska.

I turned the entire stack over and began at the bottom, gingerly uncovering one page at a time in what turned out to be a photocopy parade of Josephine's past. There were old documents, including her birth certificate and baptism record, yearbook photos, and even a copy of her local library card, complete with girlish signature. After that were voter registration cards—one in Illinois and one, a year later, in Missouri. Both were decades old. Next was a photograph of Josie at a protest rally. She carried a sign with the word *SORGHUM* in dripping red letters, under a superimposed skull and crossbones. As I stared at the picture, her flashing eyes and curled lips caught by the photographer midshout, I could almost hear the noise of the crowd and the rising cries of the passionate young activist.

The next several pages contained names and addresses, including a lot of O'Malleys and Milannis. I experienced a little jolt when I saw my own name and address. There was a large red asterisk beside it.

As I flipped through the pages, a postcard fluttered to the floor. I picked it up and knew right away it was one of Josephine's, even though it wasn't signed. Her handwriting was unmistakable. It was addressed to Gil Johnson and postmarked from South Dakota one month ago. The front featured an iconic image of Devils Tower. The back contained few words, but they were so weighty I had to sit down.

> *Coming to E. in October. I'm going to make one last pitch for your cooperation, then I'm coming clean. It's time, G. I know you don't agree, but I have to do it.*

I blew out a breath. *Incredible.*

I straightened the papers, returning them to their folder, and stacked the files as best as I could. In a daze, I picked up one of the loose papers lying on the desk. It was a fuzzy copy of a newspaper article from a 1978 edition of the *New York Times.* The headline cut like a razor: "Sorghum Bombing Claims Two Lives." I skimmed the article, halting when I reached a section that was highlighted in florescent yellow and circled in red. It was the names of the slain security guards: Robert Treeleaf and Alphonse Mendona.

A scraping sound on the window wrenched me from the past. It was a tree branch, buffeted by the wind. I stood up, suddenly conscious of where I was—in the midst of committing my own crime. I wondered what the penalty was for trespassing.

With a backward glance at the desk, I hurried to the front door. After making sure the coast was clear, I let myself out—only to realize the lock was a dead bolt. I wouldn't be able to relock it without a key. No matter. I needed to get away from here. I ducked around the corner and leaned against a picnic table.

My mind whirred. The papers I'd seen suggested Josephine had some connection with the Sorghum bombing, just as I had speculated. At a minimum, Levi must have thought there was a connection. Apparently, Gil was involved, too. I couldn't imagine how Levi obtained the postcard meant for Josephine's old pal. Did Gil even receive it?

More importantly, *why* did Levi have all those papers? Was he writing a book about the bombing? Perhaps a historical fiction novel, or a nonfiction account of the incident?

Or did he have a special interest in the victims? Maybe he was related to one of them. Maybe he was out for vengeance.

One thing was clear: he didn't happen to innocently meet Josephine on a hiking trail. He came here to track her down. He followed her—just like in my dream.

And now he was taking Farrah to the scene of the murder.

CHAPTER SIXTEEN

The wind whipped my hair as I stood under the trees next to Levi's cabin. I needed to call Farrah to let her know she could come back. I looked at my phone, then slapped my forehead. There was no signal.

The more I thought about Farrah alone in the forest with a man who wasn't who he said he was, the more worried I became. I had never thought of Levi as dangerous, but what did I know? What if he was one of those psycho writers in a Stephen King novel?

Without further delay, I took off down the hiking trail. Clouds blotted the noonday sun, making the forest dark and dreary. I tried to comfort myself with the knowledge that Levi should have nothing against Farrah. She wasn't named in his list of people related to Josephine. Still, I walked faster and faster until, before I knew it, I was jogging, and then racing, down the trail. I dodged branches and jumped over rocks and roots, picking up steam as I ran. At first, I thought I would approach them silently, see what was going on, and try to get Farrah's attention. Now, I was so worked up, I threw caution to the wind and tore through the trees like a madwoman.

Suddenly, I was upon them—so abruptly, I almost ran right past them. I skidded to a stop, panting and red-faced. I must have looked wild and crazy. They both gawked as if they'd just witnessed me land before them in a flying saucer. Clutching my side, I bent over to catch my breath.

Farrah found her voice first. "Keli? What—what on earth are you doing here? Are you okay?"

As my heartbeat finally returned to normal, I looked at them again and realized I had worried for nothing. They stood next to each other as comfortably as old friends. Levi, leaning on a walking stick and looking cute in his plaid flannel shirt, gazed at me with a mixture of curiosity and concern.

"I'm fine," I said, trying to sound casual. "I just . . . that is, I—I wanted to catch up with you. I wanted to see the place again, where my aunt was killed. I ended up taking the day off from work, so I thought I'd join you."

"Oh," said Farrah, still looking confused.

"I tried to call you," I said, "but you must not have phone service out here."

"It's real spotty," said Levi. "And it's worse in bad weather. It's very frustrating."

"That must be it," I said, motioning toward the sky. The clouds looked like they could break open at any second.

"We were heading back," said Farrah. "I didn't want to get caught in a storm. Are you sure you really want to see the site now?"

I hesitated. Although it was only an excuse before, now that I was here, I found that I *did* want to see the spot again.

"Are we very far from it?"

"It's about a five-minute walk from here," said Levi.

"Well . . ."

"All right," said Farrah, seeing that I was serious. "Let's make it quick."

I turned to Levi. "You don't have to come with us. I think we can find it from here. It's by that cairn, right?"

"I don't mind," he said, falling into step behind us.

We hurried along the twisting path without speaking. Before long, Levi signaled that we'd reached the place. It was a good thing, because I probably would have missed it. You had to know precisely where to look to see the stacked stones.

"I'll just be a minute." Leaving Farrah and Levi on the trail, I hurried over to the spot Levi had shown me before. For a moment, I stood motionless, feeling the breeze on my face and listening to the trees creak and whistle overhead. I didn't know what Levi was up to, but I felt sure he'd told me the truth about this place. This was where Josephine had died. Of course, I could always ask Detective Rhinehardt for confirmation.

I took out my phone and snapped a few pictures of the stones and trees. Belatedly, I wished I had an offering or memorial to leave here, such as flowers or, better yet, seeds.

I glanced at the dark clouds overhead and knew I should get back. Yet, still I lingered. It was almost as if a magnetic pull kept me rooted to the place. I felt a strange sense of expectation, as if I was waiting for something to happen. What it was, I didn't know.

Reluctantly, I finally began walking back toward the trail. Peering ahead, I didn't see Farrah and Levi where I'd left them. I figured they must have started back. As I picked my way through the brambles, the wind shifted and the air became cold. Out of the corner of my eye, I thought I detected a swift motion. When I looked, there was nothing. I took another step, then froze. I had a strong feeling that something was behind me, but when I looked over my shoulder, I saw nothing but trees and rocks. I turned my head again, and this time I did see something, a few feet away. Then, just like that, it was gone. It had been fleeting, like a shadow or a trick of the light. It was probably just my imagination. Whatever it was, it looked an awful lot like a petite, gray-haired woman. Like Aunt Josephine.

I ran the rest of the way back to the trail and found Farrah and Levi sitting on a boulder a short distance from the path. Farrah hopped up to meet me halfway and gripped my arm, as if she thought I might keel over. "Keli? You okay? You look like you've seen a—"

"Don't say it." I held up my palm. "Please. Don't say it."

* * *

Farrah plied me with questions, but I refused to answer until we were safely ensconced in my car and driving away from Briar Creek Cabins. If Levi wasn't already on to us, I figured he soon would be. As we emerged from the forest and approached his cabin, he glanced around as if wondering where I'd parked. Before he could say a word, I tossed off a quick good-bye and practically dragged Farrah away. I didn't want to be present when Levi noticed his cabin was unlocked.

"Girl, what happened back there?" she demanded. "First, you come running up into the woods like a jackrabbit on fire, then you can't wait to get out again."

"I was afraid you were in danger. I can't believe I let you go off by yourself with a murder suspect."

"Wait. He's a murder suspect? Since when?"

"I don't know what's going on," I admitted. I told her about all the documents I'd seen in Levi's cabin.

She took a moment to process the information. "So, he could still be writing a book. Is that what you're saying? The articles, all those artifacts, that sounds like research material to me."

I sighed. "I guess it could be. But what about this?" I reached into my jacket pocket and pulled out the postcard Josephine had sent to Gil. I handed it to Farrah.

"Jeez, Kel! You stole this from his cabin?"

"I didn't mean to. I was in such a hurry to get out of there, I slipped it in my pocket without thinking."

"I suppose," Farrah said doubtfully.

"It doesn't belong to him anyway," I argued.

"Unless Gil gave it to him."

I considered the possibility. Josephine had written that she was "coming clean," and that she hoped for Gil's cooperation. Evidently, he didn't support her decision. Would he have tried to talk her out of it? Could he have employed Levi to talk her out of it? Or worse?

"Let's swing by Gil's canoe shop. Do you mind?"

Farrah consulted her watch. "I've got time. Go for it."

As soon as we turned onto the gravel road leading to Gil's place, fat raindrops splattered on the windshield. I switched on the wipers, and pulled up to the dark, shuttered cottage. All the vehicles and canoes we'd seen the last time we were here were now gone, presumably stored away for the season.

"What does that say?" asked Farrah. She squinted at a handwritten sign hanging in the window.

"'See you in the spring,'" I read.

"That was fast. We were here, like, two days ago. That kid made it sound like they'd be open for a while yet."

"Yep." Unlike Levi, Gil apparently wasn't going to keep hanging around.

We watched the rain pour down, dripping from the gutters of the shack and filling the potholes in the small parking lot. After a minute, I put the car in reverse and headed home.

"What are you going to do next?" Farrah asked.

"I guess I'll find out who owns that property Fern wants to buy. Apparently, that's the only way she'll talk to me."

"I'll conduct the title search for you."

"You will?"

"Yeah. You've been through enough today. You look like you could use a nice, long nap."

After a hot shower and a change of clothes, I decided a soothing cup of tea was in order. It was what Mila would prescribe anyway. I'd add in a bit of kitchen witchery for good measure.

While the water heated on the stove, I gathered an assortment of dried herbs and tea leaves. Standing at the counter, I whipped up a concoction that seemed to suit my current state of being. Starting with a base of loose black tea leaves, I made up a little rhyme as I went along:

> *A cup of black tea . . . for courage and pluck,*
> *Petals of rose, for protection and luck,*
>
> *A sprig of rosemary to sharpen my mind,*
> *For psychic skills . . . some dandelion,*
>
> *A pinch of lavender to ease my stress,*
> *A couple of bay leaves to ensure success.*

I ground my ingredients with a mortar and pestle, dumped them in a mug, and topped them with boiling water. While the tea steeped, I took up a broom and engaged in some moving meditation. I swept the floor with slow, purposeful brushstrokes, imagining the energy swirling beneath the broom. *Clear house, clear mind. As without, so within.*

By the time the tea was cool enough to drink, my floor was clean and my nerves were at least slightly calmer. I lifted my mug in a toast to the Goddess, took a sip—and promptly spewed a mouthful into the sink.

Blech!

It was awful. Good intentions aside, some herbs just weren't meant to be mixed. With a disgusted sigh, I dumped the tea down the drain and had a glass of water instead.

Now what?

I wandered into the living room, where the cat was curled up on the back of the couch. For a creature who used to have the run of her neighborhood, she seemed perfectly content to stay inside.

"What do you think, Miss Kitty? Willow? Mittens?"

She blinked at me slowly, and I blinked back. I felt like we were communicating, but I had no idea what either of us was saying.

What I needed was answers, but not the kind that came from within. I needed to go out again, this time to a place where answers were plentiful. I needed to pay a visit to the public library.

CHAPTER SEVENTEEN

Every time I entered the Edindale Public Library, I felt like I was stepping back in time. Built in the early 1900s with funds from a Carnegie grant, the old library still inspired a sense of civic pride and lofty ideals. It was a quiet bastion of knowledge, a haven of culture and learning. Or maybe that was just me.

At the gleaming, oak circulation desk, I asked if Zeke Marshal was available. The librarian directed me upstairs to the staff office behind the stacks. Zeke was waiting for me.

"What a fantastic surprise! I'm supposed to be here for another hour or so, but it's not a big deal if I take off early. Want to go grab a drink?"

"I don't want to get you in trouble, Zeke. I was just hoping to borrow a minute of your time."

"Come on in." He ushered me into the staff room, which was plastered with posters of baby animals and motivational quotes. "This is a shared space," he explained. "They wouldn't let me redecorate."

I smiled and sat at an empty desk next to Zeke's workstation. He hopped on his wheeled office chair and rolled over, until our knees were inches apart.

"My office mates are gone for the day," he said. "So, we're all alone."

So, it's Zeke the flirt today, I thought. Out loud, I said, "My boyfriend worked here for a while, a couple years ago. He really liked it."

Zeke raised his eyebrows. "The bartender? I didn't think books were his thing."

"Part-time bartender," I corrected. "He's actually a photographer, but he also likes to read."

Zeke shrugged. "I take it you're not looking for books today."

"No. I was hoping you could tell me more about Fern Lopez."

He groaned. "Again? I already told you her terms. Look, she's a tough nut to crack. But if you can help her out with that property, you'll be first-rate in her eyes. Trust me."

"I'm working on it. In fact, I'd like to tell her I'm working on it. She's going to have to talk to me if she wants my representation. I can't make a purchase offer without a few details from her."

For a moment, Zeke remained as tight-lipped as a clam. I waited. With a sweet smile and a hopeful gaze, I tried to use some very subtle, innocent magic on the boy—otherwise known as my feminine wiles. It didn't take long for him to cave.

"I can't make Fern talk to you, but I do know where you can find her this afternoon. There's a fall festival out at the Valley Farm Pumpkin Patch. She said something about selling her jewelry at a booth there."

"Thank you, Zeke!" I was so grateful for the information, I almost hated to press him for more. But I did it anyway. "Say, can you help me find a guy's address? I know he lives in Edindale, but he's unlisted."

"Can I find a guy's address?" Zeke repeated the question in his cocky, know-it-all voice. "Have you forgotten who you're talking to? Give me the name, and I'll find the address in less than two minutes."

"You're the best." I figured a little flattery couldn't hurt—especially since I had nothing else to offer him.

I was anxious to drive by Gil's house, but I didn't want to go alone. As I descended the steps of the library, I thought about calling Farrah. I really didn't want to bother her again, even though she was always up for adventure. Perhaps I'd wait a bit.

The late afternoon sun cast a golden tint over the glistening trees. After the earlier rainstorms, the air felt clean and refreshing. It felt good to be outside. It was perfect weather for a trip to the pumpkin patch.

As I headed to my car, I heard someone call my name and turned to see Crenshaw approach with long strides. His slim gray suit with matching silk tie and neatly trimmed hair exuded lawyerly competence.

"This is fortuitous," he said. "I need to speak with you."

"Hi, there. On your way to court?"

"I'm returning to the office now. I had a status hearing on the McCauley matter. I was nearly late for it, too, because of the disturbance this morning."

"What disturbance?"

"That woman came looking for you again, the one who sought you out last Friday evening at the haunted barn."

"Fredeline Paul? What did she want?"

"According to Julie, she wanted to make an appointment with you. When she learned you wouldn't be available until next week, she began asking questions about your practice and your caseload."

"Polite conversation?" I asked, hopefully.

"More like a fishing expedition."

"What do you mean?"

"She was exceedingly nosy. Besides asking about you specifically, she wanted to know about the firm: our success rate, profit margin, pro bono caseload."

"Oh, my. How did Julie handle her?"

"She called me for assistance. And that's when things got really interesting."

"I'm afraid to ask."

"She began crying and wailing. She said she can't go back to Haiti unless she raises some funds, and she doesn't know how to do it. Then she said something about praying to the Loa and making sacrifices to someone called Papa Legba. It was quite a scene. Luckily, no clients were in the lobby at the time."

I frowned, but not because I related to Crenshaw's apparent irritation. I felt sorry for Fredeline.

"We can't understand what it's like for her back home," I said. "It sounds to me like she feels frightened and alone. I wish I could help her."

Crenshaw scowled. "You don't even know if you can trust her. In any event, surely there are agencies she can turn to. If she shows up again, I'll refer her to the Red Cross."

I thought for a moment. There was one thing I could do. I could introduce Fredeline to Fern. Maybe Fern's Sisterhood could help. First, I'd have to get Fern to talk to me.

For a weekday, the Valley Farm Pumpkin Patch was more crowded than I expected. When I arrived, a shrill-voiced chaperone was rounding up a troop of rowdy fourth graders, informing them that their field trip was over. Once they loaded their school bus and took off, the place was a little more peaceful. It felt odd to be out and about in the middle of the week, when I'd normally be inside at work. I kind of liked it.

Following a well-worn footpath, I strolled past artful displays of wild-shaped cucurbits and jolly scarecrows. Along the way, cute signs pointed to a corn maze, a hayride, and a petting zoo. Up ahead, a snack shop sold popcorn and taffy apples—and, based on the luscious aroma permeating the air, cinnamon and sugarcoated apple cider donuts. I doubted if they were vegan, but I could still enjoy the smell. Before long, I was stopped by a laughing young couple.

"Would you mind taking our picture?" asked the girl, looking sweet in a sundress and a jean jacket. They poked their faces through a plywood cutout painted like *American Gothic* and tried, without much success, to remain straight-faced for the photo.

As I returned their camera, I found myself missing Wes. Pumpkin patches were meant to be enjoyed by friends and families, not solo visitors. *Kind of like haunted barns.* I recalled the first time I encountered Levi, when he was by himself at Fieldstone Park. Now that I knew he had my name written in a file on Aunt Josephine, I wondered if his appearance at the park was more than mere coincidence.

Remembering my purpose, I cut over to the row of vendors manning tables beneath a striped canopy. Fern's table was toward the front, between a guy selling hand-carved wooden toys and a woman offering soy candles and glycerin soaps. Fern was sitting in one of two lawn chairs situated next to a wide display of beaded ornaments and jewelry.

"Hello, Fern," I said brightly.

She seemed surprised to see me. "Good afternoon." Her demeanor was reserved but polite.

I looked at her offerings and noticed a gorgeous beaded dreamcatcher in red, orange, yellow, and teal. I decided it would look great on the wall above my bed.

As Fern rang me up, I said, "I spoke with Zeke

Marshal. I'm happy to look into the availability of the property you're interested in. If you decide you'd like to make an offer, I'll need you to come by my office and fill out some paperwork."

She looked over my shoulder at a mother pushing a baby carriage. They strolled by without stopping. Finally, Fern said, "That land can't be built on because of the wetlands. I figure I should get a good deal."

"I'll look into it," I promised. I glanced at the empty chair behind her table. "Mind if I sit with you for a minute? I really need to talk with you about Josephine. It's important."

She shook her head. "This is my daughter's chair. She'll be back shortly."

"Okay." I could stand. I moved closer to the table and lowered my voice. "Will you please tell me what was going on with Josephine? Was she in some sort of trouble?"

Fern frowned and looked away. I wasn't giving up. This time she couldn't walk away from me. "Did Josephine have something to do with the Sorghum bombing? She and Gil Johnson?"

Now Fern stood and put her hands on the table. "Shh! Not here."

A pair of older ladies walked up and gushed over Fern's collection of beaded bracelets.

"Then where?" I asked.

Glancing at her potential customers, Fern heaved a resigned sigh. "Come back at six. We can talk while I pack up."

With time to kill, I moved down the line of

vendors, buying gifts at almost every one: a curvy, wooden candlestick for Mila, scented soaps for Farrah and my sister, and hand-stitched tea towels for my mother and grandmother. At the end of the row, set apart from the other tables, was an open-sided tent. Stylized lettering on a purple banner read, "Gypsy Rose: Fortune-teller."

Curious, I waited for my turn, as a woman with a rose in her hair spoke intently with a couple of college-aged girls. Though she probably wasn't much older than the young women, Gypsy Rose was dressed like a wise woman, complete with peasant skirt, pashmina shawl, and a Celtic amulet around her neck. I wondered if she was the real deal, like Mila, or only an entertainer.

When the girls left, I went inside. The ground was covered with a fringed oriental rug, ringed by four square folding tables. Red and green apples hung from strings tied to the tent's canopy, and sandalwood incense burned next to an oversized palmistry hand. A small sign fastened to a mason jar said, TIPS WELCOME.

"Hi, there. Care for a glimpse into the future?"

"What is all this?" I asked, gesturing to the tables.

"Ancient forms of divination. In the old days, Halloween was known as an optimal time for fortune-telling. Divination games were especially big in Ireland, from hundreds of years ago all the way up through the early 1900s. That's where a lot of our Halloween customs originated, like bobbing for apples and carving jack-o'-lanterns."

I took a quick look at each table. One contained

nuts and pumpkin seeds on a velvet-lined tray; another had a number of saucers filled with various objects next to a blindfold. I stopped at the table with a basket of apples and a basin of water.

"Is this for apple bobbing?"

"Nothing that messy," said Rose, good-naturedly. She brought out a sturdy-looking, rubber-handled vegetable peeler. "This is for learning the identity of your true love. Select an apple, and peel one, long strip. Then turn around and toss it over your left shoulder into the basin of water. The peel will form the initial of the person you'll one day marry."

I smiled. "Okay. Why not?"

I followed her instructions and tossed a strip of apple peel into the water. She took the peeler from me and wished me luck, then left to help another curious visitor.

As I watched, the apple peel curved itself into a sideways C-shape and remained floating in that position on top of the water. I snickered. How could a peel ever form any other shape?

On the other hand, there could be more to see in the basin. I sometimes gazed into a bowl of water as a scrying technique. While a crystal ball might be more traditional, any reflective surface could work. I'd never tried it in public, but the atmosphere in the tent seemed conducive to clairvoyance.

Without further thought, I stared into the clear water surrounding the apple peel and allowed a question to surface in my mind. *What was Josephine's secret?* My aunt had been vague and mysterious. The one time I spoke with her, she mentioned not trusting anyone. Was she as paranoid as Fern? Was she scared?

I continued to look into the water until my vision blurred. With my eyes half closed, I began to perceive random images: an apple, a book, a tree. Holding the question in my mind, another, clearer image took shape. It was a person carrying a gun. For a moment, I felt a jolt of fear, but I willed myself to keep watching. It was a person of authority, I realized. Someone in uniform, wearing a ranger hat and holding a ticket book. She turned, and I saw who it was: Ricki Day, the environmental inspector.

"How we doing over here?" The peppy voice of Gypsy Rose, Fortune-teller, snapped me out of my reverie.

"Fine," I said. "I think."

CHAPTER EIGHTEEN

It was after 5:00 p.m. when I left the fortune-teller's tent. I decided to grab a bite to eat, so I headed to the snack shack and purchased an apple slushy and a bag of popcorn. On my way out, I ran into Pammy Sullivan, from the firm.

"Why, Keli! What a surprise. Meet my nieces, Maddie and Bea. They're visiting from Chicago."

Instead of her usual polyester dress suit with co-ordinating makeup and jewelry, Pammy wore pressed denims and a Western-style plaid shirt. I guessed she must have taken the day off work, which meant she missed the excitement with Frede-line. We chatted for a few minutes. The girls were eleven and eight and full of giggly energy. I shared my popcorn with them and told them about Gypsy Rose's fortune-teller games.

"How fun," said Pammy. "What letter did you get?"

"What letter?" I echoed.

"With the apple peel. What's the initial of your future husband?"

"Oh," I laughed dismissively. "It was a *C*."

Pammy looked perplexed. "*C*? Like . . . Crenshaw?"

"What? Goodness, no. My boyfriend's last name is Callahan, so maybe the prophecy will turn out to be true. Who knows?"

"Let's go, Aunt Pammy!" said Bea, the younger of the two girls. "I want to have my fortune told."

"Okay, we'll go there next, right after we get our snacks. I could go for some hot cider. It's starting to get chilly."

"It was nice meeting you," I said to the girls. To Pammy, I said, "I'll see you next week. My aunt's funeral is Tuesday, so I should be back on Wednesday."

"So, I won't see you Friday at the Jameson party?"

I had no idea what she was talking about. My confusion must have shown.

"Didn't Beverly tell you? You know who Neal Jameson is, right? He owns a couple restaurants and hotels in Edindale and nearby towns. He's also big into philanthropy. He hired Beverly to develop his estate plan. Anyway, he's throwing a benefit party on Friday. It's going to be a masquerade ball. The firm is a cosponsor."

Now I recalled Beverly mentioning the "Jameson opportunity." She must have been talking about the party.

"I already got roped into playing a wicked witch at the haunted barn," I said. "I think it's okay if I sit this one out."

"Oh, that's too bad. This is going to be a great

networking opportunity. Lots of bigwigs will be there. Plus, it should be a great time. It's being catered by a celebrity chef out of Memphis, who specializes in vegetarian fare. We all thought of you when we heard."

I had to admit this sounded a lot more interesting than the haunted barn. "What's the cause?"

"Something to do with the local organic food movement and expanding the farmers' market. Tadd Hemsley will be there, and some other Farmers Union people."

"Farmers, huh? That does sound like a good cause. Maybe I'll try to make it after all."

This could be a good opportunity for more than one reason. Perhaps I'd meet someone who knew Josephine. Speaking of which, it was time to follow up with one person who definitely knew her.

"Fern, please tell me what you know." I sat in a chair behind Fern's display table as she carefully packed her bead jewelry in cloth-lined traveling cases. The last of the pumpkin patch visitors walked past pulling wagons laden with fat orange pumpkins. Ignoring them, I plied Fern with questions. "Did Josephine have a house someplace? Does she have bills that need to be paid? Will creditors be looking for her?"

Fern shook her head. "She didn't own a house."

"You're sure?"

"There won't be creditors. I'm sure."

I waited for her to go on, but she didn't. "Okay, well, what about a will? If she made a last will and testament, where would it be?"

"With no property and few personal possessions, I doubt if she had a will. She lived a simple life."

"Where was she going when she stopped through Edindale? You said she was going out east. Was she visiting someone? Is there someone who should be notified of her death?"

"I've already let folks know of her passing."

"Through your network?"

She gave me a sharp glance, but I didn't flinch. After a mini-staring contest, Fern relented. She held her finger up as if to ask for one minute, then walked over to speak with her daughter, who was chatting with another vendor. She handed the younger woman a case of jewelry and asked her to take it to their car. Then she sat down next to me and leaned forward with her hands on her knees. She spoke quickly and in hushed tones.

"There is a sisterhood of women," she began, "who are so attuned to the rhythms of nature and the needs of Mother Earth that they grasp the urgency in protecting what we have before it's too late. Understanding that there's strength in numbers, they—we—banded together to fight the destructive forces of industrialization—in small ways and big. It all started at the Happy Hills Homestead in 1969, before Josie arrived. When she moved in, it didn't take long to see that she was one of us."

I nodded to encourage her to keep talking. I wasn't about to interrupt.

"One of our most ambitious projects was the creation of a secret seed bank. We took upon ourselves a sacred contract—to preserve and spread heirloom seeds. This was critical, as the rise of modern industrial agriculture has resulted in a devastating loss of plant diversity. And it has only worsened as companies like Sorghum have begun patenting hybrid seeds and GMOs."

She paused, so I steered the conversation back to the subject of my aunt. "So, that was Josephine's mission? To distribute heirloom seeds?"

"Yes."

"She really was like Johnny Appleseed, wasn't she?" Fern didn't respond, so I asked another question I had been pondering. "What ever happened to Roger, the guy who came to the commune with Josie?"

Fern wrinkled her forehead. "That dope? He didn't stay long. He thought his draft card was about to be picked, so he headed to Canada. The dummy didn't realize the war was practically over by that time."

"So, he just left Josephine behind?"

"It was her choice. She could have gone with him, but she'd lost interest. He didn't share her passions."

"Fern, the other day, you said Josephine had made enemies. What did you mean by that?"

She looked away, and I was afraid she was done talking. Then, she looked at me again with fire in her eyes. "Josie was hungry. Itchy. Change couldn't come fast enough for her. She was more aggressive than the other sisters. At some point in her travels, she met up with a group of radicals who pushed the bounds of peaceful activism. Instead of sharing seeds and spreading hope, they made targets. Who were her enemies? It runs the gamut: Big Oil, Big Ag, timber companies, chemical companies."

"But she did continue to distribute seeds," I pointed out. "Isn't that what her business, Sister Seeds, was all about?"

"That came later. A couple years ago, Josie decided she wanted to get back in touch with her original mission."

"Oh." I was quiet for a moment as I tried to decide what else to ask. I knew my time was running short. "So, this group of radicals that she joined up with. Can you give me any names? Did she keep in touch with any of them, or mention anybody in any of her visits?"

"There is one person. When she left the commune, she didn't leave alone."

"Who did she leave with?" I asked, though I already suspected the answer.

"Gil Johnson."

By the time Fern and I wrapped up our conversation, the last of the pumpkin patch patrons had left, and workers were picking up litter and emptying garbage cans. I walked with Fern to her car, helping her carry some of her merchandise. I was happy she had finally warmed up to me. While she didn't know the details of all Josephine's past activities, she did tell me she believed it was Gil's fault Josephine became involved with the "troublemakers," as Fern called them. According to Fern, Gil was a gregarious and charismatic man with big ideas, but little patience, and she didn't trust him as far as she could throw him. She didn't keep in contact with him, even after he moved back to Edindale, and Josie didn't say much about him. She had no idea what he was up to these days.

On a more promising note, Fern agreed to meet with Fredeline. She even offered to explore ways the Sisterhood might be able to support Fredeline's efforts in Haiti, picking up where Josephine had left off.

As Fern slammed her trunk shut, I thought of one more thing I wanted to find out. "By the way," I said, keeping it casual. "I'd like to thank you for the book."

"What book?"

"Josephine's book. *Silent Spring*."

Her confusion appeared genuine. "I've read that book, but it's been decades. I assume Josie read it years ago, too, but I don't know for sure."

"Then it wasn't you? Somebody left an old copy of the book on my front porch. Do you have any idea who might have done that?"

"No. I have no idea."

Oh, well. It was worth a shot.

I waved at Fern and her daughter as they pulled out of the parking lot, then I headed over to where

I'd left my car. As soon as I got there, I realized something was missing. *My bag!* I had set down the shopping bag with all my purchases when I was talking with Fern. It was probably still on the ground beneath the table.

I jogged up to the entrance, which was now blocked with a rope. Seeing no one around, I stepped over the rope and retraced my steps to where the vendors had been set up.

It was dusk now, and the gray clouds had returned. The atmosphere at Valley Farm was completely changed—whereas before it was festive and lively, now it was quiet and desolate. Even the scarecrows seemed to take on a more sinister mien.

My bag was still where I'd left it, with the contents untouched. *Whew!* I snatched it up and hurried back to the exit. As soon as it came within view, I saw that the way was now blocked by more than a rope. A semitrailer had pulled up to the entrance. Veering from the path, I decided to cut straight to the parking lot from the side near the corn maze.

As I walked along, my bag jostling in my hand, I suddenly felt the strange sensation of being watched. This had happened before and turned out to be true. I stopped to listen. The wind rustled the tops of the dried cornstalks. A flock of crows lifted from a nearby field, their cries sounding sad and eerie. Then I heard something else, in a whisper.

"Keli."

I jerked my head around, but there was no one in sight. I shook it off and started walking again, a little faster now. I was hearing things.

But then it came again. A woman's voice. "*Keli. Help me.*"

Again, I looked around. The place was deserted. Before I could hear it a third time, I took off at a run and didn't stop until I reached my car. When I made it, I almost laughed at myself. What did I think, I was being chased by a ghost?

I fumbled in my purse for my car keys—and then screamed as a strong hand clamped down on my shoulder.

CHAPTER NINETEEN

"Whoa! Take it easy!"

This time the voice that spoke to me was masculine, and it was one I knew well.

"Wes! What are you doing here?"

"Looking for you. You never answer my texts, so I had to do a little detective work of my own to track you down."

I was dumbfounded. "I do so answer your texts!" I reached for my phone to prove it, but it wasn't in my purse. I looked through the driver's side window of my car and saw it sitting in the cup holder. *Oops.*

"I've been a little preoccupied lately."

He reached out and lifted the hair from my neck. "I know."

As we looked into each other's eyes, I felt a rush of love—followed by regret for how distant I'd been. I vowed then and there to treat Wes more like a partner and less like a part-time lover.

"How did you find me?"

He smiled. "I have my ways." He took my keys from me and unlocked my car. "Want to go to the Loose? Jimi's been experimenting with new veggie burger recipes. He could use your expert opinion."

"He wants me to be his guinea pig, huh? Fine by me. I could use some food. And a drink."

Wes followed me in his car as we drove back to town. When we arrived at the Loose Rock, the bar was half-full with college kids, but they were a mellow crowd. I was forever grateful to Jimi, the owner and an old friend of Wes's, for not installing TV screens in his place. The focus here was on music and friendship.

We found a table in the back and settled in with beers and burgers. I caught Wes up on everything I'd learned so far. He expressed dismay when I described my caper in Levi's cabin, but he knew better than to scold me. Before long, he seemed as intrigued as I was.

"Can I see the postcard?" he asked. After reading it, he raised an eyebrow. "She wanted to 'come clean.' This makes it sound like we were right—she was on the run from the law. She committed some kind of crime."

"Yeah. That seems clear. And I suspect she might have been planning another crime. I think she was scoping out HAPCO, this company that deals in synthetic pesticides and other chemicals. It's just the kind of thing she'd be against. In fact, Ricki told me that she filed complaints about the company.

Of course, she was using an assumed name at the time, but I'm sure it was her."

"Do you think she was caught breaking in or trespassing?"

I shook my head. "I don't know. She was at least a mile or two from the facility when she was shot. Still, it might be good to know more about the business. When I ran into Tadd Hemsley yesterday, he said no one had seen her in the area. But I don't see how he could know for sure. He didn't make it sound like he'd asked his employees. I wonder how many people work there?"

"You want to know more about Tadd? Maybe I can help."

"How so?"

"You know that feature the paper is doing on various townspeople? I get a say on who we feature next, and Hemsley is on the list."

"Hey, you were supposed to pick Beverly for that."

"Sorry, babe. She's not on the list. But Hemsley is. Besides all his work for farmers and local businesses, he apparently has an unusual hobby."

"What kind of hobby?"

"I don't know. I didn't read that far into his bio." I made a face, and Wes grinned. "I'll find out," he said. "Got any other assignments for me?"

"You're cute when you play detective," I teased. "And you still haven't told me how you knew I was at the pumpkin patch."

He gave me a coy grin and took a swig from his beer bottle. My phone rang, and I saw that it was

Zeke. I showed Wes the display, then answered. "Hey, what's up?"

"I found something," he said. "Meet me at the Loose?"

"Uh, I'm already at the Loose."

"Say no more." He hung up, leaving me to shake my head. I wondered if he lived nearby, or if he was still at the library.

"So, back to your private-eye skills," I said. "Did you see Zeke this afternoon? He's the one who told me where I could find Fern."

Wes scoffed. "That bozo? I wouldn't even know where to find him."

"Now, be nice. He'll be here—" I broke off, as the door to the Loose opened. "Now," I finished.

Zeke scanned the room, then moseyed over when he saw me. He stopped short when he got to our table. "Oh. I thought you'd be with the blonde."

"Zeke, have you met Wes?"

Wes flashed his pearly whites and held out his hand. "Pull up a chair," he said to Zeke.

Deflated, Zeke shook Wes's hand and grabbed a nearby chair.

"What did you find?" I asked.

Brightening slightly, he retrieved a piece of paper from the inner pocket of his snazzy blazer. "The other day you asked me about unsolved ecocrimes, and I told you about the Sorghum bombing."

"Yes, I remember."

"And I told you the feds had some suspects at the time, but then the investigation fizzled."

"Go on."

"Well, I was curious about those supposed suspects, so I did a little digging. And I found this."

He handed me a printout of a news article, which mentioned the FBI was looking for a "person of interest" by the name of Davey Winslow. The name rang a bell. I was pretty sure it was one of the names on the folders in Levi's cabin, though I didn't feel the need to share that tidbit with Zeke.

"Then I found this." Zeke handed me a second article. The headline read: "Sorghum Bombing Person of Interest Found Dead."

"Uh-oh," said Wes. I could tell his line of thinking followed mine.

"Apparently, the guy had agreed to meet with the agent heading the investigation," said Zeke. "But before the meeting could take place, he wound up knocked upside the head in some alley. I don't think they ever found out who did it."

"That was a long time ago," I said, half to myself. "But if there is a connection here . . ." I trailed off, as the two guys looked at me expectantly.

"What are you thinking?" asked Wes.

"I'm thinking Gil might be in danger."

Back at home, Wes and I discussed what we should do with the information about Gil. A few people I'd spoken with recently, such as Fern and Tadd, seemed to think Gil was a shady character. But Josephine had trusted him. And if he really was involved in something illegal with both Josie and Davey . . . then it stood to reason that he could be the next target.

"What does your instinct tell you?" asked Wes, as he emptied his pockets and tossed the contents on the bureau.

I dropped onto the edge of the bed and sighed. "My instinct hasn't been talking lately. I don't know what's going on. It's like I've lost touch with my inner guide."

"I'm sure that's not true. It's been a rough week, that's all."

As I twisted the end of my nightshirt, the cat sauntered in and rubbed up against my legs. "At least I made the right call with Kitty, here. You're sure you don't mind having her live with us?"

"Nah, I like cats. I don't mind. She needs a name, though. How about Buffy?"

"You're kidding, right? Does she look like a vampire slayer to you?"

"Phoebe? Piper?"

"Ha-ha. No, I need to wait and keep my eyes and ears open. I think her name will come to me in due time—assuming I'm not completely cut off from the divine spirit. I still don't know what to do next, Wes. And my family will be here in just a few days."

"There you go again. Look, you should check in with Rhinehardt tomorrow. Tell him you're worried about Gil and let him figure out what to do."

"Yeah, I suppose. But I think I'll go by Gil's house, too. I really want to talk to him again."

"Then I'm going with you. I can take the morning off, since I'm going to Memphis tomorrow afternoon."

"You're going to Memphis? As in Tennessee?"

"Didn't I tell you? The paper is doing a piece on this celebrity chef who might open a restaurant here in Edindale. There's a cooking award ceremony, or something. They're putting us up for the night, then I'm supposed to get some city shots the next morning."

"Okay, then it's settled. We'll go see Gil in the morning."

I only wished I knew what to do after that. I crawled up to the head of the bed and looked over at the dreamcatcher I'd hung on the wall. It reminded me of a dream I'd had shortly after Josephine's death. In it, she had attempted to give me a Native American talking stick.

What were you trying to say?

I fell back onto my pillow and closed my eyes, as a rush of images washed over me: Gypsy Rose and her divination games, Fern's Sisterhood, a distraught Fredeline, Josephine's face in a murky looking glass . . .

Then, a whispered plea carried on the country wind.

Wes flicked off the light and got into bed. Shivering, I cuddled up next to him. I didn't want to admit it, but a troubling notion had begun to creep into my consciousness—a terrible feeling that I was being haunted by the spirit of Aunt Josephine.

CHAPTER TWENTY

Gil Johnson lived in a part of town known as the Hills. The neighborhood was semi-woodsy and peaceful, with the homes widely spaced and set far back from the road. Gil's house was a charming wooden cottage built, appropriately enough, into the side of a hill. As we pulled into the long, steep driveway, I half-expected a dog or two to come out and greet us. But when we climbed out of the car, the only sound was the soft, sorrowful coo of a mourning dove.

"Looks like nobody's home," remarked Wes, as we walked up to the front porch. He knocked on the door, and I angled for a glimpse between the curtains.

"His car could be in the garage," I pointed out.

"Could be," said Wes, knocking a second time.

We both spoke quietly, as if we were doing something surreptitious. I tried to tell myself we were merely dropping in on an acquaintance, a friend of a friend. It was perfectly normal to peer into a window when no one came to the door. *Right?*

In truth, I was trying to get a feel as to how long he'd been gone. Had he just stepped out to the grocery store? Or had he shipped off to Tibet again?

"Let's check the back," I whispered.

We rounded the house and came upon a new deck. I recalled the kid at the canoe shop saying Gil had been working on his deck. Cautiously, I crept up the stairs to peek in the patio door. That's when I noticed the missing pane from a side window.

"Wes, look at that!"

He crossed to the window and assessed the damage. "Someone broke in. They removed the glass and reached inside. Check the patio door—I bet it's unlocked."

He was right. I turned the knob and pushed the door open.

"We should call the police," said Wes.

"I will. But what if Gil has been hurt? If he needs help, every second counts."

Wes didn't argue. He followed me in and scanned the room.

"Gil?" My voice sounded hoarse. I cleared my throat and tried again. "Gil!"

There was no answer.

My heart beat a steady cadence as we tiptoed through Gil's living room. The place was cluttered, but not torn apart. The TV was still on the wall. The kitchen was mostly clean—just one glass in the sink and a few crumbs on the counter. Overripe bananas sat in a bowl on the table.

We continued to call his name as we crept upstairs. In the bedroom, a few clothes were strewn about, but it was hard to tell if this was the work of a burglar or the normal untidiness of a bachelor. I stood in the center of the room, thinking. I was curious to know if any clothes appeared to be missing, but I was reluctant to leave my fingerprints on any knobs. Then I had another idea. Moving into the bathroom, I looked all around the sink for a toothbrush. There was none.

"He's skipped town."

"You think?"

"Yeah. Maybe he left in a hurry, but it looks to me as if he left of his own free will. Let's check the mailbox."

"Don't you think we should call the cops now?"

"Yeah . . . in a minute. I don't think it's an emergency now."

"I'm not so sure."

Wes stood at the front door, while I jogged down the path to check the mailbox. It was empty. I told him as much, as I slipped back inside.

"I guess that means he left today, unless he doesn't get much mail."

"He could have put a hold on it."

I wandered back into the kitchen, where a built-in desk was covered with papers, most of which appeared to be junk mail and hardware store receipts. The cubby above the desk was filled with pens, Post-its, and something else. A postcard. Considering postcards were Josephine's preferred means of communication, I carefully extracted the card. It featured a picture of the Edindale County Courthouse and was addressed to "JJ, c/o Fern Lopez."

"JJ," I murmured. "Josie June." It was a sweet nickname, but there was nothing sweet about the brief message: "Don't do it. Remember what happened to Davey." It was signed "G."

I shivered involuntarily. There was no postmark and the note was undated. The postcard had never been mailed. Still, I felt sure this was Gil's intended response to the postcard Josephine had sent to him—before she came to Edindale for the last time. When I found her postcard in Levi's cabin, I hadn't known if Gil had ever received it. Now I knew. Seeing his reply confirmed that he not only received it, but he also knew Josephine was in town. He had lied.

"Keli, we really gotta get out of here."

"Okay." I replaced the postcard and let Wes usher me out of the house. We circled back to the front and stood in the driveway, where I placed a call to Detective Rhinehardt. His voice mail picked up, so I left a message, saying only that I had stopped by Gil's house and noticed the broken window.

After hanging up, my eyes wandered the property. A piece of litter on the edge of the driveway caught my attention. I walked over to pick it up.

"What's that?" asked Wes.

"An old receipt. It looks like it's been stepped on. It was probably on the floor of someone's car and stuck to the bottom of their shoe."

Wes joined me and read over my shoulder. "One burger, one large fry, and a large soft drink. From a place in . . . Virginia?"

I nodded. "Levi drives a car with Virginia plates."

"Not exactly a smoking gun," said Wes.

"No, but . . . if he was here, that might explain how he obtained the postcard Josephine had sent to Gil."

"Why would he take that one and not the one Gil wrote in return?"

"Maybe Gil hadn't written his response yet?"

Wes looked doubtful. "In that case, if Levi was here before Gil wrote the message to Josephine, that would mean this receipt has been blowing around on the ground here for a few days. Right? 'Cause I assume Gil wrote that note before Josephine was killed."

I studied the crumpled receipt. It was slightly damp, but not soaking wet. Other than the year, most of the date was too blurred to read. I didn't know what to think.

Wes squeezed my shoulder. "I think you're right that Gil left in a hurry. Maybe he came to the same conclusion we did and figured he might be in danger. Or maybe not. Either way, there's nothing we can do about it."

I glanced back at Gil's darkened house. "I wish we would have snapped a photo of that postcard."

"It didn't say much," said Wes. "Just, 'Remember Davey,' and 'Don't do it.' Something like that."

"You're right. I guess it's the tone I really wish I

could read. You know what I mean? Was Gil's message meant as a concerned plea? Or was it a threat?"

For the rest of the morning, I cleaned house and helped Wes pack for his trip. When my family arrived in a couple days, they'd likely stay in a hotel. Still, I wanted the house to be presentable. My grandma would want the grand tour.

After Wes left, I called Beverly to get the details on the Jameson party the following night.

"I'm glad you can make it," she said. "We've rented out an entire mansion. We need a good showing. Invite friends if you'd like. Tickets are forty dollars at the door. Oh, and don't forget to come in costume."

"Right. No problem."

I hung up and looked in my closet. I had no costume. I'd already returned the one Crenshaw had rented for the haunted barn—which I wouldn't have worn anyway. I'd never been one for the vampy, mistress-of-the-night look.

What to wear, what to wear? I was about to call Farrah, when my phone rang. Once again, it was my neediest client, Grace Hammerlin.

"Hello, Mrs. Hammerlin."

"Keli, is that you?"

"Yes, Mrs. Hammerlin. This is Keli. What's the matter?"

"I'm calling you from the Cadwelle Mansion Bed

and Breakfast. I can't stay in my house another night. I didn't get a wink of sleep last night."

"Oh, dear."

"I'd like you to call Mr. Friedman, or his lawyer, as soon as possible and tell them what's going on. He's going to have to pay for those city ghost-busters, and if that doesn't work, the whole deal is off. He can have the house back and return my money."

"Oh, dear," I repeated. "Mrs. Hammerlin, it doesn't work like that. We can't ask for a refund. These sounds you're hearing, I don't think they qualify as a home defect the seller was obligated to disclose."

"Well, can you at least ask? Maybe he'll agree. He probably knew the place was haunted when he sold it."

The cat jumped up onto the couch next to me and tried to nudge her way onto my lap. I patted the top of her head.

"Mrs. Hammerlin, let me ask you something. Have you heard any scratching or thumping since I took the cat home with me? Have any more gloves or other items gone missing?"

"No. That's not the problem. It's the overnight noises. For a couple days, there was nothing. It was blissfully quiet. Then, last night it was back again. That's the thing—I never know when it's going to happen! Just when I think it's gone, it starts up again. It's like the spirit is toying with me!"

"Well . . . what if I stay the night in your house? Maybe I can get to the bottom of this."

The words were out of my mouth before I could stop myself. Mrs. Hammerlin jumped on my offer.

"Fine. You're welcome to try. But I'm not going back there until I'm sure these ghosts are banished for good. I'll meet you at the house at six to let you in, then I'm going back to the B&B—which, by the way, I think Mr. Friedman should pay for. You can add that to our list of demands."

I suppressed a sigh. "I don't think that will be necessary, Mrs. Hammerlin. I'll see you this evening.

I couldn't believe I'd volunteered to spend the night in a haunted house. And I wasn't even promised a huge inheritance or awesome prize money! I laughed at the absurdity of the situation as I strolled through Fieldstone Park on my way downtown. I had decided I needed some fresh air—and a quick confab with the wisest witch I knew.

Mila was helping a customer when I entered Moonstone Treasures, so I amused myself by browsing the newest additions to her collection of spell books and witchy fiction. Without planning to, I gravitated to the section on evil spirits and dark energies. I was particularly drawn to a glossy hardcover, whose cover featured a medieval rendering of a nasty, scarlet-skinned demon. It looked like it flew straight out of Dante's ninth circle of hell.

"Trying to scare yourself?" asked Mila, coming up behind me.

"No." I replaced the book onto the shelf. "That's the last thing I want to do right now."

"Come sit up front with me," she said. "Catrina is off today, so I need to stay close to the cash register and telephone."

She brought out a velvet-cushioned stool, set it next to the checkout counter, and ordered me to sit. While she unpacked a box of candles, I filled her in on the latest from Mrs. Hammerlin. I also told her about seeing Josephine's image in the mirror—or, at least, what I imagined was her image.

"Interesting."

"Mrs. Hammerlin is so frightened of whatever it is causing all the noise at her house. She calls it a 'banshee.' But if it's really Aunt Josephine—which seems very unlikely, but assuming it's her for the sake of argument—she would be a benevolent spirit. She's not evil."

Mila didn't answer right away. I could tell her mind was working to select the right words. I spoke up again. "A banshee is an evil spirit, right?"

She glanced toward the book section we'd just left. "In Irish folklore, a banshee is a female spirit that flies through the night wailing, or keening, a warning."

"A warning?"

"A warning that someone is going to die."

"Of course."

"She's not always considered an evil creature. It depends on the story."

"It sounds like you don't think banshees are real."

"Well, I'm not saying there's no truth to the stories." She smiled. "Spirits and energies can manifest in many different ways. As for your aunt, it sounds to me like she's crying out for help. She's trying to get your attention however she can. The most likely reason would have to do with her unsolved murder. I doubt she's a harbinger of more death to come."

"I would agree, except for one thing." I told her about Davey and Gil and my suspicions about the Sorghum bombing. Mila didn't ask me where I'd derived my information, but a look of concern crossed her face.

"You might have something there. Besides dealing with her sudden, violent death, she might have other unresolved issues—like guilt."

I nodded grimly. Aunt Josephine had wanted to turn herself in and was never able to follow through. Perhaps she was the haunted one.

"Do you have a plan for tonight?" Mila asked.

"Yeah, sort of. I'm going to make a protection amulet and bring along some salt and fennel."

"Let me get you some crystals." She turned to the glass case behind the counter. "You'll want some tourmaline, for sure. And some quartz, too, I think."

I watched with admiration as Mila filled a velvet pouch for me. She pulled the drawstring and raised the pouch to her lips. She blew softly, then brought the pouch to her heart. I knew she was infusing the crystals with her own positive energies.

"Thanks, Mila." I placed the pouch in my purse.

"Hey, on a more fun note, I need a costume for a masquerade party tomorrow night. Think you can help me out?"

"Absolutely! I have several options that would look great on you. Did you have something specific in mind?"

"Not really. I'm up for anything—as long as it's not a banshee."

CHAPTER TWENTY-ONE

Mrs. Hammerlin was waiting for me on her front porch. She unlocked the door and flipped on the lights.

"Make yourself at home. I just want to water my plants while I'm here. I forgot to do it before I left."

I followed her to the conservatory and watched while she tended to her plants. "Were any of these here before you moved in?" I asked, to make conversation. "Or did you bring them all?"

"They're all mine. This solarium is one of the things I love best about this house." She looked out the window at the setting sun. "I do love it here. I truly hope you can work your magic and get rid of that lonely spirit—or whatever it is."

"Me too."

She put away her watering can. "Come on upstairs. I'll show you to your room."

At the top of the staircase, trepidation set in. It was made worse when Mrs. Hammerlin opened the door to the room with the flowered wallpaper. She walked inside and fluffed the pillow. I stood in the doorway.

"Is there another room available, by chance?"

She looked up in surprise. "This is the only guest room that faces the cemetery. If you want to see a ghost, this is your best option."

"That's what I'm afraid of," I said under my breath, knowing I was being silly. I told her it would be fine and thanked her for letting me give this a try.

A short time later, she left in a flurry of last-minute instructions. "Don't go outside without a key or you'll wind up locked out. Don't use the fireplace, because the chimney hasn't been cleaned. Don't run the microwave and dishwasher at the same time, or you'll blow a fuse. The fuse box is in the basement."

When the door clicked behind her, I turned to face the empty house and gulped. I wished I'd thought to bring the cat with me. *Millie, for familiar? No, that's not it. Amie, with the French pronunciation, for friend? Maybe not.* Whatever her name was, she would have been good company.

I'd been through Mrs. Hammerlin's house before, so I already knew my way around. The first order of business was to shore up its energetic shields. Beginning in the dining room, which was roughly the center of the house, I spread my supplies out on the table, cast a magic circle, and thought about my protection strategy. I would place crystals on the ground outside, at the four cardinal directions around the house. Inside, I would sprinkle salt across each threshold (with the intention of sweeping it up before I left tomorrow), and I'd use herbs and incense in the bedroom overnight.

Using a handful of black and white ribbons I'd brought from home, I formed a pentagram around the items on the table. I arranged black and white candles at each of the five points, lit them, and took a deep centering breath. Standing in front of the table, I softened my gaze and visualized a glowing orb of silvery, white light. The light formed a bubble that held me softly—much like Glinda the Good Witch. I imagined the light pulsating with energy as it expanded to surround the table and fill the room. It grew brighter and flowed throughout the whole house, from floor to ceiling and corner to corner, until it seeped out the windows and stretched to form a giant, protective sphere around the entire house.

I raised my hands to recite an incantation . . . and found myself at a loss for words.

What, exactly, did I want to accomplish? Did I want to banish and repel? Or attract and communicate?

I realized it was both. I wanted to stop the harassment of Mrs. Hammerlin. And I definitely wanted to expel any malignant spirits that might be lurking about. But if someone, or something, was trying to communicate from the beyond, I wanted to hear the message. I wanted to be open to hear and receive . . . and maybe even to help.

When in doubt, call upon the Great Mother. She'll know what to do.

I decided to invoke the Mother Goddess in her guise as Tara, one of the oldest creator goddesses, sometimes called the mother of Buddha. Appropriately enough, she presented herself in two aspects.

In a voice that sounded more confident than I felt, I called out:

Oh, White Tara, Goddess of Peace,
By your power, the stars increase,
Love is your light, compassion your power,
Protect me now, in this place and in this hour.

Oh, Green Tara, Goddess of Night,
You wield great strength, a loving might,
Help goodness speak and evil leave,
That Grace's fears shall be relieved.

Goddess Tara, bless this home,
Let restless spirits no longer roam,
Darkness banish, light be free,
As I will, so mote it be.

I stood at the table for a few more minutes, directing my energy outward into the house and beyond. Then I closed the circle and headed outside to place the crystals on the ground, propping open the back door with a terra-cotta flowerpot.

I was glad I remembered to bring a flashlight. Otherwise, I might have bumped into a birdbath or tripped over a garden gnome. The waning moon was mostly hidden by clouds, making the yard— and the cemetery—darker than I'd ever seen it before. I rushed to finish the job and hurried inside to sprinkle some salt.

Once the house was fully protected to the best of my magical abilities, I flopped into a tufted chair in the front parlor and gave Farrah a ring. Like Wes, she was currently miles away living it up in a swanky hotel—only she was even farther away, in Atlanta, where her company was headquartered. I reached her in her hotel room, where she'd just returned from her conference dinner.

"Why do they have to have so many courses at these things?" she complained. "I'm so full, I'm gonna be up 'til midnight digesting."

I laughed. "You couldn't restrain yourself, could you?"

"Not to mention all the cocktails beforehand. Ugh."

"And you have, what, two more nights of this?"

"Yeah, I come back Sunday. I'm so bummed I'm gonna miss the Halloween party! Randall asked me to go with him, and he totally would have agreed to wear any couples' costume I'd choose. I was thinking Adam and Eve. Or maybe Pebbles and Bamm-Bamm."

"Um, yeah. I'm not so sure about that."

"Well, keep an eye on him for me, will you? Not that he can't freely mingle with other women. I'd just like to know about it, that's all."

"You got it, girlfriend."

"Hang on, I'm getting a text. I'm being summoned downstairs for after-dinner drinks. As if I have an ounce of room left in this dress. Never mind—they can wait. How are you doing in that big, old spooky house all by yourself?"

"It's not that bad. Just super quiet."

"I wish you could've postponed for a week. I'd totally be up for a slumber party in a haunted mansion. What a lark!"

I looked around at the heavy, polished Victorian furniture, crocheted doilies, and blown-glass figurines lining the mantel. Not exactly a party atmosphere.

"I'm still confused, though," Farrah went on. "Why would your aunt be haunting Grace Hammerlin's house? Did they know each other?"

"No. I asked Mrs. Hammerlin, and she said she's never even heard of Josephine O'Malley. Anyway, I still think there's going to be a logical explanation for everything."

"Is that the lawyer in you talking? Or the witch? Oh, hang on. I'm getting buzzed again. I only see these folks once or twice a year, so . . ." She trailed off, presumably answering the text.

"You go have fun," I said. "I'll fill you in later."

"Okay, stay safe. And, say 'hi' to the ghosts for me!"

I hung up and sat for a moment longer in the parlor. The ticking of the grandfather clock echoed somberly. It was going to be a long night.

After checking in with Wes, who was also too busy to talk long, and then aimlessly flipping channels on the TV, I decided to go ahead and get settled in the guest room. I didn't expect to sleep much, but

I put on pajamas anyway and crawled under the covers with a paperback. I read for the next hour or so, until my mind wandered and I no longer had any idea what was going on in the story. I closed the book, stood up, and stretched. I walked over to the oval mirror and stared at my reflection.

"Aunt Josephine?" My voice sounded small and tentative. I hadn't intended to summon her tonight. I wasn't even sure how to do that. I was accustomed to calling on gods and goddesses, not the ghost of my recently murdered aunt, whom I hardly knew.

I moved to the window and stared outside at the dark cemetery. The night couldn't have been quieter. I was afraid this whole plan was going to be a bust.

As I stood before the window, I recalled a childhood game I'd played with my neighborhood friends. It was a hide-and-seek tag game called Ghost in the Graveyard. Just for fun, I whispered the words from the game, in a slow, rhythmic chant: "One o'clock, two o'clock, three o'clock . . ." When I reached midnight, I said, in a jokey way, "Come out, come out, wherever you are!"

Something crashed behind me.

I thought my heart would leap out of my chest. I whipped around and saw what had caused the jarring noise. A full-length mirror had fallen off the back of a closet door. The glass splintered in the frame, but luckily it didn't shatter. With my hand to my chest, I went to investigate.

How did it fall?

Carefully, I lifted the edge of the mirror to look

at the back. The nails appeared old and bent. Examining the door, I saw an outline where the mirror had been. It must have hung there for years. Then I noticed something else. There was writing on the door.

I grabbed my flashlight and shined it on the door. There were tick marks, like on a yardstick, and dates. This was a child's height marker, I realized. I'd had one on my kitchen wall when I was a child—that is, until my parents decided to update the kitchen and painted over it.

Some of the lines had extra information, such as "Lost a tooth today!" and "Training wheels off." The last one, at the top, was labeled "First day of second grade."

And that was it. The child—the girl, if this was her bedroom—was no longer measured. The mirror was hammered onto the door, and there it stayed. Until now.

I dragged the mirror to the side of the room so it wouldn't get stepped on. I was about to take another look at the dates, when I became conscious of another sound. A faint wailing.

I ran to the window and saw nothing. I dashed to Mrs. Hammerlin's bedroom, since that's apparently where she usually was when she heard the noise. The sound stopped, then started again. Listening carefully, I followed it to the small dressing room attached to her bedroom. A brocade curtain covered the entire back wall. Hesitating for only a second, I pulled it aside to reveal a high window. It was open a few inches. The wailing was louder now. It was coming from outside.

I tried to open the window farther, but it wouldn't budge. It had probably been stuck in this position for ages. Wasting no time, I flew downstairs and out the back door, pausing only to step into my tennis shoes.

I still had the flashlight in hand, but I kept it turned off. I wanted to remain hidden. Staying low, I scuttled over to the fence separating the yard from the cemetery.

The wailing had stopped, but I heard something else. It was a scuffling sound, like footsteps, and then the crack of a twig. I followed the fence to the opening the kitty had shown me and slipped inside the cemetery. I was running on adrenaline, excited to be on the tail of the so-called banshee. I was also scared out of my mind.

I kept close to the fence as I made my way back to a point directly behind Mrs. Hammerlin's bedroom, except on the cemetery side of the fence. The screeching wail pierced the air once more. This time it came in a short burst, followed by what I could have sworn were voices. Human voices. They were coming from an old mausoleum, bordered by overgrown weeds and untrimmed shrubbery.

I darted from tree, to tombstone, to monument, trying to make myself invisible behind each one. A stone's throw from the mausoleum, I stopped and hid myself behind a large double headstone. There were definitely people in there. I strained to make out what they were saying.

"Cut it out with that whistle! You're overdoing it."

"Then where is he? He should have been here already."

"Just wait. He's probably nervous."

It was two guys. I couldn't tell their ages, but they didn't sound very old. Or very smart. I waited for what felt like an eternity but was probably only five minutes. Then the sound came again, echoing from the door of the mausoleum. It *was* a whistle, I realized. Some sort of bird call that mimicked the sound of a barn owl or a sick crow. I supposed it was a hunter's whistle, which could make a variety of sounds depending on the whistler's hand grip and breath control.

I was so fascinated by the eerie sound, and how it traveled through the night air to Mrs. Hammerlin's bedroom, that I almost failed to notice the figure approach from the other side of the graveyard. It seemed to be a thin man in dark jeans and a gray hoodie. As he came closer, I ducked behind the headstone once more and remained still as a statue.

Seconds ticked by in silence, until a whisper sounded close by.

"In here."

More footsteps. More whispers. Then someone raised his voice. "A deal is a deal!"

"Keep it down!" hissed a second voice.

"But we had an agreement! I ain't turning over the smack 'til he turns over the cash."

My eyes grew wide in the darkness. It was a drug deal. And, unless I was mistaken, it was a drug deal about to go bad.

"Hey, hey, hey! You don't gotta show that. I'll get your money."

"Keep it down!"

"He's lying. He didn't come here with the dough!"

I was beginning to sweat. I had to get out of here and call the police. My cell phone was back in the house next to the guest bed. As the strained voices grew louder, even as the cautious guy kept telling the other two to "keep it down," I started to back away. As before, I tried to stay behind trees and larger grave markers, but my priority now was speed. That turned out to be a mistake. I had retreated only a few yards when I tripped over a wooden cross. I landed with an *oomph*.

As I scrambled to my feet, I sensed the men peeking out of the mausoleum.

"There's someone out there!"

"What is this, a setup?"

"Hey, you! Get back here!"

I ran like my life depended on it, not daring to think it really might. I made it back to the hole in the fence, squeezed in, and ran all the way up to Mrs. Hammerlin's back door. I grabbed the knob and pulled. It didn't budge.

I was locked out.

CHAPTER TWENTY-TWO

It was like a bad case of déjà vu. I flashed back to that moment in Levi's cabin when I realized the closet door was locked and I had to scramble for a hiding place. Only this time, the consequences seemed much more dire. Fearing armed and angry drug dealers were hot on my heels, I sprinted to the front of the house. Of course, the front door was locked, too.

Standing on the porch, I looked to the street, where my car was parked along the curb. It was useless as an escape vehicle. My keys were in my purse, which was next to my phone in the house.

Goddess help me. Tara protect me. I clasped the amulet around my neck together with my pentagram necklace and envisioned the white orb of protection surrounding me as before. Soon I began to breathe a bit easier—because I hadn't been followed to the front of the house.

Now that I didn't fear for my life, I realized the full extent of my current problem. I had no phone, no car keys, and no way back inside. I shivered, suddenly feeling the coolness of the air.

With a sigh, I walked to the sidewalk and looked down the street. All the houses were dark, both the vacant and the occupied ones.

Oh, well. I have no other choice. I started off down the pavement. I'd made it only a few steps, when something compelled me to look back. I glanced up at Mrs. Hammerlin's house, dark and quiet. The bedroom lights I'd left on weren't visible from the front, but there was a dim light in an upstairs window on the side of the house. As I looked, the curtain moved. I gasped. I was sure it had moved. It had rustled and then fallen still.

I took off at a jog down the street. Several blocks later, I finally came to a house with its lights on. I crossed my fingers and rang the bell. A minute later, the door was opened by a startled-looking teenager. He wore ripped jeans and a T-shirt, and his hair was in need of a trim, but his face was sweet.

"Hi," I began. "I was wondering if I could borrow your phone. I locked myself out."

"Uh, sure." He handed me a cell phone, which I stared at, suddenly at a loss.

Who should I call?

Originally, I'd planned to call 9-1-1, but the situation no longer felt like an emergency. The drug dealers were surely long gone by now. Besides, I wouldn't be going back to Mrs. Hammerlin's house tonight anyway, not without a key. I'd have to call her, as well as the police, in the morning. All I needed right now was a place to spend the night.

According to the cell phone, it was nearly 3:00 in the morning. Who was I willing to disturb at this hour? I didn't want to bother Mila. Her husband worked in construction and always had to get up at the crack of dawn; plus, she would have to be up early to open her shop. So many of my friends had families or jobs or both. I knew I could call Wes's parents in a pinch, but this whole situation was not going to be easy to explain.

Only one person's name came to mind. Someone whose number I knew by heart, and who I knew well enough to ask such a big favor. One person who already thought I was weird anyway. That was okay. I thought he was weird, too.

I called Crenshaw.

The kind teenager sat with me on his stoop as I waited for my ride. He told me his name was Pete, and the reason he was up so late was that his mother had gone into labor. His father had rushed her to the hospital, leaving Pete in charge of his two younger siblings, who were upstairs sleeping.

I introduced myself and explained that I was house-sitting for Grace Hammerlin. I also told him I'd heard strange noises in the cemetery, which was how I ended up locking myself out of the house.

"Aw, man. That was kind of crazy. I mean, you must be really brave. But kinda crazy."

"Yeah." I chuckled. "You're probably right about that. I think I interrupted a drug deal."

He nodded. "For sure."

"Wait, do you know something about it?"

He shrugged. "Just rumors."

"Well, I guess the rumors are true. Hey, do you happen to know what smack is?"

"Oh, you know. Dope. Like, heroin, I guess."

"Yikes."

"Yeah. Bad stuff."

A few minutes later, Crenshaw pulled up and left his car idling as he walked up to the house. He wore a blue dress shirt, unbuttoned at the collar, with black pants and tennis shoes. His beard was slightly longer than usual and his hair bordered on shaggy. It was the most casual I'd ever seen him.

I stood and thanked Pete for his help. "Good luck with your new baby sister!"

"Thanks." He grinned mischievously. "Good luck staying away from drug dealers."

"Amen to that."

Crenshaw lived in a modern, luxury duplex not far from the university. As we neared his place, I started to have second thoughts about the imposition.

"You know, you can just drop me off at the office. You'll have to unlock the building for me, but I can spend the night there."

He raised an eyebrow in a look that told me he thought I was daft. It was a look I knew well. "Don't be silly. I have a perfectly serviceable guest room."

When we arrived, he unlocked his house and removed his shoes at the door. I followed suit, then stood in his foyer and took in the striking minimalism of his decor. Everything was all sleek lines and shiny surfaces.

"Wow," I said. "Your place is so . . . clean."

"I have a maid service. Who has time to clean?" He walked to a slim white and chrome bar cabinet and pulled out a bottle of single-malt scotch whiskey and two tumblers. He poured a finger of the amber liquid into each one and handed me a glass. "You look like you've been to hell and back."

"Thanks," I said drily. We sat in matching leather club chairs and sipped our whiskey. I was beginning to wonder if this whole night was one long Dalí-inspired dream sequence.

"Did you and what's-his-name have a fight?"

"Who, Wes? No. He's out of town."

"Ah. So, you decided to go to a pajama party, and the other girls kicked you out? Left you out in the cold to fend for yourself?"

"Funny." I gave Crenshaw the short version of what had happened.

"I have to hand it to you. You do go above and beyond for your clients."

"Well, the whole thing was so baffling. I wanted to know what was going on. I like to have answers." We were silent for a moment. Then, I said, "Is being partner what you expected?"

He raised his brows at the question. "For the most part. Is the position failing to meet your expectations?"

"I don't know."

"It's more responsibility, of course. Perhaps

you're feeling uncertain because you haven't yet found your niche."

"What do you mean?"

"You know. Randall handles financial matters for the firm. Kris oversees human resources and management of client relationships. Beverly is grooming me to take over business development. I believe she's hoping you'll take on the role of pro bono coordinator and public relations."

"She is?" This was news to me. But maybe it shouldn't have been. I recalled all the recent public speaking engagements. There was almost always another partner present. They were probably reporting on my performance to Beverly.

I yawned. I was too tired to think about it anymore.

First thing I did after I woke up was call Mrs. Hammerlin at the B&B. Then I had to lean on Crenshaw once more to get me to her house. On the way, I asked him to stop at the vegan bakery for scones and pastries. I waited in the car. Even in his borrowed trench coat, I was too embarrassed to be seen in public. We parted somewhat awkwardly on the street in front of Mrs. Hammerlin's house.

"Thanks for everything. I'll return your jacket at the party tonight."

"Keep it. That is, keep it until you come back to the office. No need to bring it along tonight."

"Okay."

"And, Keli? Be careful, will you? You have a habit

of poking your pretty little nose into some dangerous business. I know you're loath to heed such warnings, especially from me, but I feel it needs to be said. Leave police work to the police."

I nodded without a word. All I could think was: *Pretty little nose?*

He took off, and I hurried up the steps of the painted Victorian, looking all bright and innocent in the morning light. Mrs. Hammerlin made coffee, while I used her guest bathroom to shower and get dressed. Then we sat together at her kitchen table. I told her all about my night—minus the part about my spell-casting and impromptu chanting. As it turned out, she didn't mind the broken mirror or the salt on the floor, or even the "drug house" mausoleum behind her backyard. She was just thrilled to learn there wasn't a banshee haunting the neighborhood.

Besides leaving out the part of my story where I might have inadvertently summoned a ghost, I also didn't tell Mrs. Hammerlin about the curtain moving in the window. I never told her about the face in the mirror the other night either. *What is it with mirrors in that room?* For all I knew, those occurrences might have been more about me than the house. Maybe they were manifestations of my own anxieties over Josephine's death. It was my own guilty conscience for failing to catch her killer.

Detective Rhinehardt arrived just as I was pouring myself a second cup of coffee. He let me finish drinking it, as I repeated the tale of my overnight adventure in the graveyard. His normally impassive face betrayed a flash of anger. And something else—resolve.

"This heroin epidemic is getting out of hand. It's everywhere, and it's destroying lives. These dealers in the cemetery, I'm sure they're on the bottom of the heap. They probably don't know who's bringing the supply into Edindale. But we'll watch them and see where it leads."

The detective and I took a walk outside, and I showed him the mausoleum. We found cigarette butts and other litter, but that was all. Rhinehardt thanked me again for the tip and said the cops would take it from here. But instead of heading back to the house, we strolled through the cemetery toward the main entrance. I took the opportunity to raise the issue at the forefront of my mind.

"Any progress on Aunt Josephine's case?"

The detective stopped beneath a willow tree and looked me in the eye. "Ms. Milanni—"

"Please," I interrupted. "Call me Keli."

"Keli. From what we've been able to gather, it appears your aunt was a drifter."

"A drifter?"

"A transient. Basically, a person who wanders from place to place, jobless and homeless."

"She wasn't jobless," I countered. "She had a business, Sister Seeds. Didn't you talk to Fredeline Paul?"

"There's no record of any legal business in your aunt's name. And that microloan organization that funneled the original donation to Ms. Paul in Haiti?

It's since been dissolved. For all intents and purposes, its records are gone."

I didn't like the defeatist tone in his voice. "What about the hunters' cabin and the stolen gun? Have you figured out why Josephine's fingerprints were in that house when there was no evidence of a break-in?"

"Someone left the door unlocked. That's the most likely explanation. The owners told us they sometimes let friends and acquaintances borrow the cabin in the off-season. They also have a cleaning service go through every couple of months. Someone must have forgotten to lock the door when they left, and Josephine took advantage of it. Free accommodations."

"That doesn't explain how she ended up shot in the woods," I retorted.

"My guess is she hooked up with another vagrant and realized that person was dangerous. It's not uncommon for these drifters to be drug addicts or mentally unstable. She took the gun for protection. This other person took it from her, used it, then hopped on a freight train and left town. Unfortunately, we may never catch him."

I couldn't believe what I was hearing. "So, you're giving up?"

"I didn't say that. The case is still open. I'm only trying to manage your expectations."

I thought about the postcards I'd seen and the proximity of HAPCO to the place where Josephine's body was found. That was no accident. She wasn't just "drifting" through that forest. She was there for a reason.

"What about Gil Johnson?" I asked. "Did you search his house? Doesn't it seem suspicious that he's disappeared so soon after Josephine's death?"

As my voice rose, the detective's grew softer. "Now, Keli, you know we can't search his house without a warrant. There's no probable cause here. Besides, his neighbor reported that Johnson lives in Edindale primarily in the summertime. Recently, he asked the neighbor to collect his mail and keep an eye on his place, just like he does every fall. That's not exactly suspicious behavior."

I shook my head, too frustrated to keep arguing. I couldn't accept the fact that Josephine's murder might go unsolved. And I was beyond disappointed that Rhinehardt appeared to be done questioning people.

Well, not me. I would keep digging. I'd keep asking questions. There had to be someone out there who knew the truth about what had happened.

CHAPTER TWENTY-THREE

On my way home from Mrs. Hammerlin's house, I stopped at Mila's for my costume. I wanted to talk with her about my experiences the previous night, but she was too busy with customers to take a break. She wished me a blessed Samhain and asked me to call her later.

At home, I saw Wes briefly when he returned from Memphis. He had to turn around and leave again for his appointment with Tadd Hemsley for the newspaper profile. Before he left, I asked if he'd like to go with me to the costume party that evening. He made a face.

"As fun as that sounds, I think I'll take a pass. Jimi said he could use a hand at the bar tonight, if I want to make some extra cash. I think I'll take him up on that."

"Too bad," I said. "I'm going as a woodland fairy. I thought you could be my elfin king."

He snorted and took me in his arms. "We don't

need a party for that. I can be your elfin king right here."

I laughed and told him I'd miss him. But, inside, I figured it was just as well. I was on a mission tonight—and it wasn't to have a good time.

I spent the rest of the day napping and getting ready for the party. When evening came, I drove myself to Honeycutt Manor, a sprawling private estate often rented for weddings and parties. As I walked up to the stately front door, I felt a bit like Cinderella arriving at the ball—all alone without an escort, dressed like a princess, and harboring a secret unknown to all the other guests.

As I soon discovered, everyone else had a secret too—the secret of their identity. Since this was a masquerade party, masks were required. I already had one, an emerald green eye mask adorned with jewel accents and feathers to match my shimmery, layered dress, so I was allowed to enter. Partygoers who arrived with bare faces were stopped at the door. They couldn't proceed until they'd made a selection from a large basket of assorted half-masks. "All in good fun," said a gatekeeper dressed like a medieval knight.

I followed the sound of music and laughter down a long hall to the grand ballroom at the rear of the mansion. A few steps in, I paused, impressed by the variety of costumes on every person in sight. Some of the partiers went the formal route, with tuxedos and ball gowns paired with ornate Venetian masks. Others chose more playful outfits. There were lots of superheroes, along with a handful of comic book villains. With a nod to the purpose for the event, there were also several guests with farm-related costumes, from famous country music singers and masked cowboys to scarecrows and farm animals. I was completely dazzled.

As I stood on the fringe, a few people began to notice me. A pirate in a gold half-mask waved at me. The Phantom of the Opera tipped his felt cap. And an uncomfortable-looking werewolf stared at me from across the room.

A dapper Zorro approached with a wineglass in hand. "You look lost, Milanni," he said.

"How did you know it was me?"

Instead of answering, he handed me the glass. "I take it you recognized me, as well."

"Your beard gives you away. Why didn't you dress as a vampire again?"

"Dracula doesn't wear a mask."

"Ah."

Crenshaw offered me his arm and led me to a motley group of people standing around a tall cocktail table. It took me just a second to figure out that Marie Antoinette was Beverly, the lovely Catwoman was Kris, and Prince Charming was Randall. Randall's choice of costume wasn't as cutesy as Farrah would have picked, but I was sure she would approve. I made a mental note to send her a photo or two.

"Love your wings," said Kris.

"Thanks. I have to keep reminding myself they're back there. I'm afraid I'm going to bump into somebody and knock them crooked. The wings, I mean."

Crenshaw peered into the crowd. "I do believe I see another befuddled damsel from the firm. I'll go fetch her."

Beverly and Randall appeared not to hear him, but Kris and I exchanged a look. "Just when I think there's hope for him," I said.

Kris laughed and rolled her eyes.

When Crenshaw returned, he was accompanied by Little Bo-Peep. She wore a hoop skirt, blonde ringlets, and a red half-mask. She handed Crenshaw her crook and grabbed a glass of wine from a passing waiter. I wasn't entirely sure it was Pammy until she spoke.

"Nobody told me masks were required! I might have chosen a different costume. Whoever heard of Little Bo-Peep in a mask?"

"Don't answer that," said Randall in a jokey way, though I wasn't sure who he was talking to.

I gazed around the room at the kaleidoscope of colorful costumes. My mission seemed hopeless. How was I going to bring up Aunt Josephine in casual conversation—especially if I had no idea who I was even talking to?

Beverly touched my arm. "There's Neal Jameson. Come with me and I'll introduce you."

I followed her across the room where a short, slim man in a tux and a Mardi Gras mask held court with a merry bunch of revelers. He shook my hand warmly.

"I think it's wonderful you're doing this," I said. "I'd love to see more local, organic food in the area."

"Keli is a vegan," Beverly informed him. "Vegetables are very important to her."

"Is that so?" said Neal. His eyes seemed to twinkle behind his sequined mask.

"No wonder she's got such a great figure," said a voice at my elbow. It was the gold-masked pirate, doing a passable impersonation of Captain Jack Sparrow, drunken slur and all. Ignoring him, I turned to speak to Beverly and discovered she was gone. She had moved on without me.

"Only kidding," said the pirate, in a more staid voice. "Vegetables are important to me, too. You could say my business relies on them."

I squinted at him. Who was this joker?

He laughed and held out his hand. "Tadd Hemsley, at your service."

"Oh! I didn't recognize you, Mr. Hemsley." I shook his hand. "This whole masquerade thing is a little disconcerting."

"That's what makes it so much fun."

"I guess." The awkward werewolf appeared behind Tadd and seemed to be staring at me again. I moved an inch closer to Tadd. "So, did many of your employees come to the party?"

"Yeah, sure. We got a good showing. My workers all support the cause."

"How many people actually work at HAPCO?"

"Hang on a minute, babe," he said, touching my shoulder. "I see a guy I gotta talk to." He walked away, leaving me both irritated at the brush-off and glad he was gone. *Only Wes is allowed to call me "babe."*

The weird werewolf took a step in my direction,

so I turned quickly to move away—and almost bumped into the Phantom of the Opera. With his theatrical black cape, white gloves, and satin vest, he cut a dashing but mysterious figure. His white mask covered the top half of his face, instead of one side as with the iconic phantom mask.

"Hi, there," he said. "Want to dance?"

I was so startled, I nodded in agreement. There was something familiar about the man. I took his hand and we proceeded to the dance floor. Instead of the classical music one might expect at a masquerade ball, tonight's event featured fast-paced Halloween party music. The DJ played "Don't Fear the Reaper," a 1970s melancholy rock number about death's inevitability and undying love. It had a spooky feel in spite of the cowbell. Somehow it seemed appropriate.

The stranger and I faced each other and danced to the music. When the song ended, I did a little curtsy and took off to find my colleagues. This whole scene was turning out to be weirder than I'd expected.

As I waded through the throngs without seeing anyone I knew, I ended up at the French doors leading to a sparkling, decorated terrace. Evidently, the party had begun to spill outdoors. I spotted Tadd smoking a cigarette in a grassy area beyond the veranda, but no one from the firm. I moved along, wondering where everyone had gone.

"Ooh, love your costume!" said a female voice. I turned to see a woman dressed like Neytiri from the movie *Avatar*, with a blue, animal-striped jumpsuit, pointy ears, and braided wig with beads. Her face paint was so professionally done, it distorted her own features—and apparently got her past the front door without a mask.

"Thanks," I said. "Your costume is awesome."

She grinned and twirled her tail. "Any chance to be a Na'vi."

We were joined by a couple of guys in skeleton masks. "Hey, Ricki," said one. "Who's your pixie friend?"

"No idea," said Neytiri with a laugh. I studied her face behind the paint. Was this Ricki Day, the environmental inspector? She looked so different.

"You both are so *cute,*" said the other skeleton. "But not very Halloweeny. Where are all the witches and zombies? I thought Halloween costumes were supposed to be scary."

The next song from the DJ's booth was "Monster Mash." The skeleton man raised his hand in the air as if the song proved his point. "See!"

"Spooky stuff doesn't impress me," said Ricki. "I spent my childhood living next to a cemetery. Got my fill of the morbid."

Huh. That was interesting. I wanted to talk with Ricki some more, but the phantom showed up again.

"Hi," he said. "You don't recognize me, do you?"

I stared at him. *Of course not!* I wanted to say. *You're wearing a mask!*

He lifted the mask to show me his face, and my heart began a tap dance in my chest. It was Levi Markham.

I tried to play it cool. It was entirely possible he

didn't know I'd snooped around in his cabin. After all, he was a distracted artist-type. Supposedly.

"How's the book coming along?" I asked.

"Pretty good."

"What's it about again? You told me before, but I forgot."

"Actually, I don't like to talk much about my works in progress. I'm kinda superstitious that way."

"Uh-huh." I was finding it hard to keep the distrust out of my voice. I cast a glance at Ricki, but she seemed to be happily flirting with the skeleton men. "So," I said to Levi, "how'd you find out about this party?"

"There was a flyer in one of Jameson's restaurants," he said. "I thought it would be good to get away from the cabin for a little while. Of course, I don't know anyone here. Besides you."

I narrowed my eyes. He knew me, all right. He knew me so well, he had my name on a list of people associated with Aunt Josephine. I wanted to bring up the Sorghum bombing, but I didn't know how. I also didn't know if that was the wisest thing to do.

Then I noticed Levi wasn't paying attention to me anymore. He was looking at someone near the French doors. I followed his gaze and spotted the werewolf, standing alone and surveying the crowd. He was quite a sight with his brown rubber claws, furry chest hair sticking through a ripped shirt, and whole-head wolf mask, complete with pointy ears and a gaping, toothy mouth. As we watched, the werewolf was approached by a masked butler, who handed him a slip of paper.

"What's this—a love letter from his she-wolf?" I joked. Levi didn't answer. The werewolf read the note, then crumpled it in his fist. With a last sweep of the room, he swung around and headed outside.

"And it's not even a full moon tonight," I said. "Who is—"

Levi didn't let me finish. "Say, I'm gonna go find a bite to eat. I'll catch you later." He squeezed my arm in farewell and took off.

"What is going on? Did you see that?" I turned to Ricki and her friends, only to find that they had left as well.

Crenshaw appeared at my side. "Having a nice time, Milanni?"

"Uh, yeah."

"I'd ask you to dance, but . . ." he trailed off, waving his hand in the air. The song now playing was "Spooky," sung by Dusty Springfield.

"Hey, is that a real sword?" said a passing knight.

"I beg your pardon?" said Crenshaw.

"I bet mine is bigger than yours. En garde!"

I glanced over at the doors again and saw Levi hurry outside. *So much for getting food*, I thought.

"I'm gonna go get some air," I said to Crenshaw, who seemed to be scuffling with the knight.

By the time I reached the doors, Levi was nowhere in sight. I looked around. Most of the guests out here mingled on the terrace, but a few had wandered onto the lawn. These outliers seemed to be the smokers, including Tadd and a couple wearing square-dance apparel.

I rubbed my bare arms against the cool, damp air. *Where did Levi go?*

A minute later, I spotted a figure in a long dark cape heading to a grove of trees at the edge of the lawn. I took a few hesitant steps, then decided to follow. The ground sloped upward for several yards. When I reached the crest, I noticed a gazebo in the distance, nestled under the trees. Someone was standing by the rail—or maybe it was two people. I paused, not wanting to interrupt a lovers' tryst.

I turned to leave when three things happened at once: a low yelp arose from the gazebo, a gust of wind lifted my wings, and someone cried my name. I tried to hold onto my wings while looking to see who had called for me. There was a man near the trees at the bottom of the hill who seemed to be looking my way. He wore a black suit, long cape, and a hat. Was it Crenshaw or Levi? Or someone else?

I faced the gazebo again, uncertain what to do. The lovers were gone, so I tripped up the steps to get out of the wind. As I adjusted my fairy wings, I caught sight of something on the ground behind the gazebo. I leaned over the railing to get a closer look—and gasped. It was a body, a man, crumpled in a heap.

"Hey!" I yelled.

The man didn't stir. In an instant, I was at his side. I found his wrist and checked for a pulse. It was there, but faint.

"Hey!" I called again. Then, into the wind, I yelled, "Help!"

Carefully, I tried to turn the guy over to give him some air. He was heavy and solid, but I managed to push him onto his side. That's when I realized who he was—the weird werewolf. As gently as possible, I lifted the mask from the front of his face. Even in the darkness, I now recognized who he really was. Not Lon Chaney Jr., but Gil Johnson. And he was bleeding profusely from the back of his head.

CHAPTER TWENTY-FOUR

The rest of the night was a blur—people running and shouting, paramedics and police weaving through the crowd, barking orders. It was after midnight when the officer in charge finally allowed me to leave. Crenshaw insisted on driving me home, even though I kept assuring everyone I was fine. In the end, I gave him my car keys, if only so he'd stop making a scene. Beverly followed to give Crenshaw a ride home.

On the way, I called Wes to let him know I was all right. Knowing how fast lurid news traveled, I figured someone would come into the bar and start flapping their lips about trouble at the masquerade party. I didn't want Wes to worry. Even so, he decided to come home and see for himself that I was okay. He met us on the street in front of our house.

Crenshaw scurried around the front of the car to open my door, then stepped aside when Wes approached. "She's had quite a shock," he said, in a sonorous tone.

"I'm fine," I said for the thousandth time. It must have been the fairy costume, I decided, that made me appear vulnerable. "It's Gil I'm worried about."

We headed up the walkway to our house, as Crenshaw climbed into Beverly's car. Wes paused and watched them take off. "You know, I don't care for the way he looks at you."

"What are you talking about?"

"He has feelings for you—which, who can blame him? It just bugs me sometimes."

"Wes, I can't even think about that right now. Crenshaw is the least of my worries."

"You're right. I'm sorry." He opened the door and stepped back to let me in. "So, you were right, then? About Gil being in danger?"

"It sure seems like it. I'll call Detective Rhinehardt first thing in the morning. I only hope Gil makes it through the night."

As it happened, the detective beat me to the punch. He showed up at our front door before I'd had my first sip of coffee.

"Trick or treat." His straight face threw me off, leaving me at a loss for words. "Sorry," he said. "Bad joke. Got a minute?"

"Sure. Come on in. Would you like some coffee? Or something else to drink?"

"Nah—well, unless you already have it made. That coffee smells good. Black is fine."

"I'll get it," said Wes, from the kitchen doorway.

"Cute cat," said Rhinehardt. "What's his name?"

The cat lolled on the windowsill, pretending not to notice us. I smiled. "She doesn't have a name yet, but we're working on it."

Wes handed the detective a mug and invited him to have a seat at the small dining table in the corner between the kitchen and the living room. I opened the blinds on the patio doors to let in some light, and Wes brought out a plate of cookies Mrs. Hammerlin had sent over. It was all a little too cozy, given the circumstances.

"How's Gil?" I asked. "Any word from the hospital?"

"He hasn't woken up yet, but they think he'll make it." Rhinehardt pulled a small notebook from his pocket and flipped it open. "Now then, I've read the statement you gave to the responding officer last night. If you don't mind, tell me again how you happened to find Johnson on the ground?"

I explained that I was following someone I believed to be Levi—who, in turn, seemed to be following Gil. I also told Rhinehardt about the note Gil had received.

"And you have no idea who this butler character might have been?"

"No. I asked around last night, and no one even remembered seeing that costume."

"Anyone could have walked into the party, right?" asked Wes. "You didn't have to have an invitation."

"That's right. All you needed was money and a mask."

"Which presents a challenge," said the detective.

Except, in my mind, we already had a prime suspect. "I think Levi is hiding something," I said. "I overheard him tell the cops he was nowhere near the gazebo, but I don't think that's true. Is there any chance you could make him take a polygraph test?"

Rhinehardt's expression betrayed a mixture of amusement and regret. "Afraid not. You said you saw him go outside and then lost track of him. There's no evidence he was involved. Anyway, I hope Johnson will have something useful to say when he wakes up, but don't hold your breath. With everyone running around in a mask, he might not know who hit him. Plus, he was hit from behind."

"Did you find the note on him? Or on the ground at the gazebo?"

"No. I'm going out to Honeycutt Mansion from here. It might have been missed in the dark last night."

I was itching to go out there myself. Rhinehardt must have guessed as much.

"Look, Keli, I know you might not have much faith in me—"

"Sure, I do," I said.

"Well, listen, I do appreciate your candor and all the information you've managed to uncover. In light of what happened last night, I did some more research on Gil Johnson. Turns out he has a record in Texas. Nothing too major—vandalism, petty theft, disturbing the peace. This was years ago and doesn't necessarily have any bearing on the present. But there was one other thing."

"What is it?" I expected him to say something about the Sorghum bombing, which occurred in Texas.

"Evidently, he was wanted as a person of interest in connection with the murder of a guy by the name of Davey Winslow. And he wasn't the only one. Josephine O'Malley was wanted for questioning as well. I guess their stories checked out, and they were never charged. Still, it's an interesting piece of info."

I was rattled by Detective Rhinehardt's news. In spite of Josephine's sketchy past, I didn't honestly think she'd turn out to be a killer. For that matter, this was the first time I'd heard Davey's death officially referred to as a murder. It gave me an icky feeling.

When Rhinehardt left, Wes came over to me and rubbed my back. "What do you want to do today? This is your holiday."

He was right. Today was October 31. Halloween to the masses, Samhain to Wiccans like me. It was not only the last of the harvest festivals and the start of the darker half of the wheel, it was also considered the Witches' New Year. Normally, I'd do a special ritual and meditate on my goals for the coming year. But now I couldn't see past Monday, when my parents were due to arrive.

I leaned into Wes and closed my eyes. Then I promptly opened them as a thought occurred to me. "Hey, you haven't told me about your interview with Tadd Hemsley! I guess we both saw him yesterday, you in the afternoon and me in the evening."

"It wasn't my interview. Jason, the reporter, interviewed him. I just took the pictures. Anyway, there's not a lot to tell. We got a tour of his facility. It was a lot cleaner than you might expect. Everything seemed to be stored nice and neat, with lots of clear signage for safety. Oh, and get this. He said he's been experimenting with organic fertilizers. He wants to reduce the environmental impact of his products."

"Wow. Ricki told me his business complies with all relevant regulations. It sounds like he's going above and beyond."

"Yeah, he seemed pretty progressive."

"Wait, what about his unusual hobby?"

Wes grinned. "See for yourself." He reached for his laptop, pulled up his most recent pictures, and turned the screen toward me. I found myself looking into the eyes of a tiger.

"Whoa! Seriously? You were this close to a tiger?"

"Yeah. With bars between us."

"So, Tadd's hobby is . . . ?"

"Collecting exotic animals. He has several tigers, lions, even a bear."

"And this is legal?"

"I guess so. He's got a permit as an animal refuge on a couple acres behind HAPCO. Oh, and he told us the reason he has such a high barbed-wire fence around his facility is not to keep the animals in, but to keep people out. He doesn't want hikers wandering onto his property and getting too close to the cages."

"Good idea."

"He also said he lets a couple of his tigers roam the warehouses at night, instead of security dogs. But I think he was joking about that."

"Wow. You were right—Tadd does have an unusual hobby."

"Yeah. But it doesn't help you any, does it? Did Josephine have anything against private zoos?"

"I have no idea. It doesn't really fit in with everything I know about her. Anyway, from what you learned, it seems unlikely that she could have gotten onto his property, even if she wanted to."

"Well, Tadd seems to really love his animals. He said he's considered a wild animal sanctuary."

"Interesting guy." I took my cup to the sink and looked out the window. It was a beautiful day. The sun shone brightly through the treetops, and the leaves on the ground glistened like strewn confetti.

"I'll rake today," said Wes, behind me.

I turned around and smiled. "I don't mind the yard as it is, but you can rake if you want. Looks like a great day to be outside. I think I'll go for a run."

A short time later, dressed in running shorts, a bright T-shirt, and running shoes, I jogged through Fieldstone Park, then hopped onto the rail trail, a moderately traveled path that ran through town and out toward the river. Though it crossed a couple roads and passed behind neighborhoods, it was largely shady and quiet. It was easy to imagine I was in the middle of a forest.

I loved running, not only for the exercise and endorphins, but also as a meditation practice. The repetitive motion of my footfalls and even rhythm of my breathing almost always brought me into a calm mental state. I was able to focus on the present moment and quiet the chatter in my mind.

Of course, my thoughts still wandered now and then. Even so, things seemed clearer out here in the open air with only the trees to keep me company. As I ran, I thought about Aunt Josephine. I really did have a lot in common with her. We both cared about the earth and tried to live in harmony with the environment. But our approaches were vastly different. Whereas I adopted a vegan lifestyle and tried to reduce my carbon footprint, she went out into the world to promote organic farming—and to stop things she believed were destructive to the environment. If my suspicions were correct, she was willing to commit crimes to advance her cause. I'd never do that.

As soon as I thought it, a wave of guilt coursed through me. I *had* broken the law. I illegally entered Levi's cabin and Gil's house. I trespassed. I invaded their privacy. My intentions were good, but that was no excuse. I knew what I was doing was wrong. That was why I never told Detective Rhinehardt about the postcards. I was embarrassed. I told myself the correspondence between Josephine and Gil didn't necessarily tie in to her murder. Rhinehardt probably couldn't do much with them anyway—except ask Gil what he and Josephine were referring to. And now Gil couldn't talk.

But those postcards *did* tell me something. They told me Josephine felt guilty, too. After all these years, she wanted to come clean.

I reached the two-mile point and turned back. Heading in the other direction, it occurred to me that if Josephine wanted to confess her past crimes, it wouldn't make sense for her to want to commit another one. So, what was she doing in the woods around Briar Creek Cabins?

I'd hit my stride and was running faster and faster now. With my heart pumping and the wind in my hair, I realized I couldn't outrun the decision I had reached. Because, above all the confusion, one thing had suddenly become crystal clear. It was something I should have realized a long time ago. Deep down, I probably always knew it: The only way to find out what had happened to Aunt Josephine was to ask her myself.

I was going to have to communicate with her spirit. And I had to do it tonight.

CHAPTER TWENTY-FIVE

As soon as I got home from my run, I called Mila for advice.

"I know about ancestor veneration," I said. "That's not a problem. But, what is the best way to receive a message back from Josephine? Use of a Ouija board seems a little too hokey. Do I need to hire a psychic medium? I mean, I don't actually need to host a séance, do I?"

"Oh, no. You're perfectly capable of being a channel yourself. You've already heard from your aunt in dreams and visions. You just have to remember the language of Spirit. Spirit speaks in symbols. No Ouija board required."

"Oh. That's good."

"You sound disappointed!"

"I'm not. It's just that symbols require interpretation. I was hoping for some clear answers."

"Don't sell yourself short. You can do it. Although . . ."

"Although what?"

"It might help to have a bit of magical support."

"You mean like a talisman or a potion?"

"I mean like an extra witch or two. One witch can certainly cast a spell, but when you have multiple witches chanting and raising energy, the effect is that much more powerful."

I was silent for a moment. I'd always been perfectly happy as a solitary Wiccan. I didn't feel a need to join forces with others. Now, I wasn't so sure. With everything that had been happening lately, having some extra help didn't sound like such a bad idea. Truth be told, I was a little frightened about the whole thing.

"I'm going to be at Oak Grove Cemetery tonight," she went on. "Isn't that where your aunt will be buried?"

"Yeah, but she isn't there now," I said, with a twinge of alarm. "The burial isn't until Tuesday." It had never occurred to me to do the ritual outdoors, much less in a cemetery. I had planned to summon Josephine at my altar. Mila's suggestion was making me nervous.

"I think you've already established she's not with her body," she said, without a trace of sarcasm. "Calling her to the cemetery might be beneficial for two reasons. First, the energy there is conducive for making contact with ghosts. It's a transitional place where lots of crossing over happen. Second, by showing her where her body will be laid to rest, you might make it easier for her when it's time for her to let go and move on."

"Okay, but I think they lock the gates at dusk.

Wouldn't it be trespassing to sneak in?" Not that I'd let that stop me before, but I was trying to be good now.

"Oh, we'll have permission. I know the caretaker. He lets me in after dark a couple times a year. He knows I'm always quiet and respectful."

I was running out of arguments. "I don't want to take you away from your own celebrations."

"You won't be. I've been celebrating with Circle all week. Tonight, I'll honor my own ancestors early in the evening. After that, I'm all yours."

I was so touched by her offer, I couldn't refuse. But there was still one problem. I wasn't public about my Wiccan religion.

"Mila, I'm pretty sure the police are watching that cemetery, at least the old section. There's been drug activity in one of the mausoleums. Granted, it usually happens after midnight and in the early morning hours, but still."

"We'll be in the new section, but we can certainly let the police know we'll be there. That's not a bad idea."

I imagined Detective Rhinehardt's reaction if he learned I was a witch. It might not faze him, but, then again, it might lower his opinion of me. I hated thinking that way, but it was true.

"What is it, dear?" asked Mila.

"I don't want to be recognized," I said, in a small voice.

"Oh, that's not a problem," she said lightly. "Leave everything to me."

* * *

And that's how I found myself, several hours later, dressed like a medieval monk. The long black robe with large, rounded hood was heavier and more masculine than I was used to. It was a little awkward.

On the other hand, I couldn't deny the excited flutter in my solar plexus chakra. It was quite a rush to stand under the moonlight in the middle of a graveyard on Samhain night. I had never done anything quite like this. But I was a witch, dammit, and this was a very witchy thing to do.

It was all the better to be surrounded by other, similarly clad figures—strong, fierce women. With my permission, Mila had asked Catrina Miller, Max Eisenberry, and Fredeline Paul to join us. Fredeline wore her own colorful caftan and head scarf, and made it clear that she was there to worship the Loa rather than any Pagan gods. But she also wanted to honor Josephine and didn't mind hanging out with a handful of American Witches for an evening, especially since Max offered to give her a ride.

We had met at the cemetery gate at sundown. Mila had already been inside at her own family's plot and had seen the headstone I'd purchased for Josephine. She showed us the way, and we gathered in a cluster to admire the stone. It was an upright granite marker with an engraving of an angel next to Josephine's name.

"That's a nice touch," said Mila, tracing the angel. "I'll bet your mom will like this."

"Yeah. My grandma will, too."

We all chatted for a few minutes, and Max showed

us a picture of her toddler in her pumpkin costume. She'd had a busy day, with a Halloween parade, family cookout, and trick-or-treating. She was so tuckered out, she'd fallen asleep watching cartoon specials with her papa.

With that sweet image in mind, we all had smiles on our faces as we formed a half-circle facing Josephine's headstone.

I recalled what Mila had said about liminal times and places being conducive for contacting spirits. At Samhain, which literally means "summer's end," we were transitioning from the light, warm half of the year, to the dark, cold half. And the cemetery itself felt very transitional tonight, with the half-bare trees and sharp chill in the gentle breeze. Even the moon was transitional. As a waning gibbous, it was less than a full moon but more than a half moon. Just a curvy body in between.

I wasn't sure what to expect tonight, but I was grateful for the support. It seemed appropriate that we were a group of five, like the five classical elements and the five points on a pentagram.

I asked Mila if she would open the ritual. As high priestess of her coven, she was a natural leader who instilled confidence and trust.

"I would be honored," she said. For Fredeline's benefit, she explained that she would first cast a protective circle to contain our magical energy and keep negative energies at bay. Though this was familiar territory for me, I couldn't help envisioning dark spirits swirling in the sky like deathly ghouls in a gothic horror novel.

I shook myself. This was supposed to be a solemn, sacred ritual, not a "haunted barn" experience. I tuned in to Mila, who was chanting a blessing as she walked in a wide circle around the headstone, scattering yellow and red leaves as she went. Then she called the quarters, beginning in the east and working her way around the four directions:

> *Spirits of Air, lovely sylphs, we call on you to grace*
>   *us with your presence.*
> *Spirits of Fire, mystical salamanders, we call on*
>   *you to grace us with your presence.*
> *Spirits of Water, charming undines, we call on you*
>   *to grace us with your presence.*
> *Spirits of Earth, sturdy gnomes, we call on you to*
>   *grace us with your presence.*

She stood beside the headstone, lit a pillar candle, and held it high. "This flame represents the light of life that continues burning even after death, like the spark in our souls. It is hope; it is love. It is a beacon calling forth all those who have lost their way."

She placed the candle on a plate in front of the headstone and picked up a bundle of sage, lavender, and other herbs. "Now, we will each leave an offering for Josephine O'Malley, Keli's aunt, her mother's sister, friend and benefactor to Fredeline Paul, and steward of the earth. May she join us here in this safe space, knowing that we honor her. We welcome her in love and peace."

She placed the herbs on the ground near the candle and motioned for me to follow. I picked up the small potted chrysanthemum I'd brought and placed it next to the herbs. Fredeline came next with a handful of sunflower seeds. Catrina sprinkled water, and Max contributed pumpkin seeds.

After we made our offerings, we resumed our places in the half-circle. Mila closed her eyes, her lips moving soundlessly. I watched the flame of the candle dance in the wind. A moment later, I glanced at Mila, and she opened her eyes and smiled. I nodded in return, not sure what to do next. She stepped forward.

"Let us now join hands as we invite Josephine into our circle." She took my left hand, and Fredeline grasped my right. Mila continued in a strong, authoritative voice:

Josephine O'Malley, spirit, soul, spark of Divine,
Come now, to this place, give us a sign.

Josephine O'Malley, restless one, spirit in the air,
Come now, join us, in this space we share.

Across from me, Max's curls fluttered outside her hood. Tree branches swayed overhead. Mila continued:

Come now, Josephine, enter our sphere.
Make yourself known, right now, right here.

Mila's voice drifted into silence. In the gap, I picked up the call.

Aunt Josephine, if you're here,
Join us now. Please come near.

Fredeline spoke up then, chanting something in Haitian Creole. The only word I understood was *Josephine*. Next, Catrina raised her voice in supplication:

Spirit of the night, hear our plea!
Retreat from the shadow, set yourself free.
Show yourself here, please speak now.
Cross the veil. Please speak now.

Max echoed Catrina's last words. "Speak now!"

Then we all joined in, chanting the words like a mantra. "Speak now, speak now, speak now!"

As one, we halted, listening. The wind had died down. The air felt prickly on my face. The darkness seemed to thicken as clouds rolled in, blotting out the moonlight.

I couldn't say how long we stood there, hovering on the edge of expectancy. It might have been seconds or minutes. However long it was, I knew right away when a new presence had entered our midst. All at once, I had a strange urge to count the hooded figures around me, as if another might have joined our ranks. The others felt it, too. Catrina gasped. Fredeline began swaying and babbling in Haitian Creole. Max hummed a low, melodic drone. Only Mila and I remained quiet and watchful.

Out of nowhere, a gust of wind snuffed out the candle. At the same moment, an icy finger of cold penetrated my robe. I shivered, and my eyes fell closed.

In a flash, I was transported to a dark forest. At first, I felt as if I were watching a silent film. Everything was in black-and-white, with a silvery sheen. The absence of sound was cottony and complete—until, suddenly, a noise burst through like feedback in a microphone. Then, amplified breathing.

Someone was running, crashing through the underbrush. I felt her fear and desperation, the pain in her ankle, the thudding of her heart.

The sharp pop of a gunshot rang out, freezing her in time. She fell. And when she hit the ground, a swarm of bats erupted from the trees, screeching into the night.

For a moment, the bats blocked my view. When they dispersed, the scene was an old film reel of black-and-white trees once more—with one exception. One tree stood out from the rest. It was outlined in gold and appeared to be hollow. A fiery glow lit it from within.

The next thing I knew, there were hands on my shoulders and back. I opened my eyes and found myself looking into the serene face of Mila Douglas.

"She's back," said Max, from somewhere nearby.

"That was awesome," whispered Catrina.

Mila handed me a bottle of water. "Have a sip."

I obeyed, then looked around to get my bearings. The moonlight had returned, casting a dim, bluish light on the tombstones in its path. My hood had fallen back. I pulled it up, feeling self-conscious.

"Let's give her some space," said Mila. She took my hand. "Would you like to sit down?"

I shook my head. "I'm okay. Did you close the circle?"

"Not yet. You're sure you're okay?"

"Yes."

We took our places in the circle for a final blessing. Mila thanked all the spirits who had joined us and told them they could leave now. Then she thanked the deities, the Lady of the Moon and the Lord of the Sun, and dismissed the quarters, one by one. Once finished, she clapped her hands together softly, as if sealing our return to the physical plane.

"Would anyone like to come to my house for a late-night snack?" she asked, as she collected the candle and tidied the area around the headstone.

"I should get home," I said. I was feeling a bit spacey and detached, like someone who had just woken from a deep sleep. I doubted I'd be very good company.

"Don't you want to talk about what you saw?" asked Catrina. "I thought you were possessed there for a minute."

I smiled, sorry to disappoint her. "Maybe another time. I think I'm still processing."

Mila squeezed my hands, and the other women hugged me and said good-bye. We removed our robes, piled into our cars, and went our separate ways.

As I pulled away from the cemetery, I flicked the radio on to anchor myself to the material world. It didn't work. I kept finding myself back in the eerie forest of my vision. Before I knew what was happening, I had passed the turn for my street and was heading to River Road, which led out of town.

"What am I doing?" I muttered. But I didn't turn back. Something compelled me to keep going. I drove all the way out to Briar Creek Cabins. There was something I needed to see.

I left my car on the side of the road near the lane leading to the cabins and continued on foot. This time, the owner's cabin was lit up, and another guest cabin, besides Levi's, had a car parked in front. Avoiding detection, I slipped into the trees and circled behind the cabins to pick up the trail Josephine had traversed only a week and a day earlier.

Without the ritual robe, my only barrier to the cold was a long, thin cardigan sweater, but I hardly noticed. I hurried onward, wearing the darkness like a blanket. Leaves crunched under my boots. Mysterious rustles sounded close at hand, but I wasn't afraid. I felt close to Aunt Josephine. She was leading me, I realized. Or, more accurately, she was pulling me.

I came to a point where the trail curved. Instead of following it, I went straight, abandoning the path. I had no idea if I was anywhere near where Josephine had been shot. The darkness was impenetrable. I would never see the cairn, even if I tripped over it—which was a distinct possibility since I couldn't see a thing. I walked with my arms held out in front of me like an animated mummy. Branches slapped my arms, and twigs caught in my hair. Still, I forged onward.

Eventually, I slowed to a stop. Shards of moonlight cut through the canopy above, revealing a strange tangle of shapes all around me. For a split second, I came to my senses and almost panicked.

I'm lost in the forest!

Before I could start hyperventilating, I became aware of a squeaking sound and more rustling. Something flew toward me. A bat! I remembered the bats in my vision and tried to keep this one in sight. After some mad fluttering, it disappeared into a wide, gnarly tree, possibly an oak. The tree wasn't glowing, but it was reminiscent of the golden tree in my vision.

I pulled my cell phone from the pocket of my sweater. Even though there was no signal, the light still worked. I held it near the tree, looked up and down—and spied a hollow. Standing on my tiptoes, I tried to look inside. I saw nothing but blackness.

Feeling a bit like Audrey Hepburn in *Roman Holiday*, I shut my eyes and stuck my hand in the hole—the Mouth of Truth. As I did, I whispered a fervent prayer: "Please don't let there be any biting, stinging, or squishy creatures in here."

My fingers touched something cold and hard. I reached in farther, scraping my wrist on the bark, and finally grasped an odd-shaped object. It felt like plastic and metal. After a couple of false starts, I managed to extract it from the tree.

Now that I held it in both hands and could feel its shape and heft, I knew what it was. As the realization sank in, I began to tremble. I had the answer. In my hands was the answer to my question. *What had happened to Josephine?* She had seen her killer. She took a picture of her killer.

And this was her missing camera.

CHAPTER TWENTY-SIX

By some miracle, I found the trail and managed to stumble out of the forest without losing my mind. Strange sounds had echoed in the darkness, and I kept trying to explain them away. *Probably just an owl. Or a fox. Or an insect.* At one point, I swore I heard footsteps behind me and convinced myself it must have been a deer. Still, I walked faster and faster until I was practically running when I finally emerged from the woods.

I clutched the camera to my heart. The lens was smashed and the body was cracked, but the film compartment was closed. And it appeared the film was still inside. I had to get it to Detective Rhinehardt right away. He would know what to do.

The sharp snap of a twig wrenched me from my thoughts. I was so focused on watching my step and protecting the camera, I failed to notice how close I'd wandered to the cabins. I looked toward the sound and felt my blood run cold. A man was there, facing my direction. In one swift movement, he emerged from the shadows, drew an object from his waistband, and pointed it right at me in his outstretched hand.

"Stop!" he shouted.

"Don't shoot!" My voice was a high-pitched yelp.

"Keli?" The weapon disappeared and Levi stepped forward. "What are you doing back there?"

My knees gave out. He rushed forward and caught me before I hit the ground. Feeling as if I could dissolve into a puddle of frayed nerves, I held onto his neck with one arm and let him help me to the front of the cabin. But when we reached the door, I pulled away.

"Come inside and sit down," he said, as he tried to guide me through the doorway. "I'll get you some water. Or coffee. Whatever you want."

"N-no, thanks. I'm okay. Just—just startled, that's all."

He looked at me with mingled concern and disbelief. "What are you doing here?" he repeated. "Can I call someone for you?"

Speaking fast, I tried to give him a coherent answer. "I was just heading to my car. I was thinking about my aunt tonight and wanted to go for a walk on her trail. I got a little turned around, but I found my way out." I mustered up a smile and tried to smooth my hair. My fingers caught on a leafy twig, which I pulled out and tossed on the ground. "Well, thanks again. Happy Halloween!" With that, I abruptly took off, hobbling down the lane.

"Wait!" Levi called.

"Have a good night!" I responded.

When I reached my car, I placed the camera on the passenger seat next to me and peeled out. I didn't care how late it was—or how much I resembled a girl who'd been raised by wolves. I was going straight to the police.

The closer I got to town, the safer and calmer I felt. *What a night!* And what an incredible feeling to have been guided and protected in that forest. I didn't know if it was angels, fairies, or ghosts, but I sensed it was more than the spirit of Aunt Josephine who helped me find my way.

I was elated to have her camera. Now, I might actually be able to provide some answers for my grieving mother.

As I came to a crossroads, where one street led to my house and another led downtown, I decided to make a pit stop at home. I needed to use the bathroom and wash up. I'd make it quick. Wes was bartending tonight, so I wouldn't have to explain myself.

Standing on the stoop, fumbling for my key while cradling the camera, I felt my phone buzz in my pocket. With a sigh, I grabbed it to check the message. It was from Farrah, and it said, "Look behind you."

I whipped around.

"Boo!"

"Oh, my gosh! You're back!"

Laughing, she ran up the sidewalk. "Yeah, I had a chance to switch flights and decided to take it.

I was tired of Atlanta and wanted to be here for Halloween. Want to go to the Loose? Let's go inside and conjure up some costumes."

"Actually, I have a thing . . ."

"Wait. Where have you been?" She squinted at me in the porchlight. "Is that dirt on your face? Are your jeans ripped, and not in a trendy, artful way?"

I looked down at my pants. "Dang."

"Did someone attack you?" she exclaimed.

"No, no. Nothing like that."

"Give me your keys, girlfriend. Let's get you inside."

I complied and followed her to the living room. In a rush of words, I told her about my vision and experience in the woods, ending with my brief encounter with Levi. Her mouth gaped in a large, round *O* the whole time.

"Hold this," I said, handing her the camera, "while I use the bathroom."

When I rejoined her a couple minutes later, she was still in awe. "So, this is what happens when I leave you for three nights!"

"I haven't even told you about the excitement at the party yesterday, or the ghosts at Mrs. Hammerlin's house. But there's no time now. I gotta get this camera to the police."

"But, but," Farrah sputtered. "Why can't Wes develop the film? Aren't you dying to see what's on this camera?"

"Wes doesn't have a darkroom. He might be able to borrow one at the university, but I don't want to risk it. The camera is damaged. The police forensics unit will know what to do. Want to come with me?"

"Of course! I'm never leaving your side again. Let me just use your bathroom first. I came straight here from the airport."

While waiting for Farrah, I went to the kitchen for a glass of water. I'd taken one gulp when there was a knock at the door. I frowned. What now?

I looked through the peephole and saw a huddle of people in costume. They were too tall to be children, and besides it was much too late for trick-or-treating. I figured they must be teenagers, especially since their masks tended toward the macabre. I noticed a couple of skull faces and a deformed zombie. I opened the door to tell them we had no candy—and was immediately knocked to the floor.

I tried to call out, but someone clamped a hand over my mouth. Another person held me down. I struggled with all my might, twisting and writhing on the ground, but I was pinned under the weight of one of the monsters. In the midst of the tumult, I thought I heard the cat hiss. I gnashed my teeth, trying desperately to bite the flesh pressed to my mouth. It was no use.

Then, as suddenly as it began, it was over. The weight lifted, and I was free. I pushed myself to my hands and knees and looked up in time to see four men—not teenagers, I was pretty sure—barrel out the door. At the same time, Farrah came out of the bathroom and shrieked.

I ran to the door. The ghouls ran down the street toward the park and disappeared from sight.

"Oh, my God!" screamed Farrah. "What just happened? Are you okay?"

I swallowed the bile in my throat and managed to nod.

"Should we call 9-1-1?" She reached for her phone.

"It's too late for that," I said. "There's nothing the cops can do now."

I looked at the table where I'd left Josephine's camera, already knowing what I'd see. An empty space. The camera was gone.

CHAPTER TWENTY-SEVEN

We called the police anyway. I realized it was best to report the attack right after it happened, especially with those creepy, masked goons on the loose. I didn't know the officers who responded, so I didn't mention Aunt Josephine. I told them a camera was stolen without telling them where I'd obtained it. I still planned to follow up with Detective Rhinehardt in the morning.

When the officers left, Farrah asked me if I was up for going to the Loose for a nightcap. Wes would still be working for another hour or so until closing time. But I was in no mood to be around any more costumed revelers—and probably wouldn't be for a very long time. Farrah was fine with that. She rummaged in my freezer for snacks and found a vegan pizza. As she switched on the stove, she ordered me to go put on my pajamas and wait for her in the living room. For the next hour, we sipped wine, ate pizza, and speculated about who was behind Josephine's murder.

"It's definitely a conspiracy," said Farrah. "It was six men who attacked you, right?"

"Five or six. Yeah."

"That means Gil is still a suspect. He could be the mastermind. In fact, if it's a conspiracy, anyone with an alibi is now fair game."

I took a sip of wine and leaned my head back on the couch. I had brought Farrah up to speed on everything she'd missed the past couple of days. Her reasoning matched my own. It now seemed as if we were looking for not just one culprit, but a whole group of people. The first thing I thought of was all those folders in Levi's cabin. Maybe the group of criminals we were after were the ecoterrorists from Josephine's past.

"You know who leads a whole big secret society of people," Farrah continued. "Fern Lopez. Didn't Zeke say her 'Sisterhood' was all over the world? She must have been pretty unhappy when Josephine went off and formed her own group. Maybe there was a rivalry there."

"I don't know that Josephine formed her own group, necessarily. But Fern does seem to have mixed feelings about Josephine. Could just be hurt feelings."

"Or jealousy or resentment. Or anger, if Josephine stole Fern's trade secrets."

"Hmm. I suppose it's possible. Speaking of Fern, did you happen to find out who owns that property she wants?"

"Yeah. I emailed you the info. It's bank-owned."

"Oh, I guess I haven't checked my email lately. Thanks a million. Maybe I can coax Fern into telling me more now. Like who else Josephine worked with. There has to be someone else. Doesn't there?" I closed my eyes. I was becoming too sleepy to think anymore.

Farrah got up and took my plate and glass. "You go to bed," she said. "I'll hang out here until Wes comes home."

"You will?"

"You bet."

I went upstairs and crawled into bed. As I drifted off to sleep, a disturbing thought swam to the surface of my mind, like a shark in murky waters. Someone knew I'd found that camera tonight. Someone who knew what the camera signified, knew where it was hidden, and knew where I lived.

I was exceedingly grateful Farrah had stayed.

The next morning, Wes and I took a walk through the neighborhood. Along the way, I picked up discarded candy wrappers, imagining it was what Aunt Josephine would have done. We talked a little about my experiences the previous evening. Wes expressed his concern, as I knew he would, but he was remarkably calm—especially about my decision to head into a dark forest by myself without telling anyone. I figured Farrah must have warned him not to lecture me. There was a time and a place for cool reflection, and I wasn't there yet. I was too nervous about my parents arriving the next day. And that Josephine's killer was still running around scot-free.

When we returned home, Wes tagged along behind me as I washed up and straightened the house. He was supposed to go help his dad with a home improvement project today, but he didn't want to leave me. "Why don't you come along?" he suggested. "You can hang out with my mom. She's been wanting to have us over for dinner anyway."

"I'll stop by later," I promised. "You go ahead. I need to go see Detective Rhinehardt first."

Wes wasn't happy about leaving me alone, but I finally convinced him that the police station was about the safest place I could be. Since it was Sunday, I gave Rhinehardt a call first to find out if he'd be in his office. He said he'd be there a little while longer and could meet with me if I came now.

As eager as I was to speak to him, I found myself dragging my heels. By the time I parked in front of the station and headed to the entrance, I was almost ready to turn around and go back home. How could I explain the fact that I'd found Josephine's camera in a tree last night? Was I really going to tell him I was led to the forest by a psychic vision—after summoning my aunt's ghost?

No. No, I was not. I couldn't do it.

I would make up an excuse about not feeling well. I walked up to the front desk to leave a message with the officer on duty, when Rhinehardt came out to the lobby. He looked so haggard, I immediately set aside my own anxieties. With his puffy eyes, unshaven jawline, and rumpled suit, it was obvious he'd been up all night.

"Come on back," he said.

"Is this a bad time? We can talk later."

"Nah. Halloween is always a pain in the neck. Almost as bad as New Year's Eve. Did I hear right that you had a run-in with some punks at your house? There was an alert issued to be on the lookout for a gang of creeps fitting the description you gave. Sorry to say, they weren't apprehended."

"I'm not surprised. They probably removed their costumes right away. About that—"

"About Gil Johnson," Rhinehardt cut in. "I have some good news and bad news."

"Oh?" For a moment, I forgot all about Josephine's camera. "Did he wake up?"

"Affirmative. He came to early this morning. He had a concussion, but the doctor said he's recovering nicely. Problem is, he's refusing to talk. Johnson claims he doesn't know who hit him and doesn't know anything about a note—which we never found, by the way. To all our other questions, he only said, 'Sorry. Can't help you out.' Tough nut, that one."

"Shoot," I said, unable to hide my disappointment. So, Gil was still mistrustful of the police. "He *has* to know something. He could still be in danger."

Rhinehardt smiled grimly. I wasn't telling him anything he didn't already know.

"Can he receive visitors?"

"Sure, I believe so." He eyed me carefully, then stood up and touched my arm as he opened the door. "You learn anything from him, you be sure to let me know ASAP."

"I will." I'd call Rhinehardt at home, if I had to. I had no more time to lose.

The Edindale Medical Center was a modern, six-story hospital serving all of Edin County. Wes's mom's cousin, Sharon, worked at the intake desk, so I stopped by to say hi. She looked up Gil's room number for me and told me visiting hours started at 11:00, which was in ten minutes. We chatted for a minute, then I left to find my way to the fourth floor.

The second I stepped off the elevator I could tell something was amiss. People were running and yelling. At first, I assumed it was a medical emergency, until I heard someone holler, "Call security!"

With increasing alarm, I made my way down the hall toward Gil's room—which seemed to be at the center of all the commotion. A wide-eyed candy striper stood in front of Gil's closed door.

"What happened?" I asked. "Is Mr. Johnson okay?"

"A nurse is with him now," the girl answered. "I'm not supposed to let anyone in except the doctor or the police."

"The police?"

"Yeah." She bit her lip, clearly unnerved. "There was a guy in here messing around the patient's bed. He wore a skeleton mask! When the nurse came in, he punched her and ran out."

"Oh, my God!"

"I know! A bunch of people ran after him, but he was fast."

"Which way did they go?"

"That way, probably to the back stairs." She pointed down an empty hall.

Without hesitating, I took off in pursuit. I knew I was at the tail end of the chase, but I hoped to at least catch a glimpse of the intruder. I heaved open the door to the stairs and trotted down four flights, my footsteps echoing in the stairwell. When I reached the bottom, I burst through the steel exit door and found myself in the employee parking lot.

I ran a few steps, then faltered, blinking in the sunlight. There was no one in sight. No hospital personnel, no police, no masked bandits. Either they'd outrun me, or they didn't come this way.

I turned back, only to find the door had locked behind me. I'd have to walk around to the front entrance. I headed around the side of the building, past a landscaped hedge bordering the parking lot. I hadn't gotten very far when I heard someone sneeze. I paused, looking around. Was someone behind the hedgerow?

Curious, I walked to the end of the row and peeked around. A man was blowing his nose into a cloth handkerchief. It was Levi Markham.

"Oh, hello," he said, when he spotted me. "These darn allergies."

I narrowed my eyes. "What are you doing back here?"

He acted confused by the question and slightly defensive. "I'm taking a walk, getting some fresh air. Though, I don't know that I owe you any explanations. You never tell me what *you're* up to."

How do you like that? Levi Markham, Mr. Mystery himself, thinks I'm holding back.

We glared at one another. Maybe it was the broad daylight that emboldened me, or the fact that we were next to a hospital full of people—not to mention the fact that the police were supposedly on their way. Whatever the reason, I felt more irritated than afraid.

Who was this guy? Was he a shy author conducting research about the Sorghum bombing for a book he planned to write? Or did he have a personal connection to the bombing? Was he a relative of one of the victims, intent on seeking vengeance, one bomber at a time? Maybe he was a relative of one of the coconspirators, such as poor, unlucky Davey.

Levi turned his head and sneezed again, ending our staring contest. Slowly, like clouds parting on a mild, windless day, another possibility came to mind.

"Who are you really?"

"What?" He appeared startled.

"I know you're not who you say you are. You might as well fess up. You're not really a writer, are you?"

"What are you talking about?" He looked around in exaggerated disbelief. He really wasn't a very good liar.

"Why do you have a file on my aunt Josephine?"

"I *knew* you searched my cabin!"

"You didn't answer my question. Why were you after her? What's your interest in the Sorghum bombing?" I recalled my earlier theory that Josephine had been running from the law. And I remembered the authoritative way Levi had held a gun and ordered me to "stop." When he reached into his inner jacket pocket, I didn't even flinch.

"Special Agent Len Martinwood," he said, showing me a very real-looking badge. "FBI."

CHAPTER TWENTY-EIGHT

I was having some difficulty adjusting to Levi's real name. He didn't look like a "Len Martinwood" to me. When I asked him if I could continue calling him "Levi," he said, "Please do. I'm still undercover."

We sat on a bench in the flower garden next to the hospital. He told me he had been tracking Josephine for months. She was wanted as an ecoterrorist in connection with the Sorghum bombing. He was also investigating Gil.

"The bombing happened decades ago," I said. "Why now?"

"The case was never closed," he answered. "Every now and then, new administrations will assign agents to take a fresh look at cold case files. I was assigned to this one."

"Does Detective Rhinehardt know about you?" I asked.

He nodded. "I try to work with local law enforcement whenever I can. This time, I had to identify myself when Josephine turned up dead."

"No wonder Rhinehardt said you were okay. I kept trying to tell him you were hiding something."

"You suspected me in your aunt's murder?"

"Well, you were obviously lying. What was I supposed to think?"

He opened his mouth as if to respond, then thought better of it.

"Never mind," I said. "Tell me about Gil. Who do you think attacked him? And what was he doing at the costume party anyway? I thought he'd gone into hiding."

"You might be right about that. I can think of two reasons he might've come out of hiding. Either he was trying to track down Josephine's killer and thought he could get a lead at the party—"

Kind of like me, I thought.

"—or else someone lured him there with an offer he couldn't refuse."

"Hmm. I wish I knew what was in that note he was given."

"Actually, I have that." Levi patted his pocket. Seeing my raised eyebrows, he explained. "I tipped the groundskeeper last night and asked him to keep an eye out for it. I just met up with him before coming here."

"So much for working with the local police."

"I'm heading over to the police station next," he said, a touch defensively.

"Okay. So, what did the note say?"

He hesitated, and I gave him a *pretty please* look until he sighed. "The note was written in plain block letters. It said, 'I know what happened to JO. Come to the gazebo behind the mansion.'"

I bit my lip as I pondered the message. It was consistent with both of Levi's theories. Gil could have innocently seeking information about Josephine's death. Or he could already know what happened to her because he was involved. In that case, maybe someone was trying to blackmail him. Or punish him.

On the other hand, if someone was targeting people involved in the Sorghum bombing, Gil could have been summoned to the party for an entirely different reason.

I met Levi's eyes. He raised his shoulders in a subtle shrug. He didn't know the answer either.

"Tell me something," I said. "You've been following Josephine around for quite some time. Where did she live when she wasn't in Edindale? Who did she associate with?"

"She moved around a lot. She seemed to know people everywhere. For the longest time, she was always one step ahead of me. Then I tracked her to this retreat center in Sedona, Arizona, run by a wealthy new-age guru type. I suspect he funded her business."

"Sister Seeds?"

"Right. I think it was based there at the center. But when I started asking questions, I got the runaround. Everyone denied knowing Josephine. Or even seeing her. It felt like *The Lady Vanishes.* You know that old movie?"

"I do. Yeah." Levi was full of surprises. I wouldn't have figured him for a classic movie buff like me.

"Anyway, then she came to Edindale. I figured she was here to see you, but she kept going out to the forest."

"What do you think she was doing out there?"

"I think she was scoping out HAPCO. She was planning something."

I shook my head. That couldn't be it. At least, not in the way Levi meant.

I started to argue with him, then noticed the tears in his eyes. My heart immediately softened— until he screwed up his nose, turned his head, and sneezed.

On the off chance I'd be allowed to see Gil, I made my way up to the fourth floor once more. However, he was sleeping, and since I wasn't family they wouldn't even let me go in.

From there, I went straight to Wes's parents' house. It was time for a little normalcy.

Bill and Darlene Callahan lived in a lovely Crafts-man on a historical street in Edindale. We spent a nice afternoon talking about their renovation projects, offering our opinions on their paint samples, and, later, making and eating pumpkin pie. It turned out that Darlene and Bill had dinner plans, so Wes and I snacked on food from their fridge and left their house in the late afternoon.

It had been a nice little respite from the mystery, but as soon as we left, my mind began puzzling once more. We were home for only a few minutes before I started pacing the living room. The cat mewed nervously as she prowled about underfoot.

"Sorry," I said to her. "I can't help it. I'm on edge."

"Did you say something?" called Wes, from the kitchen.

"I was just telling the cat how restless I feel." I glanced out the window. "There's still some daylight left. Want to take a drive out to Briar Creek?"

"You're kidding, right?"

Instead of answering, I went upstairs to the bedroom and pulled out the envelope of jewelry Detective Rhinehardt had given me. I slipped one of Aunt Josephine's rings on my finger. Wes came up behind me.

"You're not going out there again." It wasn't a question.

"Not alone," I agreed. I turned to him with pleading eyes. "Aunt Josephine has been communicating with me, Wes. There's no denying it. I need to hear from her one more time. Please. Go out there with me."

With a sigh, he grabbed his jacket from the bedpost. "We'd better hurry," he said.

We were quiet on the drive out of town, each lost in our own thoughts. I didn't believe Levi was right about Josephine. He thought she was doing reconnaissance at HAPCO in preparation for another bombing. But that made no sense—not if she wanted to come clean about her past crimes.

So, the question remained: What was she doing out there in the forest?

We pulled into the lane leading to the cabins, when suddenly: *Boom!* A loud bang jerked me from my thoughts. I was so startled, I screamed. Wes swore and steered the rattling car to the side of the road. Luckily, we hadn't been going very fast.

We both got out to examine the front tire. It was completely flat.

"Do you have a spare?"

Wes popped the trunk and cursed again. "I have a spare, but no jack. I lent it to a buddy the other day and didn't get it back."

"Looks like Carl is home," I said, pointing to the office cabin. "Let's go see if he has one."

Carl had already come out to see what had caused the loud noise. He was a nice guy and immediately offered to help. While the men discussed tires, I cast an anxious glance at the sky. I was fast losing my daylight hours.

When Carl jogged over to his Jeep to get a jack, I pulled Wes aside. "I'm going to go ahead and take a little walk while you do this. Okay?"

"Okay. Wait. Not in the woods?"

"Yeah, it'll be fine. I know my way around these trails really well now. I won't get lost."

"Come on, Kel. Be reasonable. It's gonna be dark soon."

At that moment, a couple of middle-aged

women with hiking sticks emerged from one of the trailheads.

"Look," I said. "People are still out here. I'll be perfectly safe." I hitched my purse on my shoulder and waved at Carl as he rejoined us. "Be back soon."

I walked quickly and soon found myself under the dark vault of the trees once more. As I trod deeper into the forest, I twisted Aunt Josephine's ring on my finger.

"Speak to me," I whispered. "Speak now."

As I followed the familiar trails, I recalled the day Levi had showed me the place where Josephine was killed. Scanning the landscape now, I spotted it: the stacked stones. I left the trail and stood next to the cairn.

"Aunt Josephine? Are you here? Send me a sign."

Nothing happened. I observed only the ordinary autumn evening sights, sounds, and smells. Frustrated, I returned to the trail.

It was dusk now. I knew I should go back. But instead of turning around, I continued down the trail until I came to a fork I recognized. The offshoot led to the sandbank where Farrah and I had parked the canoe the other day. That meant the HAPCO fence was near here.

Follow in my footsteps.

The thought came to me like a directive from beyond. I needed to retrace Josephine's steps—but not her last running, limping steps. Her first steps. Where did she go first?

My mind flashed to the list in Josephine's pocket and her plan to "see Ricki." Ricki was on the good side of the law. Maybe Josephine *was* scoping out HAPCO, but not for nefarious purposes as Levi suspected. Maybe she hoped to catch the business in an environmental crime. She had her camera to take pictures, then show the pictures to Ricki.

I spotted the fence at the top of the incline on the side of the trail. I climbed up to it and looked through the links. Then I followed it all the way to the front entrance like Farrah and I had done before. When I reached the end, I hid behind a tree and studied the scene.

How did Josephine get on the property? From what Levi said, she must have been trying to find a way on for several days. Did she watch the gate and wait for an opportunity to sneak in? In the movies, heroes always snuck past guards by hiding in the back of a truck. But the only trucks entering HAPCO were tankers and semis carrying drums of chemicals. No place to hide there.

Then I thought of the private zoo behind the facility. All those animals had to eat. I figured there must be routine meat deliveries. Of course, those trucks would be refrigerated. Again, no place to hide.

How about the old wait-for-someone-to-open-the-gate trick? Could she have slipped in unseen in the wake of an authorized vehicle? I dismissed the idea as soon as I thought it. The area around the front gate was totally exposed, with no place to hide.

Anyone tailing another car or truck would certainly be seen.

How did you do it, Josephine?

Slowly, I retraced my steps along the edge of the fence. This time I studied the fence from top to bottom, looking for any weaknesses. I had nearly reached my starting point, when a gust of wind shook the branches overhead, causing a rain of leaves onto my head. Brushing them off, I looked up. The branches were awfully low here. *Was it possible?*

It was. Channeling my inner child, I climbed the nearest tree and crawled, hand over hand, along the lowest branch. It brought me within inches of the HAPCO fence. Like an aspiring trapeze artist who wasn't quite up to snuff, I clutched the branch, lowered my legs, and swung my body toward the fence post. After a couple of tries, I finally managed to plant my feet on the metal post. Fearing I'd fall into the barbed wire, I wasted no time. I jumped to the ground.

The moment my feet hit the uneven berm below, it dawned on me. This was how Josephine had sprained her ankle. She was injured even before she was chased. Luckily, I didn't suffer the same fate. I landed on my hands and knees, evenly distributing the pain. I hopped up and ran to the nearest building.

The place was quiet, but well lit. Floodlights bathed the front gate, while security lights cast small pools of light throughout the facility. In addition to

the semitrailers I'd seen before, a small pickup truck
was parked next to one of the buildings.

Josephine wanted to get inside. Was she looking
for a place to plant a bomb, like Levi suspected? Or
did she just want to find evidence of illegal chemicals, like I believed? Either way, where did she go
from here?

Like me, she surely wanted to remain out of sight.
I darted to the back of the warehouse, so I wouldn't
be seen by anyone who happened to enter the front
gate. I passed loading docks, and garbage bins, until
I reached a grassy area between two buildings. I
paused, uncertain which way to go, when a strange
whistling rang through the air. A familiar whistling.
It sounded exactly like Mrs. Hammerlin's banshee.

Following the sound, I climbed up an embank-
ment at the back of a warehouse and noticed a gap
between the berm and the building. Looking down,
I saw a row of dingy windows along the wall near
the ground. They must be basement windows. One
was broken, leaving a splintered gash just large
enough to peek through.

Kneeling on the ground, I looked through the
hole. I gasped and drew back. There were people
inside, bustling about in a frenzy of activity. Cautiously, I took another look. I tried to make sense of
what I was seeing. It was a large room with cinder-
block walls and several metal tables. One table
contained what looked like laboratory equipment.
Another table held stacks of clear plastic bags in
assorted sizes. The men below were filling some of

the bags with pill capsules, and others with a white substance. The bags were then being weighed on a small scale.

This wasn't an environmental crime. This was a drug operation.

CHAPTER TWENTY-NINE

I pulled my phone out of my purse and snapped a couple pictures through the hole in the window. Though it was dark outside now, the underground room was well lit. I hoped the pictures would turn out.

This must be what Josephine photographed with her camera. Only she was caught.

With that sobering thought, I dropped my phone into my purse and backed away from the window. Now, to make my escape. I couldn't very well leave the way I came in. I had no means to get over the barbed wire from this side of the fence. I'd have to exit through the front gate.

Was that Josephine's plan, too? Was that when she was seen, and then chased through the forest?

Heart pounding, I hugged the building as I inched my way toward the front of the facility. When I reached the corner, I ducked behind a semitrailer and gauged the distance to the front gate. I'd have to cover at least forty yards, all out in the open.

Then I discovered another problem. The gate was electronic with a motion sensor for exiting vehicles. I couldn't just lift a latch and walk out.

Headlights sliced through the darkness on the road outside the facility. As I watched, the gate opened and a black sports car drove in. It was Tadd Hemsley's car.

Suddenly, I remembered the evening of the haunted barn opening. As I stood chatting with Vampire Crenshaw, Tadd had come out to take a phone call. It was a call that seemed to annoy him and caused him to leave the event. That was Friday night, just hours before Josephine was shot.

Oh, God. Was I still walking in her footsteps? Was this turning into a repeat of that night?

I had to get out of here.

I ran back toward the warehouse buildings, in the opposite direction Tadd's car had taken. Avoiding the building with the drug lab, I rushed to the next one. I tried the first door I came to. Amazingly, it was unlocked. I pulled it open, then hesitated on the threshold. Perhaps it wasn't wise to go inside. I felt like I was entering a dragon's lair.

Heavy footsteps drew near. Someone was coming! I had no choice. Into the lair I went.

It turned out to be a cavernous warehouse. Dim security lights lined the floor and ceiling. On the far end of the building were loading docks with half a dozen bays for truck trailers. Another end contained a process area with a conveyor belt, venting equipment, and covered vats of chemicals. The center of the building was filled with industrial-sized metal shelving, stacked with steel drums and sacks of pungent-smelling fertilizer. It was an altogether creepy place to be.

I eased my way along the wall, hoping to find a telephone. On the other side of the building, a closed door caught my eye. Maybe it was an office. I headed that way but didn't get very far. The click of a door opening echoed throughout the building.

In a panic, I ducked into a small alcove between a tall lift truck and a stack of wooden pallets. There was a hollowed-out space behind the pallets. It looked like a good hiding place. I crawled inside and shone my phone on the floor, so I wouldn't bump my head. After a couple of passes with the light, I noticed a small slip of paper. I would have ignored it, except that a word jumped out at me. It appeared to contain flight information—the date, time, airline, and number for a flight out of Port-au-Prince, Haiti.

It might as well have said, "Josephine was here."

I didn't have time to dwell on this information. Footsteps clicked across the concrete floor. Then a voice rang throughout the building.

"I know you're in here, Keli Milanni! You were seen in the window. You can come out."

I froze, not daring to breathe. I listened as Tadd seemed to swagger up and down the corridors between the metal shelves.

"You shoulda left well enough alone, darlin'! I'd already decided you didn't know anything. I wasn't sure at first. The old lady made one phone call while she was in here, so I figured somebody knew what she saw. Of course, *now* I lock the office. But she managed to make a call to somebody. The ancient phone doesn't save outgoing calls, so I didn't know who she called, except that it was a local number. I thought it might be you, until you showed me how clueless you were."

His voice grew louder, as he got closer to my hiding place. I closed my eyes and mentally deployed my glowing shield of white light. *He will not find me. He cannot see me. He will not find me. He cannot see me.*

"Then I thought it was Gil Johnson," continued Tadd. "You told me he was the old lady's friend. He acted so flighty, I was sure it was him. I put a tail on him and ordered my boys to take him out. Then, lo and behold, you show up here. So, I figure I was right the first time. It was you all along. And here you are to see what your auntie was tellin' you about."

He laughed, a raspy hacking sound. I had no idea what he was talking about. Josephine hadn't called me. Who would she have called?

"Of course, then the old lady managed to escape outta here. My boys were supposed to be watching the doors, the numbnuts. I have to do everything myself. But she didn't get far before I found her. Fortunately for me, she was too chicken to use her little rifle. She had her chance and couldn't pull the trigger. I grabbed it right outta her hands."

He laughed again. I shook with anger and disgust— and sorrow. In the end, Josephine chose not to take a life. And she had paid for it with her own.

"You can't hide forever, ya little sneak! I'll tell you what. How about if I go open the tiger cages? What do you think? Serve a trespasser right."

A door slammed. I backed out of my hiding place and peered around the corner of the stack of pallets. The room appeared to be empty. I didn't know if he'd really open the cages or if it was a ploy to lure me outside. Either way, I had to take my chance. I bolted for the exit and tore through the night all the way to the front gate—where I stopped short and looked up.

How could I get it to open? I ran back and forth in front of the gate hoping to trigger a sensor. It didn't work. I also realized I was probably being recorded on a security camera.

Suddenly, headlights blazed at me from both directions. Behind me was Tadd's black sports car, the engine revving. Ahead of me, a black Jeep flashed its brights behind the gate. I scarcely had time to react before Tadd plowed toward me. I dove out of the way in the nick of time. He switched his car in reverse and pulled back to try again. However, his car had activated the sensor. The gate slid open, and the black Jeep came roaring through. Three men jumped out and ran toward me.

I met them halfway. "Get me out of here!" I cried.

Wes, Levi, and Carl rushed forward to help me. Then Tadd zoomed up and opened his car door.

Levi jumped in front of me with his hand on a holster. "Got any federal offenses on this guy?"

"He admitted he killed Aunt Josephine! And he

has a drug lab in that building right there. I have photos in my phone."

The moment Tadd emerged from his car, Levi stepped forward. He flashed his badge in one hand and his gun in the other. "Tadd Hemsley, you're under arrest."

CHAPTER THIRTY

It was a long night full of explanations, statements, discussions, and endless Q and A—and that was just my conversation with Wes. I also spent several hours with Detective Rhinehardt and other members of the Edindale Police Department, along with Special Agent Len Martinwood, alias Levi Markham, of the FBI.

I had Levi to thank for my timely rescue. When I didn't come out of the forest by nightfall, Wes had gone in after me. However, he soon realized he would end up lost in the darkness before he ever found me, so he went back to the owner's cabin for help. Carl enlisted Levi, who immediately—and correctly—guessed I'd be sneaking around HAPCO. "Like aunt, like niece," he'd said.

Detective Rhinehardt was astonished, but thrilled, to learn about Tadd's drug operation. He figured Tadd must be responsible for providing heroin, not only to Edindale, but to the entire region and beyond. Now I understood how he was able to afford his ultra-expensive hobby. All his animals would have to be relocated to new wildlife sanctuaries as soon as possible.

When we finally returned home after all the excitement, I was able to catch a few hours of sleep before my family arrived. At half past noon, they rang the bell and poured inside, bearing gifts, gossip, and yet more questions. Happily, I was able to provide some answers.

We all gathered in the living room: Wes and me, my mom and dad, my oldest sister Megan, and my Grandma O'Malley. After the usual catching up, all eyes turned to me to recount the events of the past week, and to tell them what I knew about the ever-elusive Josephine.

It was a little tricky to tell my story without mentioning magic spells, psychic visions, and ghostly apparitions, but I decided it was best to stick to the mundane facts. It was overwhelming enough for my family to learn about Josephine's life as a rogue environmental activist and fugitive from the law— who nonetheless tried to do good things her whole life. I told them about Fredeline Paul and Sister Seeds, stressing Josephine's generosity, passion, and kindness. I also told them about her light-hearted nature and her affinity for Native American culture.

My mom was mostly quiet during my tale. When I finished by informing them that Tadd was being held without bail and would be facing multiple local, state, and federal charges, my mom took an envelope from her purse and handed it to me.

"This came in the mail a couple days ago."

It was a postcard from Josephine. It had been sent from Missouri two weeks earlier and must have been misdirected before it finally reached my mom. On the front was a picture of a wolf. On the back was a handwritten message:

I hope you'll forgive me for my long absence. I wish things were different, but I'm <u>auribus teneo lupum</u>. You're always in my heart, Little Sister.

I swallowed the lump in my throat. "Did you look up the Latin phrase?"

My mom nodded. Wes pulled it up on his phone anyway and read the translation. "It means 'I hold a wolf by the ears.' It's meant to convey a difficult situation where acting and not acting are equally dangerous."

"She knew she was in a tough spot," I said. "She wanted to turn herself in for her part in the bombings. But, in doing so, she'd not only have to face the consequences, she'd also be breaking a promise she'd made to Gil and the others who were involved."

As Levi had told me, he'd figured out there were four people who participated in the Sorghum bombing: Gil, Davey, Josephine, and a fourth man named Allen Smith. Smith, who was later arrested for other crimes, had bragged to cell mates about masterminding the bombings. He died in prison before Levi had picked up the case, but he had provided enough information for Levi to begin piecing together the facts. Levi believed that Josephine's role was to play lookout, and that she might have received a relatively light sentence in exchange for her testimony. Only, she didn't want to betray her friends.

Davey, on the other hand, had apparently decided to do just that. Gil found out and tried to stop him—and Davey ended up dead. Levi said there wasn't enough evidence to pin his death on Gil. And, there was some indication that Davey might have been the victim of a deadly armed robbery. That was one mystery that might remain unsolved.

I returned the postcard to my mom and brought out Josephine's Black Hills gold jewelry, which I handed to my grandma. I sat on the ottoman next to her rocking chair and explained what it was. She held the necklace and two rings in her clenched fist for a brief moment. Then she gave one of the rings to me and patted my cheek.

"I'd like to say one thing," she said. "Josephine was my firstborn, and she flew from the nest much sooner than I would have liked. But all birds fly away eventually. By God's grace, we bring our children into the world. We feed them and raise them as best as we can. But they don't belong to us."

"Don't tell that to my kids," Megan said, halfjokingly. My mom murmured her agreement.

Grandma smiled at them and reached for my hand. Her skin felt cool and papery and full of love. "It was a difficult period when Josephine left," she continued. "But that was a very long time ago. She wrote to me, you know. She even called me a few times. And I finally came to understand that she was not mine to own or control. She was her own person, on her own journey. I've made peace with that. I had to." She squeezed my hand. "I had to," she repeated.

I nodded, not trusting myself to speak without crying. After all I'd been through lately, I was feeling extra emotional.

"It's interesting you say she was on a 'journey,'" said Megan. "Because I always thought of her as an adventurer or a world traveler. In my mind, she was always a part of the family—just off on safari or something." She laughed at herself. "Maybe that wasn't entirely accurate, but that's how I pictured her when I was a kid. That time she visited, she wore clothes that seemed exotic to me, with lots of beads and fringe. And she gave us cool gifts. Erin and I got leather coin purses and Keli got that Johnny Appleseed book. Of course, Alec wasn't born yet."

I stared at her in disbelief. "What do you mean 'that time she visited'? I thought Grandma gave me that book."

"No, I remember it distinctly. I had just turned thirteen. So, you would have been, what, one year old?"

I remembered Josephine telling me we had met once before. I had thought she was confused or mistaken.

"That's right," Mom confirmed. "She came through town one autumn on her way to, or from, someplace else. I was so upset with her at the time—that she would breeze in like that without warning, as if it were the most natural thing in the world. And then not stay more than a couple hours!"

"I remember," said Dad. "But then she called the next day, and you forgave her."

"Yes. I couldn't stay mad at her. She was who she was."

I was stunned by all the revelations. Contrary to what I'd always thought, Aunt Josephine hadn't cut off all ties with her family. There was more to her than I'd ever imagined.

At the visitation that evening, I introduced my family to Father Gabe. He was a likable young pastor whose manner seemed to strike the right balance between solemnity and sanguinity.

When I'd met with him the other day, I was a little uncomfortable at first. It had felt somewhat strange to arrange a Catholic funeral for my free-spirited aunt—especially since I wasn't Catholic myself. Though I still sometimes attended church for weddings, funerals, and occasional holidays with my family, I always felt like a visitor. I had chosen a different spiritual path many years ago. The teachings of my family's religion simply weren't relevant to me—no more so than any other major world religion.

But that didn't mean I held no respect for my family's beliefs. That was largely why we were here today, at a Catholic prayer service.

My family was duly impressed—by Father Gabe's warmth, as well as by the general positivity of the service. They were also floored by the huge display of flowers sent from all over the world. I had a feeling Fern's sisterhood played a big part in spreading the news of Josephine's passing.

As for me, I was impressed by the turnout. I stood near the casket between my mom and my sister and introduced them to more people than I could count. Wes's parents came, as well as several of our friends and all of my coworkers from the law firm. Mila came, of course, as did Max and Catrina. When no one was listening, Catrina quietly told me she had felt a spiritual connection to Josephine ever since witnessing her "appearance" at our Samhain ritual.

Gil Johnson was also there, a little less ebullient since his release from the hospital, but chatty nonetheless. He claimed he had suspected Tadd's involvement in Josie's death. He said that, after talking with me, he got to thinking about Josie's environmental activism and what she was doing in the woods. He had planned to show Tadd a picture of Josephine and gauge the businessman's reaction. Little did Gil know, but Tadd already had Gil in his sights.

Fern Lopez came to the visitation too—with, I was happy to see, Fredeline Paul. Both women were excited about their new collaboration. Fredeline would be joining the Sisterhood, and Fern would be sponsoring Fredeline's business in Haiti. I told Fern I had information about the old commune property and reminded her to stop by my office. She said she would give me a call.

Even Levi Markham stopped by to pay his respects.

I still couldn't get used to calling him Len. He shook my hand and asked if I'd have lunch with him sometime next week.

"To talk about Josephine?" I asked.

"Oh, well, sure. I mean, not necessarily." A slow blush rose from his neck to his cheeks.

I guess his shyness wasn't part of the undercover act. I smiled to myself and ignored his awkwardness. "Are you still investigating Gil? Is there really any more you can do here in Edindale?"

"I can't tell you that, Keli. Let's just say I'll be talking to him. And I hope he decides to do the right thing. For Josephine, if for no other reason."

Farrah came up to us then, stunning in a fitted black jersey dress. "Your grandma is the sweetest thing," she said. Then she turned to Levi. "I'm so disappointed you're not an author. Now I still haven't met one."

I laughed quietly. I knew she was actually thrilled to have met an FBI agent. Levi blushed again and sauntered off.

"Hey," I said, pulling Farrah aside. "See that short, dark-haired woman over there by herself? She came through the line before, but I didn't catch her name."

"Want me to investigate?"

"Would you? I'm just curious."

"Of course, you are. Curious is your middle name."

Farrah left to chat up the mystery woman, and Crenshaw walked over. "Can I get you something to eat or drink?" he asked.

Wes appeared at my side and handed me a glass of water. "Way ahead of you buddy," he said.

Crenshaw bowed curtly and retreated. I could only shake my head.

"Say, Wes," I said, as a thought popped into my head.

"Yes, babe?"

"You never did tell me how you found me at the pumpkin patch the other day. No one knew I was going there, except maybe Zeke. *I* didn't even know I was going until after I learned Fern would be there."

Wes smiled. "Okay, I'll tell you. I wondered where you were, so I called Farrah. Even when you're not together, you two usually keep tabs on each other. As it happened, she was with Randall at the law office when I reached her. And Pammy Sullivan had just called the office after running into you at the pumpkin patch. I guess she wanted to tell them you'd be attending that costume party. So, there you go. The grapevine in action."

"Ah, I see. Lucky timing."

"Yep. Feel better now?"

"I do. Thank you." I leaned over and kissed him on the cheek.

"You really don't like secrets, do you?"

"I really don't. At least, not unless I'm in on them."

Farrah returned and inserted herself between Wes and me. "Her name's Emmy," she said, in a low voice. "She works for Moonlight Maids Cleaning Service. Said she was a friend of Josephine's."

"A maid, huh? I wonder if that's the cleaning service that handles the hunters' cabin where Josephine was staying."

"Oh, yeah! The one somebody left unlocked. Wait, does that mean Emmy will be in trouble? She seems really sweet."

"I'll go talk to her."

The receiving line was dispersing anyway, so I hurried over to the woman named Emmy before she could leave. She gave me a slightly wary look but managed a smile. "I'm sorry for your loss," she said quietly.

"Thank you," I said. "In fact, I think I have something else to thank you for."

She wrinkled her brow and took a step toward the door.

"Did you happen to leave a book on my front porch the other night? From Josephine?"

She visibly relaxed. "Yes. Josie called me Saturday morning and asked me to get her things from—the place where she'd left them. There were certain things she wanted me to deliver."

I assumed "the place" was the hunters' house where Josephine had been squatting. And the phone call must have been the one she made from the HAPCO warehouse. Did that mean she suspected she wouldn't make it out alive?

"After I left the book," Emmy went on, "I found a letter in my van and realized it fell out of the book. I wanted to give it to you today, but I didn't know how." She removed a folded piece of paper from her purse and handed it to me. "I guess this is how."

"Oh! Well, thank you again."

Emmy nodded and murmured good-bye. As she left, I unfolded the letter and read it.

Dear Keli,

I want you to have this book as a small token of my affection. It was important to me and beloved by me—as are you.

It's also a reminder of the powerful difference one person can make. One woman, against the odds, started a national movement. Follow your heart and you never know what you might accomplish.

Carpe noctem.

Love,
AJ

The next morning was crisp and sunny, a perfectly pleasant early-November Tuesday to spend outdoors. I looked out the car window during the procession from the church to the cemetery and wondered if Josephine was at peace now. It felt sort of strange not to know for sure. Was she still in the wind, as Fredeline believed? If I wanted to speak to her, could I summon her again?

The interment was sad and somber as such things always are. Afterward, the family lingered in the cemetery, strolling under the trees and admiring the more unusual monuments.

Hand in hand, Wes and I wandered toward the historical section of the graveyard. On the way, I paused midstep as something caught my eye. Sitting still as a statue on the branch of a nearby sycamore was a great horned owl.

"Look at that," I whispered.

"You don't see that every day."

"No, you don't," I agreed. And that's what made it so special.

From early Native Americans to modern-day Pagans, humans have long attached significance to the unusual behavior of birds. Owls, in particular, held great symbolic meaning, especially for Wiccans. With their gifts of insight, vision, and wisdom, owls reveal that which is hidden to others. They uncover secrets and help us see the truth.

As we watched, the owl turned its head in that uncannily deliberate way owls have. I followed its line of sight. It seemed to look straight at Mrs. Hammerlin's house.

"It's a sign," I breathed.

"A sign of what?" asked Wes.

"It's a message . . . to look more closely and listen more carefully. There's something I've been missing."

I recalled everything I'd experienced at Mrs. Hammerlin's house, from the appearance of the black cat to the unexplained sights and sounds. I also thought about all my encounters with Aunt Josephine's spirit, whether through dreams, visions, or physical manifestations. She was definitely trying to tell me something. Something more than the identity of her murderer.

I pulled out my phone and tapped the screen.

"Are you looking up the meaning of owls?" Wes asked.

"No. Something else. I'm googling the word *Shima.*"

From the cemetery, we headed to a family-style restaurant for our post-funeral luncheon. On the way, I made two phone calls. The first was to Fern Lopez to confirm my hunch. Since I'd already guessed the truth, she decided it was okay to tell me what she knew.

After we arrived at the restaurant and I'd placed my order, I excused myself and stepped outside to wait on the sidewalk. Ricki Day pulled up in her county vehicle a few minutes later. She was the second person I'd called.

"Thank you for coming," I said, as I shook her hand.

"Well, the minute somebody asks me if I'm adopted, I'm instantly going to be curious. I've been searching for my birth family since my parents died a couple years ago. My adoptive parents, I mean. They're the only parents I ever knew."

"What do you know about your birth parents?"

"Not much. My mom and dad told me my birth mother was an angel, because she brought me into the world for them. I always thought that meant she had died shortly after I was born, but recently I learned that my parents probably didn't even know who she was. It turns out I was dropped off at a hospital—not born at one."

From what Fern had told me, I was 99.9 percent sure Ricki was born at the Happy Hills commune, when Josephine was only seventeen or eighteen. Fern had admitted that Josephine gave up her baby shortly before she left town on her "secret mission." However, Josie kept coming back to Edindale to check up on her daughter and make sure she was having a good life.

But I let Ricki continue.

"The only thing I know is the date I was left and the fact that I was wrapped in a green and yellow baby blanket. The letters *JO* were stitched on the blanket. That's why my parents gave me the middle name Jo."

"And you grew up in a Victorian on Hamilton Street, right next to Oak Grove Cemetery?"

"Yes! How did you know that? I moved out when I went to college, but my parents continued to live there right up until they passed away." She looked at me expectantly.

"So, I know this must seem really weird, but you know how I was asking you about Shima the other day?"

Ricki's eyes got really wide and she grabbed my arm. "Oh, my God. You're not going to believe this, but I had a dream about her last night. She told me she loved me and was really proud of me. Are you saying . . . ?"

I smiled. "Did you know *Shima* is a Navajo name meaning *mother*?"

"Holy cow! That actually explains a few things—like how she would always ask me about my life and remember everything I'd told her." She shook her head. "Wait. You said you were related to her, right? So, if this is true, that would make you my—"

"Cousin," I answered. Her excitement was contagious. I found myself grinning from ear to ear. I nodded toward the restaurant. "How would you like to meet some more of the family?"

"I'd love to!"

CHAPTER THIRTY-ONE

By Friday evening, my life had almost settled back to normal. My family had returned to Nebraska, and I'd returned to work. After a long day, I curled up on the living room couch with a mug of tea. Wes sat on the floor playing with the cat.

"How about *Friday*?" he said, still suggesting names for our new pet.

I cocked my head. "Not bad, but not quite right."

"What's Mila's cat's name? Isn't it something strange and witchy?"

"Her name's Drishti. It's a Sanskrit word that means 'focused gaze.'" I know that from yoga, not from witchcraft."

"Oh. Well . . . how about *Tadasana*? Isn't that a yoga thing?"

I laughed. "Very good. But that's mountain pose. It doesn't fit our frisky kitty." I held up my palm before he could speak. "And don't say *Frisky*!"

Over the past several days I'd considered lots of cool, exotic, and interesting names, from Aura and

Deity to Onyx and Esmeralda. None of them seemed quite right. But now, as I sat near Wes, feeling cozy and lucky and content, it finally came to me. I snapped my fingers.

"I've got it."

"You sure?"

"Oh, yeah. I'm positive."

"Let's hear it."

"Her name is Josie."

The cat, Josie, looked up at me and twitched her ears. She seemed to approve.

Over the weekend, I pulled out my spiritual journal and wrote about the strangeness of this Samhain season. I'd lost an aunt, but I'd also, ironically, become closer to her than I'd ever been before. I'd also made some new friends and found (or was chosen by) a new feline companion. Some good came in the midst of the bad.

As the last of the leaves fell to the ground, I found myself in the mood for an even bigger change. It was the Wiccan New Year and nearing the end of the calendar year. It was time to focus on the future. It was also time to admit something I'd been trying to ignore for the past several months.

Career-wise, I no longer felt like the law firm was the right place for me. It was time to move on.

I didn't relish the conversation I'd have to have with Beverly and the other partners, but I knew this was the right thing to do. By stepping down from the firm and striking out on my own, I'd be able to make my own decisions and set my own hours. This would also give me the extra time and freedom I'd been coveting—to spend more time with Wes, to direct my own career, and, of course, to get outside, honor the Goddess, and nurture my spirit.

Now *that* was something to look forward to.

ACKNOWLEDGMENTS

Thank you, thank you, thank you . . .

To Tom, Cathy, and Jana for catching my mistakes and providing excellent feedback on my draft manuscript.

To Rachel, my wonderful agent, for her spot-on advice and steadfast support.

To Martin, my fantastic editor, for his sharp eyes and keen instincts.

To my daughter, Sage, for being an all-around awesome kid, who always makes me smile.

And to my husband, Scott, for his love, partnership, and, most of all, his great sense of humor.

Love to you all.

If you enjoyed *Samhain Secrets*,
be sure not to miss any of
Jennifer David Hesse's
WICCAN WHEEL MYSTERY series,
including

YULETIDE HOMICIDE

It's Christmas in Edindale, Illinois,
and family law attorney Keli Milanni
is preparing to celebrate the Wiccan holiday
Yuletide, a celebration of rebirth. But this
Yuletide someone else is focused on dying . . .

Keep reading for a special excerpt.

A Kensington mass market and e-book
on sale now!

CHAPTER ONE

"Blackmail? Really? Someone is blackmailing Edgar?"

Now there was something you didn't hear every day. Before I could stop myself, an image flashed to mind: Edindale's most prominent silver-haired citizen engaged in a steamy, salacious affair. Scandalous! But with whom? I shifted in my leather seat and smoothed my pencil skirt, as I waited for my boss to continue.

Beverly cast a sharp glance at the door to her dark-paneled inner office. It was still closed.

"Let's not use that word from here on out," she said. She pressed her lips together, a visible demonstration that *mum*, not *blackmail*, was the word.

"Right. Sorry," I said quickly, though I still wasn't clear as to why Beverly was telling me this—well, me and my colleague, Crenshaw Davenport III.

Crenshaw cleared his throat from the chair next to me. His long legs were crossed in an elegantly relaxed pose, but I could tell he was just as intrigued as I was. He thrust his bearded chin forward slightly more than usual.

"It's understandable that Mr. Harrison desires discretion in this matter," he said, "especially given his recent announcement." Crenshaw turned toward me and looked down his nose. "Monday was the filing deadline for anyone interested in running for mayor next fall. Edgar Harrison announced his candidacy, along with half a dozen other Edindale residents."

"I know," I said evenly, biting back the snarky comment on the tip of my tongue. Crenshaw took every opportunity he could to school me in front of Beverly. It was one of his more annoying habits—one of many. We had both been with the firm for about six and a half years, and lately Beverly kept hinting that someone might be making partner soon. This only served to ramp up the competitive wedge between us.

Beverly removed her red-framed glasses and rubbed the bridge of her nose before responding. It had been a long week at the law firm, as everyone tried to finish up as much work as possible before the holidays. Of course, Beverly still looked impeccable in her designer pantsuit and expensive makeup, even if her eyes bore telltale hints of exhaustion.

"As I said, he was contacted by an unknown person who claims to have some information that Edgar would not like to be made public. This person has demanded a large sum of money in exchange for his or her silence. Edgar has until

Tuesday to produce the cash." Beverly paused and looked from Crenshaw to me with a deadpan gaze. "Obviously, the information is not true. Edgar assured me that the person manufactured their so-called evidence. However, they must have done a convincing enough job that it could still damage Edgar's reputation should it be released."

I glanced at Crenshaw and saw him raise one eyebrow. He must have been wondering the same thing as me: *Why worry about what a blackmailer might reveal if the information is not true?*

Beverly held up her palm. "I know what you're thinking. Don't. I've known Edgar a long time. He has no reason to be involved in anything illegal. His businesses are all doing extremely well."

That was no surprise. Edgar seemed to have a knack for investing in only the most lucrative projects. He owned Edindale's only riverboat casino, its fanciest hotel, and its trendiest residential developments—among other holdings. But did that necessarily mean everything was on the up-and-up? Evidently, the blackmailer had information that might indicate otherwise. So much for my steamy affair theory.

"Here's the deal," said Beverly, twisting the silver rings on her left hand. She appeared to be choosing her words carefully. "Edgar is convinced that someone hacked into his computer. This person accessed some confidential financial records about some of Edgar's investments . . . and found a way to twist the truth about the records in a manner that might portray Edgar in a less-than-favorable light.

While Edgar has done nothing illegal, the intricacies of business law are not always easy to explain to the layperson."

Out of the corner of my eye, I saw Crenshaw nod his head and steeple his fingers under his lips. *Oh, sure. As if he already knows what Beverly means, even though she's being extremely vague.* I cleared my throat. "Is that why Edgar came to you instead of the police? Because even the police might have a hard time understanding the legalities?"

Beverly frowned. "Not exactly. It's more that the information might make Edgar look bad, in spite of the fact that his dealings were technically legal. In any event, Edgar fully intends to go to the police as soon as he has evidence. He already has a couple of suspects in mind . . . which brings me to why I asked the two of you into my office this afternoon."

"How can I help?" asked Crenshaw.

"How can we help?" I asked, at the same time. I narrowed my eyes and glared at Crenshaw, before turning back to Beverly.

"As Edgar's attorney and close friend, I agreed to help him figure out who is doing this." Beverly stood and paced to her window where she paused and looked outside. Snow was falling in slow, lazy swirls. She walked back to us and remained standing. "Of course, I immediately thought of you, Keli, because of your detecting skills. You seem to have a knack for recovering stolen objects and ferreting out criminals. As for you, Crenshaw, in addition to being one of my most trusted lawyers, I believe your acting skills may be useful in this case." Crenshaw nodded his whole upper body in a seated bow, as if thanking her for a well-deserved compliment. I fought the urge to roll my eyes.

I looked up at Beverly. "How can we possibly figure out who is blackmail—I mean, who is threatening Edgar?"

"The logical place to start is at Edgar's main office. Harrison Properties has a new IT support specialist, a young, tech-savvy guy named Zeke Marshal. Edgar thinks that if anyone could hack into his secured, password-protected files, this fellow would be the one. The only problem is, Edgar can't imagine why he would do it. The young man was just hired. He has a bright future ahead of him, in a career that will compensate him well. It doesn't make sense."

I nodded, beginning to feel more and more curious myself.

"I've arranged for the two of you to set up shop in Edgar's office for a few days. The ostensible purpose will be to conduct a thorough legal audit of his corporation's files. In fact, Edgar will be paying you to do just that. His staff will be told this is a proactive measure to ensure the company is in compliance with all relevant business laws. At the same time, you will keep your eyes and ears open, and see what you can learn about Zeke. You'll start right away. The sooner we can end this headache for Edgar, the better."

* * *

After leaving Beverly's office I headed to my own, much smaller office to gather my coat and purse. Crenshaw and I had agreed to meet downstairs in the lobby in ten minutes and then walk over to Harrison Properties to get started on our strange assignment. Shaking my head, I pushed open my office door and stopped short when I saw what was sitting on my desk: a large gold-colored box, topped with a golden ribbon.

"A delivery guy brought it while you were with Beverly," said a voice behind me. I turned to see Julie, our twenty-something front desk receptionist, peering over her trendy glasses toward the gold box. "There's a card, too."

I smiled at Julie's eagerness, then walked over to my desk to check out the package. Right away, I noticed the word *Godiva* embossed on the lid of the box.

"Did someone say chocolate?" I looked up to see Pammy Sullivan standing in my doorway next to Julie. Pammy was a fellow associate with heavily sprayed hair and a stylish, if somewhat gaudy, wardrobe. Today she wore a salmon-pink skirt suit, which matched her lipstick and fingernails. The buttons of her blazer strained ever so slightly across her plump figure.

"Come on in," I said, laughing. Pammy must have known about the delivery and was just waiting for me to return to my office.

"Ooh, Godiva," said Pammy, squeezing between the two guest chairs facing my desk to get a look at the gift box. "The nearest Godiva shop is in

St. Louis. Someone must have ordered this online, unless they brought it in from out of town. Is it from a client?"

Shrugging, I slipped the small plain card out of the white envelope and furrowed my brow. "I don't think so," I said, in answer to Pammy's question. The card simply said *Missed you.* It was unsigned.

"Aw," said Julie, looking over my shoulder. "It must be from that hunky boyfriend of yours. Hasn't he been out of town?"

"Yeah, for a week. Wes helped his brother move to Seattle. He's supposed to get back later today. I'll see him tonight."

"Well, maybe he came back early," said Pammy, her eyes still on the gold box.

"Maybe," I agreed. I lifted the lid and tore off the protective plastic covering to reveal an assortment of fancy chocolate candies. It was a somewhat odd gift, coming from Wes. He knew I wouldn't eat milk chocolate because I'm vegan. On the other hand, he would also know I'd share the candy.

I replaced the lid and handed the box to Julie. "Would you take this up front and leave it on your desk for all to share? I've got to get going."

Pammy followed Julie out of my office, while I slipped on my long black coat and tied the belt. I grabbed my shoulder bag and hurried to the elevator. It was a short ride, four flights to the ground floor lobby. I pulled on my gloves as I walked over to join Crenshaw where he waited for me by the revolving door. I almost laughed when I saw what he was wearing.

In a Victorian-style overcoat, long scarf, and short top hat, Crenshaw looked like a character straight out of Dickens's *A Christmas Carol*. In fact, as an amateur actor, he probably was. Outside his law practice, Crenshaw was active in the local theater circuit.

"Nice outfit," I said. "Where are you performing?"

"I beg your pardon?"

"The caroler getup," I said, gesturing toward his coat. "Aren't you . . . Never mind."

With Crenshaw, it was sometimes hard to know when he was being serious and what he was really thinking. At times, he could be incredibly sweet. More often than not, he was just obnoxious. My best friend, Farrah, called him the "original pompous ass."

We stepped outside into the crisp, breezy air and made our way down the sidewalk toward Main Street. We walked carefully, knowing there could be slick spots in spite of the rock salt sprinkled like breadcrumbs in our path. Snowflakes stuck to every surface, from the cars parked along the curb to the tops of signs and the large red bows decorating every light post. The bows had been up since Thanksgiving, but it was the fresh snowfall that really made the scene look a lot like Christmas. It ought to, I thought, since the holiday was only a week away.

We turned right at the corner and continued down Main Street, walking past downtown shops with cheerfully decked-out storefronts. When we passed Moonstone Treasures, I slowed down to admire the window display: gracefully draped garland and glittery five-pointed stars framed an artful arrangement of red and gold candles. Just then, the door opened and the store owner herself hurried out, raising her hand in greeting.

"I had a feeling I would see you today, Keli," she said. She approached us and gave me a hug, enveloping me in the scent of rosemary, patchouli, and orange blossoms. I smiled in return. I had known Mila Douglas for years, but we had become closer friends last February when I had helped catch the criminal who had been harassing her and breaking into her shop.

Crenshaw regarded Mila with a raised eyebrow. With her white velvet tunic over black leggings and the strands of silvery ribbons crowning her brunette shag, she looked like a cross between a snow queen and rocker Joan Jett. I ignored Crenshaw and complimented Mila on her window display.

"Thank you, dear," she said. "I can hardly believe Yule is only four days away. I still hope you'll join—" She stopped mid-sentence at my warning look. Mila was forever trying to coax me into joining her coven, but I preferred to follow a solitary spiritual practice. Only a small number of people knew I was Wiccan. Crenshaw was not one of them.

"Will you stop by later?" she asked. "I have something important to tell you."

"Um, is tomorrow okay? I'm not sure what time I'll get off today, and Wes is coming by tonight."

Crenshaw crossed his arms and tapped his foot on the snow-covered sidewalk.

"Oh, I'll just tell you now," said Mila. She took my hand and spoke quickly, her breath forming puffs of fog in the cold air. "I had a vision this morning," she said, "and you were in it. So was Mercury, the messenger god." She paused, and squeezed my hand. "There are two things you need to know. One: You will soon have a visitor from your past. Two: Someone in your midst is going to die."

Connect with Us

Visit us online at
KensingtonBooks.com
to read more from your favorite authors, see books
by series, view reading group guides, and more.